BAKERSFIELD

PIERRE OUELLETTE

BAKERSFIELD

A CRIME NOVEL

JORVIK
PRESS

ISBN-10: 0986377074

ISBN-13: 978-0-9863770-7-5

Library of Congress
Control Number: 2018948986

Cover photo: Michael Sullivan

Cover concept: Pierre Ouellette

Design and formatting: Keith Carlson

First edition

JORVIK PRESS

5331 SW Macadam Ave., Ste 258/424,
Portland OR 97239

JorvikPress.com

About the Author

Pierre Ouellette lives near Portland, Oregon and is the author of five previously published novels that span a diversity of subjects and settings. He served for two decades as the creative partner in an advertising and public relations agency focused on science and technology. Prior to that he was a professional guitarist and played in numerous pop bands and jazz ensembles, including Paul Revere and the Raiders, Jim Pepper and David Friesen.

Also by Pierre Ouellette

The Deus Machine

The Third Pandemic

The Forever Man

Writing as Pierre Davis

A Breed Apart

Origin Unknown

Dedicated to
Randy Miller
A lifelong friend and true
American Original

PROLOG

BAKERSFIELD, CALIFORNIA
1951

BEACH PARK LOOP
JULY 9, 8:00 AM

The body lay face down just beyond the sprinkler's reach, where the land came to terms with itself and went bone dry.

An old man in bib overalls stood over the lifeless figure. He waved at the patrolman, who was just getting out of his car in the parking lot. Yes, this is the spot. This is where I found her.

The cop asked the old man what he was doing here in the first place. Beer bottles. He was collecting beer bottles. Did it every morning. Picked up after those who drank and copulated in the nocturnal swelter of mid-summer. He held up a burlap bag to prove it.

The patrolman bent over the body. A female in her teens wearing a pink nightshirt and posed as though sleeping. Cheek pressed against the sandy ground. Barefoot, with white toes curled into tight little bundles, each fetal in appearance. One arm stretched toward the green of the park. No visible blood, no bruises, no contusions.

The old man waited expectantly for the cop to make some sense of it. Instead, the cop told him to stay put and went back to the patrol car. The morning sun had hit its mark and the heat ramped up. The cop shifted his gun belt to relieve the perspiration on his lower belly. He reached into his vehicle, fetched the radio mic and called dispatch at the station. Code Two. Copy that, they said, we'll get someone out there.

The old man told old tales to the young cop while they waited. He was an Okie, a product of great trouble on the distant plains in years gone past. Lived in tents, picked beans, dug ditches, got drunk, got laid. The Okies built Bakersfield, he claimed, built it from the ground up. Never got paid for it, neither. Too bad about that.

A detective from homicide soon pulled up next to the patrol car. He crossed the parking lot with a hesitant gate, pacing himself in the face of mounting infirmities. A trickle of sweat set in by the time he reached them. "So, what have we got?" he asked.

The patrolman pointed to the old man. "He found the body about thirty minutes ago. I saw him waving as I was driving by."

The detective gingerly bent over the corpse and examined the outstretched arm. The index finger pointed north, toward some location beyond mortal reckoning. "Don't see any needle marks." He grasped the shoulder and rotated the body until the limp hair fell away and the face came into full view.

"Aw shit."

He turned to the old man. "Get the fuck out of here. Right now."

The old man saw no profit in confrontation. He shouldered his gunnysack and headed out. His cargo of beer bottles clinked sporadically in protest. The detective turned to the young cop. "I'll take it from here. You move on."

The patrolman, though young, understood the subtext. It spoke of numerous layers of complication, of silent protocols, of pacts never committed to paper. He simply nodded and walked off to continue his patrol.

The detective rose on creaky knees and mopped his florid face. He'd have to do an end run. He needed to call the medical examiner directly on this. He gazed down at the body.

"You poor, dumb little thing," he said. "Look what you've gone and done."

The patrol car drove off and left the detective with nothing but the squawk of a vigilant crow and the nearby empty river. The old man had descended its bank and now shuffled along its arid bed. He left only a vague trail of footprints and the fading clink of the captive bottles.

PART ONE

LOS ANGELES, CALIFORNIA
1952

1.

NORTH HOLLYWOOD
SEPTEMBER 13

Honky Tonk Blues by Hank Williams. It didn't get much better than that, especially when he hit those falsetto notes in the chorus.

James Stone listened to it pour into the squad car over KFOX, 1280 on the AM dial. He tapped his foot to the steel guitar solo, smooth as glass with just the right touch of whine. His wife liked the pop stuff, like Eddie Fisher and Doris Day, but Stone knew better about himself. When it came to music, he was hardcore country.

The heat glued his sweaty back to his rayon sport shirt. He wore it out and over his slacks to hide his badge and Smith & Wesson .38 revolver.

Stone had a clean view down into the little park just off the brand new Ventura Freeway. His partner Murphy chose this spot in the parking lot because he'd worked it several times before while on fruit patrol. Right now, he was down in the shadows under the palms, slowly cruising the curved path, looking for the action. Earlier, they'd flipped a coin and Murphy lost, so he became Fag for A Day, as they called it. It played off the title of the TV show with Jack Bailey, the one where the women sobbed and spilled their dreams while Baily oozed sympathy.

Stone and Murphy knew the drill, knew it well. They were working Vice out of the North Hollywood Division, which extended a little farther south, but not much. Stone had been here for about a year, Murphy for three. Narcotics, porno, whores, homos. The whole nine yards – and maybe a few feet more. Stone took it all in stride. Just another rung on his way up. To lieutenant. To Robbery or Homicide.

Hank Williams ended and Slim Whitman fired up. Okay, but not as good. Stone's mental field drifted to the deal he'd made with Grace. She got the house, so he was going to get a hi-fi. Soon, Webb Pierce and Merle Travis would squeeze through the turntable, roar across a glowing set of vacuum tubes and blast out a big-ass speaker into the living room.

Stone checked his watch. It was late, just after 1 AM. And it was hot. But he couldn't roll down the windows to let any air in. If he did, the music might leak out and spoil the sting. Better to bake to a hot steel solo by Roy Wiggins than blow their cover.

The park came alive. Stone spotted a lone figure meandering in Murphy's direction. Murphy gave the figure a fleeting glance, shoved his hands in his pockets and stared down at the grass. The figure slowed but didn't stop.

Stone killed the AM. Wiggins would have to wait. He reached out, grabbed the crank and rolled down the driver's window for a better view. Murphy was shooting another glance at the approaching figure, a little come-on to keep the action alive. Stone gingerly opened the door and stepped into the parking lot. He moved out of their line of sight, and then forward. He needed to be in decent back-up position when the bust went down.

He stopped at a stand of rhododendrons where he could observe from concealment. The figure now resolved into a young man in his late teens or early twenties. Dark curly hair, powerful build, loose sport shirt, dungarees with the cuffs rolled up. The suspect halted about a yard from Murphy and started the little chat that always led up the hustle.

Stone stepped into the shadows and drifted forward, but not too quickly. He had the timing down. He and Murphy had danced this dance dozens of times. Murphy said something to the young man, who nodded and said something back. Murphy smiled and reached into his slacks for what the guy would assume was his wallet.

Stone stepped up his pace and angled to where he could do an intercept if the suspect tried to take off. Murphy pulled out his badge and declared an arrest.

The guy swiveled his head rapidly looking for an exit. His body tensed to spring, but he caught sight of Stone and deflated. Murphy spun him around and expertly cuffed him as Stone walked up to the pair.

"Good evening," Stone said to the young man, who didn't answer and stared down at the pathway.

"You got yourself in a real pickle here son," Stone said. "You done this kind of thing before?"

"No sir," the suspect said. He shifted his weight from foot to foot, like a cat on the brink of pouncing.

Stone snorted. It was not only a lie; it was a tired lie, full of boredom and resignation. "Look at me," he ordered. "I don't want to talk to the top of your head."

The young man brought his face up, and Stone looked into a world gone badly wrong. A radiant cruelty burned in the eyes. The mouth wavered between a smirk and a snarl. Stone had seen this before, but not often. Most of the hustlers out here considered a bust to be just a cost of doing business and assumed a passive stance when taken down. No need to provoke the cops. Better to play the game by the rules.

"How old are you?" Stone asked.

"Nineteen."

"What's your name?"

"Willert. Gary Willert."

"You got any ID?"

"It's in my pocket."

Stone nodded to Murphy, who plucked Willert's wallet out of his dungarees and handed it to Stone. It contained four ten-dollar bills and a social security card that verified his name.

"Okay, here's what we got. You just solicited a police officer to commit an act of sodomy. Know what that is?"

"Yeah, I know what that is. But I ain't no queer."

Stone knew it might very well be true. A lot of these guys made a weird distinction between gay sex for money and straight sex for fun. What you did at work had little impact on what you did on your own time.

Stone turned to Murphy. "I may have this wrong, but didn't Mr. Willert offer to let you suck his dick for ten bucks?"

"Indeed he did."

In the state of California, the sodomy part will get you one to ten years all by itself. Then you get a soliciting rap on top of that. Sound like fun?"

"No."

"You damn well better believe it. Now let's go."

Murphy gave Willert a tug on the arm and they headed back up toward the parking lot.

"Where you taking me?"

"Where do you think?" Stone said. "Los Angeles County Jail. Wonderful place. Absolutely first class."

The police radio squawked through the squad car's open window just as they arrived in the parking lot.

Unit Six. Code One.

Stone moved ahead, opened the door, grabbed the mic and pressed the talk button. "Dispatch, this is Unit Six."

We have a 245 at 8569 Riverside. Code Three. Copy.

Stone sighed and pressed the talk button. "Copy. We're on our way." Their whole bust was dead in the water.

"Ah fuck! Murphy exclaimed. The big, blustery Irishman had a short fuse when it came to the dictates of police command. He shoved a meaty hand into his pocket for the handcuff keys.

Stone parked the mic and got out as Murphy took the cuffs off Willert, who appeared both confused and wary. Something had just gone his way, but he didn't know what or why.

"Buddy, you just got the biggest break of your miserable little life," Stone told him. "If we ever catch you here again, you're gonna be beyond sorry. Hear me?"

"Hear you." Willert rubbed the red marks on his wrists where the cuffs had clamped his flesh. Not a trace of repentance. Not a bit of humility. He wheeled and took off across the lot at a brisk pace.

"That prick will be back on the street in an hour somewhere down in Hollywood," Murphy grumbled as they piled into the squad car. Stone fired up the Ford's V8. He liked the sound. The big engine had balls and put the old straight-line sixes to shame.

Murphy pulled out the red flasher and plunked it down onto the magnetic clamp on the dash while Stone wheeled them in a wide circle and out onto Tujunga Boulevard. He shoved the stick shift through all three gears and threaded the southbound traffic. Fortunately, it was late, and they had the street mostly to themselves.

"Maybe I should've leaned on him a little," Murphy mused. "Maybe that'd keep his dick in his pants for a few weeks."

Stone didn't comment. His views on the subject didn't jibe with the common wisdom. In the end, all this homo stuff was victimless. Nobody got hurt, and queer was queer, no matter what they did. It seemed like a huge waste of police power.

"Why are we going south?" Murphy asked as he lit up a Pall Mall.

"I'm taking the freeway. It's longer but faster."

Stone down-shifted when they reached the entrance to the newly minted Ventura Freeway. He shoved the column stick up and they swung right on squealing tires. A cascade of cigarette butts fell out of the ashtray mounted in the dash.

"Hey cowboy," Murphy said. "Let's not muss things up."

Stone slammed the gas pedal to the floor. The 110-horsepower engine howled and they rocketed down the entrance ramp. He yanked the column stick down into third as they merged into traffic. In no time at all, they were maxed out at about 85 miles per hour. Up ahead, cars were heeding their flashing light and pulling over to the shoulder.

Stone glanced out to the left, where the Hollywood Hills loomed up into the sky glow from downtown on the far side. Something was bugging him about the dispatch. A 245 code meant assault with a deadly weapon. Not that unusual around here. But they were Vice, so why did they get the call instead of Homicide? It could be that they were the closest unit, or that the other guys were tied up on another case. A little unusual, but nothing to sweat. So what was the problem?

The address. That's what was bugging him. The address on Riverside. He knew the block, he knew the place.

The Showboat. It had to be the Showboat Bar.

He shot down the Laurel Canyon exit and wheeled north toward Riverside Drive. "I got a bad feeling about this," he told Murphy.

"Oh yeah?" Murphy said as he stubbed out his cigarette in the empty ashtray.

"You hear the address?" Stone asked.

"Yeah, what of it?"

"It's the Showboat."

Murphy yanked his gaze off the traffic and over to Stone. "You're kidding?"

"Nope."

Murphy thumped the dash with his curled fist. "Aw shit! Now what?"

Every LAPD cop knew the joint. It had caused the force more grief than every other dive in the entire city put to together.

Bloody Christmas, the papers called it. All courtesy of The Showboat. Last Christmas Eve, a call came in reporting several underage customers on the premises. The two responding officers found seven Mexican Americans bellied up to the bar drinking beer. Their ID showed them all to be over 21, but cops told them to high tail it anyway. The drinkers got uppity and stood their ground, so the cops waded in and applied at little muscle to get them out the door. The action spilled out into the parking lot, and cops got the worst of it. One picked up a black eye, and another a cut on his forehead. A neighbor broke up the brawl by waving a rifle at the patrons and they drifted off into the night.

But by now, they were marked men, as they would soon find out. All seven were arrested at their houses later that night. One took a pretty bad beating right in front of his family and was carted off to the hospital. The rest were hauled off to jail.

Normally, that would have been the end of it. But on this night, there was a big, boozy Christmas party going on at the Central Station, where the defendants had been booked. Word circulated that one of the responding officers had lost an eye to the attackers, and the most fundamental rule of law enforcement quickly came into play: You touch a cop, you get touched back. The defendants were yanked out of their cells and brutally beaten for about ninety minutes by a swarm of enraged policemen, many of them drunk.

When it was over, the floors and walls were covered with blood. Amazingly, the LAPD managed to keep a lid on it for over two months. The *Times* covered the Showboat part of the story as brave officers beaten by a savage mob – and mentioned nothing about the follow-up horror at the jailhouse. But the ominous stink of it finally found its way into the papers. For the first time, the longstanding romance between the cops and the LA press fell apart. A grand jury was convened. Eight officers were indicted.

The city fought back. Mayor Bowron blamed it all on an anti-cop crusade fueled by communist agitators who wanted to bring down the system. And Chief Parker issued a reminder that his officers were all that stood between the public and total anarchy. And when brother officers were called as witnesses, their memories became very hazy and inconclusive.

After nine months, the trials were still playing out, but it appeared that the damage had been contained. One officer was cleared, another had been acquitted, and only three had received a guilty verdict. Not bad, considering that over 50 people were originally investigated. The bleeding from Christmas past seemed to be stanched.

And now this.

"We're walkin' into a minefield," Murphy muttered, "Just like when I was in Normandy."

"Maybe it's just some petty bullshit," Stone offered. "Maybe some shitfaced asshole pulled out a shiv and nicked somebody."

"You really believe that?"

Stone yanked the wheel hard right and put them on Riverside. They could already see the flashing lights parked up ahead.

"No."

2.

RIVERSIDE DRIVE
SEPTEMBER 13

The Showboat Bar fronted Riverside Drive with a red neon sign done in cursive lettering. It cast a warm glow on the cluster of young men milling on the sidewalk beneath it as Stone pulled up behind the ambulance parked in the far right lane. Back doors open, gurney gone, and attendants nowhere in sight. A bad sign.

A patrol car sat in front of the ambulance, also empty. It's flashing lights bounced off the rubberneckers in the left lane. As Stone and Murphy got out, a uniformed patrolman came out of the bar and met them on the sidewalk. "You're not gonna like this," he warned them. Behind him, the crowd of young men looked on expectantly but kept their distance.

"So what are we looking at?" Stone asked.

"Officer-involved shooting."

"Who?" Murphy asked.

"MacGregor."

Now Stone understood why they got the call, and not Homicide. MacGregor was Vice. He was one their guys. The department meant to give him every break he could possibly get.

"Where is he?"

"Inside."

Stone nodded toward the knot of young men, mostly Mexican. "We got witnesses?"

"That's what they say."

"Keep 'em here until we can get some statements."

Stone had to marvel at the situation as he pushed the door to the bar open. It was worse than he could have possibly imagined. A cop just shot an unarmed Mexican in the same bar that triggered the biggest scandal in the history of the department. It could only go downhill from here. On a very steep grade.

Inside, squalid orange light dripped from sconces and the overheads. Chocolate cigarette burns infested the red carpeting. Mirrored shelves of milky glass held rows of liquor arrayed behind a curved bar. And at its far end, two ambulance attendants in their whites bent over a body wearing baggy slacks and skinny loafers. It rested face up in a gruesome little lake of blood. One of the attendants was lifting his stethoscope's chestpiece off the man's sternum where they'd torn his shirt open.

"Dead?" Stone asked.

"Yup," the attendant answered.

"The beaner have a gun?" Murphy asked.

"Didn't see one," the attendant replied.

Stone recognized the ambulance service. A mortuary in Burbank owned it. If they found you dead, you went straight to the funeral home and became grist for the death mill. Alive, they took you to the hospital. But a case like this dictated a third path.

"Pack him up and take him down to the coroner," Stone ordered.

The attendant appeared puzzled. "No pictures?" he asked, referring to the usual practice of waiting for the police photographer to cover the crime scene.

"Just get him out of here. Got it?"

The attendant shrugged. "Got it."

Stone looked over to the bar. Sure enough, MacGregor sat at the far end, tossing down a drink and staring at the bottles on the shelves. Stone walked over and put his hand on the man's shoulder. "Hey Mac. How you doing?"

MacGregor wore a cheap suit over a lanky frame with a fedora parked on his balding head. He took another gulp before answering. "Been better."

"So what happened?"

MacGregor gave a distant smile followed by a feeble shrug of resignation. "Not much to it. I come in, I see this guy who looks underage. I ask him for ID and that sets off these guys at the bar. They start to crowd me, and I got no backup so I pull out my gun. That really gets 'em going, and they give me a couple of shoves and gun goes off. It hits the guy I was questioning and he goes down." MacGregor gulps the last of his drink. "That's about it."

Stone turned from the bar to the attendants, who were wheeling the body out. "Hold on. Anybody get a name?"

"Not us."

Stone walked over to the body, fished a wallet out of the slacks, and extracted a driver's license. "Canales. Servando Canales."

"He was underage, right?" MacGregor didn't bother to turn around as Stone asked. He'd seen enough.

Stone checked the date of birth. "Doesn't look like it." He motioned the attendants to continue on out. "We'll double check downtown. You never know."

"Yeah. You never know," MacGregor repeated.

Stone walked back to MacGregor and leaned against the bar but didn't sit. "Where's your gun, Mac?"

MacGregor swung his coat open to reveal a revolver in a small holster on his beltline. "Right where it should have been all along."

"You need to turn it in when you get back to the precinct. You okay to drive?"

MacGregor rose from the bar. "Yeah. I'm okay."

"Don't worry. We'll get this thing sorted out."

"Yeah, sure you will," MacGregor said with more than a trace of sarcasm. "See you around."

Stone wished it was true, but knew it wasn't as he watched MacGregor depart. How could a veteran cop have been so stupid? After Bloody Christmas, what was he even doing here? And why was he shaking down some kid over ID? It was like a carbon copy of the first time around, only this time, they had a kid shot dead by a cop. The press was going to go nuclear once this got out.

The front door swung open and a middle-aged guy with a loud shirt and greased back hair rushed in.

"Who are you?" Stone asked, but he'd already guessed the answer.

"Kohn, Max Kohn. I own the joint and I've just got one question: Just how fucking dumb can you guys get?"

Stone had to agree but sidestepped. "We're going to handle this just like any other investigation, Mr. Kohn. Were you present when it happened?"

"I was in my office in the back. I heard a gunshot and by the time I got out here, one of my customers is dead on the floor with one of your guys standing over him."

"Did you ask anybody what happened?"

"You bet your ass I did. Your boy got in a beef with the Canales kid over ID and shot him. Just like that. Coupla guys said your pal yelled something about Bloody Christmas before he fired. Now just how fucking dumb was that?"

"Did anybody shove or threaten the officer?"

"They all said the same thing: Nobody was near him when he fired. They're gonna roast you guys over an open fire this time."

"Yeah, maybe." Stone got out his notebook and jotted down Kohn's statement. "We'll see."

Stone found Murphy out on the street talking to one of the patrons and taking notes. "How many more to go?" he asked Murphy, who pointed to three young Hispanic males standing nearby on the sidewalk. "Those guys claim say they saw it go down."

It took Stone about ten minutes to get their names and their accounts of what happened inside. Their stories pretty much matched what Kohn had told him. He was already picturing their testimony before a grand jury. It would read as an epitaph for MacGregor's career with the LAPD.

But then again, maybe not.

3.

HOLLYWOOD PRECINCT HEADQUARTERS
SEPTEMBER 13

"You got some visitors," the desk sergeant announced as Stone came through the precinct's front doors. He nodded toward the briefing room, where two plainclothes cops stared at Stone through a waist-high window. Internal Affairs. No doubt about it. The Showboat was already pulling into port and it wasn't going to be pretty. You normally didn't see these guys for days after something bad happened, maybe even longer.

"Sergeant Stone?" the taller of the pair asked as Stone walked in.

"That's me."

"I'm Lt. Morrow and this is Lt. Jowroski."

"Let me guess: You're from Internal Affairs."

"Very perceptive of you," Jowroski commented.

"Now let me guess why you're here. It's about what happened at the Showboat with MacGregor."

Morrow raised his hands in mock conciliation. "Hey, let's not make too big a deal out of this. We're just grinding through the facts and need a little help." He gestured toward some metal folding chairs. "Let's sit down, okay?"

"Obviously, this thing is item number one for us," Jowroski said. "So for starters, we just want to quickly touch base with everyone involved."

"Have you talked with Murphy yet?" Stone asked.

"Yeah, we talked with Murphy. Said he interviewed five witnesses, and their accounts were all over the map. One guy says MacGregor hit the bar with his elbow, and that's when the gun went off. Another guy says a patron grabbed his wrist, which triggered the shooting. And so on."

"Well there you go. So what do you want from me?"

"Just a few facts," Morrow said. "Like how many people did you interview?"

"Three patrons and the club owner."

"And did their stories jibe?"

"As a matter of fact, they did. They all said the victim was nowhere close to McGregor when he fired."

Silence. Big, fat and hot. It filled the room to the brim.

Jowroski exchanged glances with his partner. He paused to contemplate the tiled floor before he spoke. "You know, truth is, stuff like this is always a matter of interpretation. You talk to some people, you take a few notes. You come back to the station and it's all a little blurred. The next day you go to write it up, and it's even more blurry. Know what I mean?"

Stone shrugged. "Yeah, I know what you mean." It meant that the department expected that his final report would line up neatly with Murphy's and exonerate McGregor.

"I did a quick check of your record before we came over," Morrow volunteered. "Very commendable. You're pretty much a cinch to make lieutenant."

"Yeah, one would hope so," Stone responded. And there was the payoff: Play along and you'll make lieutenant in no time at all.

Jorowski stood up, followed by Morrow. "Sorry to keep you past your shift, but we want to get this thing straight."

"Right."

"We'll check back after all the paperwork comes though."

"Sure."

After the pair departed, Murphy came out and watched with Stone as the IA guys departed. "So how you gonna handle this?" Murphy asked.

"Don't know."

Murphy scratched his receding hairline. "It's a tough one. Not like the old days. Back then, the chief would have killed the whole thing before it even started to breathe."

"But these aren't the old days," Stone countered. "If this thing goes to trial, we'll be put on the stand and the defense will go after us like pack of hyenas. If they can show a cover-up, we might be looking at perjury charges, maybe even conspiracy."

Murphy shook his head. "Don't think so. I'm gonna bet that Chief Parker still has the biggest balls in Los Angeles County. It'll never make it past the DA. No indictment, no trial, no nothing."

Stone simply nodded. The less said out loud from now on, the better.

4.

DOWNTOWN LOS ANGELES
SEPTEMBER 15

The world went into abrupt shade as Stone pulled into the police garage underneath City Hall and parked. He checked his watch. Ten minutes until his meeting with Chief Parker on one of the floors high above. He got out and waded through the faint odors of engine exhaust and baked motor oil to the elevator, where he ascended to the highest floor. A city ordinance prohibited any building taller than this one, so the view from Chief Parker's office promised to be unobstructed and spectacular. It looked out on a post-war LA that was bulging at the economic seams. Traffic roared, construction boomed, factories proliferated and people basked in their newfound prosperity.

A wondrous place to go on trial for his professional life.

He pondered the irony of it as he exited the elevator and headed for the rest room. The mirror above the sink reflected a face both strong and broad, with bright brown eyes, a slim nose, and close-cropped black hair oiled neatly back. The kind of face the department's PR people would choose for a photo opportunity. Or would have.

Chief Parker's secretary managed a polite smile when Stone introduced himself. She checked a calendar on her desk blotter and pushed a button on the intercom box to announce him.

Parker stayed behind his desk and didn't bother to stand as Stone entered. He gestured to a chair on the far side. "Have a seat, Stone. You know what my job is?"

Stone was caught short by the question. "You're the chief."

"That's my title, not my job. My job is to make this the best goddam police force in the world." Parker had a full face, grim jaw, conservative glasses, and a rigid bearing even when sitting down. "We live in a violent world," he went on, "full of scum just waiting to catch us in a moment of weakness. We're the thin blue line that stands between the average person and total criminal anarchy. There are forces afoot out there that would just love to stretch us to the breaking point: Communists, anarchists, mobsters, perverts in the movie business. So what do you think we should do about that?"

"The best we can," Stone countered.

"Precisely!" The chief rose and moved to the window, where the great expanse of city sprawled into the distance. "And to do that, we need people who understand the true meaning of duty and loyalty. Unless we pull together, we'll start to fall apart, which would be a disaster, both for us and the city. Each man must carry the weight of the force as a whole."

The chief returned to his desk and rifled through a thick file, ignoring Stone's presence. "As you probably know by now, I've personally assumed responsibility for the Canales investigation. I've been briefed and read all the reports, including yours, and you know what I've concluded?"

"No sir."

"The report you filed is at odds with all the other input we've collected. You're claiming that four individuals stated there was no threat to officer MacGregor, none at all."

Stone shrugged. "It wasn't a court of law. They weren't under oath. They could say anything they wanted."

The chief looked up and stared in mock disbelief at Stone. "And you believed them?"

How long have you been a cop?"

"Fourteen years."

"Let me give you the numbers on this thing," the chief went on. "Murphy interviewed five people. You interviewed four. That's nine people. You good at math?"

"Average."

"The odds are about one in fifteen thousand that you'd draw the four with the same story. Would you bet on that at the track?"

"I don't gamble."

"Ah." The chief extended an index finger with a perfectly trimmed cuticle. "But you did gamble. You gambled with the good name of the entire department. You broke ranks. You fell out of formation. You failed to join us in supporting one of our own in a moment of crisis."

He turned his back on Stone and stared out the window. "That sends a very bad message to every man in the department. It's says that when things turn to shit, we all go our own way."

He came back head-on to Stone. "And that's exactly what you did, isn't it? You went your own way, Sergeant. And since that's the way you want it, that's the way we'll play it from now on."

"I don't know quite what that means," Stone said.

"Starting next week, you're working the Harbor."

"Do you know where I live?" Stone asked.

"Yeah, you live in one those new developments up in Reseda. Five years ago, the place was a cow pasture. It should have stayed that way."

The harbor in Long Beach was 50 miles south and there was no simple way to make the trip. Stone was looking at a commute that bordered on impossible, which the chief knew full well.

The elevator down to the garage felt like a descent into a purgatory devoid of hope and light. He tried to find solace in the fact that the flipped coin was still in the air in the McGregor case. It still might come down on the side of a trial and testimony, which might trigger a departmental purge all the way up to the chief. In that case, he'd emerge as a survivor and reclaim his old job and his career as well.

Right.

He sat alone in his car in the cool, dim light for a long time before leaving.

5.

LOS ANGELES HARBOR
SEPTEMBER 26

The Marine Café smelled of dry wood, old shellac and bacon grease, all roasted by the afternoon sun that streamed in the front window and onto the lunch counter where Stone sat alone on a rotating stool. He could hear a couple's muffled screaming match coming from the upstairs floor of the wooden structure, one of many along Main Street on Terminal Island.

Outside, the cars were parked nearly bumper to bumper along both sides of the street, where a beat cop strolled the sidewalk. The twin rows of brass buttons on his uniform twinkled from the motion of his gait. A seagull, fresh off the bay, looked down on him from its perch on one of the drooping sets of telephone wires. It wasn't impressed.

Stone had no idea who the officer outside might be. The Harbor Division was ambushed by his sudden assignment and had no idea what to do with him. He just put in his hours and wandered the streets. The commute was killing him, a slow motorized death. He and Grace rarely saw each other and fought bitterly when they did.

He idly fingered an open copy of the Times, where page 7 marked the conclusion for the Canales incident. It seemed that a "specially convened" coroner's jury had ruled the death to be "excusable homicide—performed in the line of duty." In response, the grand jury dropped the case from its docket. The article itself took no issue with the ruling and the paper ran no editorial in opposition. The Mirror's coverage was pretty much the same. Canales was dead and buried in the media and courts nearly as fast as in the cemetery.

Chief Parker had won. Detective Sergeant Stone had lost. There would be no day of righteous reckoning for him. Instead, he was now a departmental pariah, cloaked in disgrace and stripped of his future.

The couple upstairs lapsed into silence. The beat cop disappeared from view. The seagull opened its wings and thrust skyward off the wire. The world moved on.

6.

"Three!"

The drunken countdown drifted over from the patio of the home next door, a ranch-style dwelling very similar to Stone's. Right now, the biggest difference was the For Sale sign posted on his front lawn, where damp blades of grass sprouted between his toes.

Fireworks snapped and popped and poked sharp holes into the cool night air. They served as a fitting backdrop for the steel guitar of Speedy West, which poured out his open front door with all the volume his record player could muster. Would it bother the neighbors? Screw the neighbors. He did a shitfaced sway to the steady rhythm that made his right arm into a pendulum weighted by his unholstered revolver.

"Two..."

He wore an unbuttoned tropical sports shirt and Bermuda shorts done in a loud plaid. Inside, the divorce papers sat on the dining room table, along with a litter of cartons containing Chinese food in various stages of decomposition. Since he'd quit the force, he'd lost track of what and when he ate and drank.

"One..."

Grace would be fine on her own. She was slim, attractive and childless, with the final innings of her youth yet to play. She would reset, retrench and rebuild.

"Happy New Year!"

Dull thuds slid in under the snaps and pops. The big artillery was now out in force. And it beckoned Stone to join the party, to become one with the celebration.

He brought his revolver up from his side. And when it reached the level of his head, he experienced a brief moment of impulse, a fleeting urge to blow his brains out.

Instead, he brought it all the way up and squeezed off a .38 caliber round into the smoky sky above Reseda, out on the far edge of the new American experience.

Where were they going? Where were they all going?

Part Two

BAKERSFIELD, CALIFORNIA
1954

7.

KERN RIVER
JUNE 13

"You ever meet Hitchcock?"

"Yep."

"I hear he hates cops. That right?"

"Wouldn't know. Never asked him."

"What about Bogart? Is he really an asshole?"

"Hard to say. He didn't talk much."

"I bet he drove a Cord or something like that."

"Maybe. Don't remember."

"Oh yeah? How could you forget something like that?"

"My feet hurt."

A year and a half gone. Stone could still feel the ache in his arches, the sweat on the back of his uniform, the blue stink of exhaust from chromed tailpipes.

"Good morning, Mr. Grant. Good evening, Miss Hepburn. Good afternoon, Miss Kelly." You had to know them all, the entire roster at Paramount Pictures as they passed through that gated arch off Melrose. The big stars were easy, you'd seen their movies. The little ones were tough – and easily offended if you got them wrong.

You smiled. You pushed the iron scrollwork open. You gave a cheerful little tug on the bill of your pseudo-cop hat. You shifted the weight on your Florsheims trying to make the hurt go away.

You longed for redemption but settled for a bar stool and a cold beer in the dolorous twilight.

"Your feet, huh?" Brainard replied. "Now with me, it's my goddam back. Too many years walkin' a beat downtown. Thank God I made sergeant before I got too crippled up." He took off his fedora and mopped his forehead. "Oh well. Doesn't matter. It's the heat that's gonna get me in the end. I'm gonna drown in my own sweat."

No comment from Stone. They turned their attention to the dead girl out in the desiccated riverbed. She lay face down in what now passed for the channel, probably no more than a couple of feet deep. Arms and legs spread like an angel, with a blue dress that billowed gently about her. The pose reminded Stone of a snorkeler paused on the water's surface with head immersed into an alternate world. Maybe those dead eyes bored through to some untold secret far below. Probably not.

"Okay, it's all yours, detective," said Brainard. He looked down at Stone's shoes. "If I was you, I'd take off my shoes and roll up my pants before I went out there. The riverbed's not as dry as it looks. Another week or two, and the farms will suck it dry, but not quite yet."

Stone got the general idea. The Kern River and all its siblings spilled down out of the Sierra Nevada and surrendered their bounty to push up potatoes, peas, beans, carrots, onions and god knows what else across the San Fernando Valley. A relentless sun beat down upon this ancient desert, and the plants fought back with water hijacked from the slopes far above. From desert to garden through hydraulic engineering on a truly massive scale. The hand of man versus the hand of God, palm to palm in an ominous stalemate.

Stone turned and watched Brainard struggle up the embankment through the scrub and dirt to the town above. Brainard was Stone's lone peer in the Bakersfield Police Department, old and tired and looking for a soft landing. They shared the workload, with the scales tipped decidedly toward Stone. Brainard could easily spend a month solid on a gas station robbery. Which left him no time to deal with the case at hand, so it went by default to Stone. His first homicide in the City of Bakersfield.

In fact, his first homicide anywhere. During his job interview, Chief Beaumont didn't seem concerned that all of Stone's plain-clothes experience was in the LA Vice Division. Stone was sure that Beaumont knew about his run-in with Chief Parker and didn't seem concerned about that, either. It had taken a few weeks to understand why he got the job: He was like an exotic animal in a third-class zoo, a big-city detective on display in a small-city police force for all to see. Even better, he looked the part, although you had to overlook the cheap suits. The divorce had drained him financially, as divorces nearly always do. And the many months of unemployment followed by twelve low-wage months as a security guard at Paramount didn't help.

"So, you ready?" Lavalle, the deputy coroner, had come up next to him. He was an old-timer, like Brainard, but still robust and almost mystically athletic. He wore a tieless white shirt, cotton slacks stuffed into rubber boots, and carried a leather bag with the tools of his trade. "You better lose that suit and shoes."

"Right." Stone peeled off his jacket and draped it on a gnarled, leafless bush. He removed his shoes and rolled his pant legs part way up his calves.

They left the river's edge and started out across the dry bed toward the body in the center. Brainard was right about the mud below the surface. Stone could feel it work its way between his toes as his feet sank half way to ankle level.

The river carved its course about thirty feet below city's ground level, and a row of gawkers had gathered on the lip of the bank opposite them. Off to the left, a second crowd lined the bridge on Highway 178. Stone felt slightly ridiculous with his rolled up pants and white legs exposed has he plodded through the mud. It presented something less than a classic cop-at-a-crime scene scenario for all these onlookers.

When they reached the water's edge, Lavalle held his hand up. "Stay here. I'll bring her over."

Stone looked upstream as Lavalle waded toward the body while donning rubber gloves. There was just enough water in the starved channel to create a lot of ambiguity about the body's origin. She didn't die here because there were no footprints, but how far had she drifted? If Lavelle could give a quick estimate of time of death, it might be helpful.

Lavelle grabbed the hem of the floating dress and dragged the body over to the water's edge in front of Stone. Without ceremony, he grasped the right upper arm and rolled corpse over, exposing the face and front side. The girl's face was locked in a death mask, eyes and mouth forever open. Lavelle did a quick, clinical scan. "No obvious signs of a struggle." Stone fought off revulsion and squatted for a closer look. No bruises, punctures or abrasions jumped out at him. But they couldn't be sure until the coroner took a closer look. "Can you tell me how long she's been in the water?"

Lavalle sloshed ashore and took a thermometer from his bag. He poked it into the water and held it there. "We've got to have the ambient temperature first. The Kern's still pretty cold, even by the time it gets down here to hell on earth. But that's not the problem."

"What problem?"

"All I'll be able to give you is a guess at how long she's been in the water. But that won't tell you how long ago she died." He lifted the thermometer up and squinted at it. "Okay, here's our ambient. Now we need to go up the old wazoo to get the body temperature." He rolled the body over so the backside was exposed and turned to Stone. "I need you to lift her dress up a little so I can do an insertion. Not much. Let's try to give her a little decency. Stone lifted the hem so Lavelle could do the procedure. He looked up at the people on the bridge in the distance. Hopefully, no one was using binoculars.

Lavelle withdrew the thermometer and took a reading. "Looks like she's been in the water for about eight to ten hours."

Stone leaned over and put his hand in the water, which was surprisingly cold compared to the sweltering heat above it. He noted just a hint of current winding around his fingers. "How far do you think she might have drifted?"

Lavelle shrugged. "That's really tough. She might have gotten hung up several times and then drifted loose. Probably somewhere up around Highway 99. You get further upstream and the channel gets really narrow with a lot of places to get snagged."

Stone stood up. "Anything else you can give me?"

"Let me take another look." Lavelle rolled the body back to its front side. "We won't really know about torso trauma until she's disrobed at the coroner's. But let's see what we can see up here." He moved in close to the head and neck. "Aha." He pointed to a spot on her throat. "Lookee there."

Stone bent over and squinted at the spot where Lavelle's gloved finger pointed. At first, he saw nothing, but then a very subtle shade of pink revealed itself. "What's that?"

"Could be an abrasion. Hard to tell after eight hours in the water – but one thing leads to another." He reached out to her face, put his thumb on one eye and peeled back the eyelid so its inner lining was exposed, all pink and raw. It sent a shudder through Stone. It felt like they were stripping off something forbidden and exposing some dark inner life.

Lavelle went in tight and nodded. "Yup." He beckoned Stone to come closer. "Take a good look at the mucous membrane. See those little red dots. They're called petechial hemorrhages. They're actually tiny blood clots."

"So what do they mean?" asked Stone.

"They mean she was strangled."

Lavelle stood up and turned to Stone. "Congratulations, detective. You've got yourself a genuine homicide. Good luck."

Stone left Lavelle and a photographer documenting the scene. He retrieved his suit coat and draped it over his arm and carried his shoes with his other hand. His mud-caked feet left him no alternative. The morning sun crept up toward that critical angle where it would begin to radiate with a vicious intensity. Searing, enveloping, unrelenting. A biblical heat burning its way into the twentieth century on its way to some future hell not yet imagined.

He could still feel how his heart sank when he first descended out of the hills above Grapevine and the San Joaquin Valley spread before him. Fifty miles wide. Hot, flat, hazy. Dirty greens and browns baked nearly colorless. Infinity to the north, distant hills to the east and west. All shrouded in a thin mist born of irrigation water floating skyward in a great cloud of evaporation. Then Bakersfield itself. Population 50,000. Oil and agriculture. A town that plunged its industrial fist into the earth and yanked out petroleum and vegetables. After a lifetime in Los Angeles, it seemed almost impossibly crude.

Stone crested the top of the drop-off to the river and headed for his car, a 1951 Chevrolet police cruiser parked on the shoulder of a gravel access road. The Bakersfield city budget didn't permit an annual turnover of public vehicles, so the cops always rolled a few years behind the times. He avoided the gravel, which was already hot enough to burn his feet. A couple of patrolmen lounged on the side of a patrol car up ahead, and gave him a silent smirk when they saw his bare feet. He glared back and they let it go. He was good at that. Other men sensed the toughness, the tightly bundled potential, and saw no profit in confrontation.

After wiping his muddy feet on the roadside grass, he threw his suit coat and shoes in the back, and drove off. The clutch and brake felt gritty from the residual sand on his bare soles, but he really didn't notice.

Who was she? There was no purse, no ID. Jane Doe, late teens or early twenties. The sooner he pegged her, the better. He'd hit the missing persons reports as soon as he reached the office.

He turned east onto 24th St, where a layer of earthen grit covered the streets and parking lots. A dust storm had passed through two days ago, a rolling wall of brown dirt scooped from the valley floor. The town had yet to shake it off.

Who was she?

He rolled past the commercial strip, all post-war and shouting for business. Motels, coffee shops, service stations. Burgers, twenty cents. Shakes, a quarter. Parking, free.

Who was she?

He turned south onto Chester Ave., the four-lane main drag that cut though the central district. Solid, sober buildings. Few higher than four stories. With awnings of striped canvas that lined the sidewalks to keep the sun at bay. Traffic was brisk. New metal surged through the town. Detroit was back to spawning cars instead of tanks.

Who was she?

He hit construction, so he went east over to the corner of 19th and K. About a half century away from Hollywood and Vine. Sears, Kress and Woolworth instead of Tiffany's, Saks and Barneys.

Who was she?

He'd better find out fast. They'd all be watching. They'd all want to see if the big-city cop stumbled his first time out.

He turned onto Truxtun and pulled into a Flying A service station. He had to do something about his feet before he got to the office. A water hose sprouted from the service island, so he opened the door, swung his feet out and rinsed them off. A uniformed attendant came over Blue shirt, bow tie, and a garrison cap. Stone waved him off. The attendant gave a cautious nod and walked away.

Stone's dignity returned along with his shoes going on. He continued down Truxtun and pulled into the secured lot behind the police station. Waves of heat boiled off the pavement as he walked to the building and took the stairs to the second story. He shared an office with a dozen other cops, each with their own scuffed metal desk, telephone and wire filing basket. Some desks held family pictures, others hunting and fishing scenes. Color by Kodak.

A secretary sat near the entrance. Mrs. Crenshaw, a pinched and wiry woman in her fifties. She clacked away at a typewriter, whose platen held a report form plus carbon copy. No mistakes allowed. She glanced up at him in sour acknowledgement.

"Any messages?" he asked.

"Not that I know of." Mrs. Crenshaw always hedged her bet. "The chief wants to see you."

"When?" Stone asked.

"Right now," she said, as if it were somehow obvious.

Stone turned around and walked down the hall to Chief Beaumont's office, where the door was open. He peeked in. The chief sat behind a substantial wooden desk. To his right, a pair of crossed flags depicted the United States and California. A large map of Bakersfield covered the wall behind him. Stone knocked. The chief looked up from a sheaf of papers.

"Stone. Come in. Have a seat." Beaumont wore a freshly pressed uniform over a solid frame. He had a Rushmore face with a blockish jaw and eagle's nose. Its effect was tempered by sad blue eyes. Not all was right in the chief's inner world, the one that most men learned to carry in solitude.

"You wanted to see me?" Stone asked.

"You just got back from down on the river?"

"Yessir."

"What do you make of it?"

"Can't really say. It's probably a safe bet that it's a homicide. So far that's all we've got. Next step is to get an ID."

"This your first murder case?"

"Yessir."

"That's what I thought. You were vice in LA. Queers and pimps instead of shooters and stabbers." Beaumont got up and went to the window. "I wouldn't worry about it. Just keep your head screwed on straight. It'll all work out."

"I'm counting on it," Stone said.

"They're all going to be watching you. You know that, don't you?"

"Yeah, I suppose I do."

"You're the big city cop. The big star up from LA. Some of them would love to see you fuck up. And you know why?"

"Why?"

"Because it would make certain little people feel like they're big people. I'm not one of them. I'd love to see you pull this off."

"Well, that's my plan," Stone replied.

The chief managed a hint of a smile. "Good. Keep me informed. That's all."

"Yessir."

Stone left the chief and went back to the main office, where he started down the row of desks. A sergeant named Bagley looked up at him, a thick man with a drooping gray mustache. "You just might be a really lucky son of a bitch."

"How's that?"

"Falworth's sick, so they put me on missing persons." He picked up the topmost sheet in his wire basket. "This came in earlier this morning." He handed it to Stone. "A Lorilee Winters. Lives up in Oildale. Seems her daughter didn't come home last night."

Stone took the sheet. "Thanks. I'll check it out."

Bagley returned to his papers. "You do that." He was a rum-soaked fifty and not too happy about it.

Stone oscillated between relief and anxiety by the time he slid behind his desk. If the report IDed the girl, it would save him considerable effort and overcome the inertia that often stalled investigations before they could gather momentum. Good. But he was about to get on the phone with a woman immersed in the deepest of dread, and suggest that her worst fears just might be realized. Bad.

He phoned the number. A woman answered after just a single ring. "Hello?" Her voice was dry and weathered, laced with an Okie twang.

"Mrs. Winters?"

"Yes."

"I'm Sergeant Stone with the Bakersfield Police Department. I'm calling about your missing person's report. I'd like to ask you a couple of questions. It says here that your daughter is eighteen, about five foot five, slim with blond hair."

"Well it's not really blond. She dyed it that way. Her girlfriend helped her."

"I see. And it says that the last time you saw her was last evening right around dark. Is that correct?"

"I do believe that's correct."

"Did she tell you where she was going?"

"We fought about that all the time." Stone could hear the woman start to unravel. "She said it was none of my business."

She doesn't know, Stone realized. She doesn't know about the girl in the river. And why would she? The paper here was a morning edition, and radio wouldn't round up the local news until noon.

"But she's always here when I get up," Mrs. Winters said. "That's usually when we start fightin'. She just don't get it. She just don't get none of it."

"I know," Stone sympathized. "People that age can be difficult. Can you tell me what she was wearing when she left?"

"She had that blue cotton dress on, the one I got her last summer."

The dress. The blue dress. Stone could still picture it billowing around the body out there in the channel. He had to level with her.

"Mrs. Winters, I'm sorry to have to tell you this, but we recovered a body out of the Kern River this morning and it pretty much fits the description you've given us of your daughter."

"Oh Lord! Oh Lordie!" The woman collapsed into fitful sobs.

Stone felt slightly sick. It was awful. You didn't have to do this kind of thing when you worked in Vice in the big city. You dealt with pimps and weasels. You didn't have to punch a gaping wound into an innocent human being. He'd come all the way to Bakersfield to become the shredder of souls.

"I'm very sorry, Mrs. Winters. I really am. But I'm going to need your help. Someone needs to identify the body. Is there anyone else besides you who can do it?"

"Maybe it's not her, right? You can't be sure, right?" Her voice floated atop a thin bubble of hope.

"No, we can't be sure. And that's why we need your help."

"I've gotta know. I just gotta know."

"I understand. You need to get this behind you. I'm going to come over and pick you up. We'll visit the county coroner and get this over with as quickly as possible. Is anyone there with you?"

Small, spasmodic sobs filled the earpiece.

"Mrs. Winters?"

"No sir. There's just me and her. We're all that's left."

Stone had no response. He knew that the tragedy on the other end of the line probably spanned decades and sent dark ripples across the inner landscapes of many lives. It would overwhelm him if he tried to embrace it. "I'll get there as quickly as I can," he said. It was the best he could do.

· · ·

He drove north on Chester Avenue, a stretch of Highway 99 that sliced through town from north to south. A squat, rectangular building on the left with two sets of double doors caught his eye. The Blackboard Cafe. He'd heard of it but never seen it. The Blackboard was the one place in Bakersfield that hadn't escaped the attention of Los Angeles.

Country music players often spoke of this wild honky-tonk out on the edge of civilization where the music was taking a strange new twist, all loud and raw. Stone made a note to return and take it in. Western music was the last thread of continuity in his rudely shuffled life.

He drove on and crossed a bridge over the Kern River that carried him out past the northern city limits.

Welcome to Oildale. Unincorporated and unforgiving. Home to the Ku Klux Klan and various spinoffs. Full of subsistence housing and a population clinging to the lowest rung on the economic ladder. Second- and third-generation Okies. Spawn of the great Dust Bowl migration in the thirties. Once confined to field labor, but now working the barren sprawl of the Kern Oil Field just to the north. All sweat and muscle and rage. Addicted to rowdy honky-tonks, cheap booze and wild women – or so said the lyrics.

In fact, it reminded Stone of South Park, where he grew up in southern Los Angeles. Only sparser and drier and flatter. In South Park, he'd watched as Southern California gradually reshaped the Okies in its own image. Twenty years after the great exodus, they drove Fords, mowed their lawns and went bowling every Thursday.

At least they did in Los Angeles, but not out here in this land-locked oven. The blue of the Pacific was a distant dream, and the dust devils out on valley floor churned up memories of failed farms, devastated crops and crushed hopes. The current residents of Oildale were better off than their parents, but still rode in the slipstream of the post-war surge. It turned out that crude oil and raw onions weren't the path to contemporary salvation.

Stone rolled along past little markets, gas stations, cafes, and dime stores, all a single story high and mostly constructed of wood. A few trees made a futile thrust into the haze, and the streets turned to dirt as soon as you pulled off the main road. Old pre-war

Packards, Oldsmobiles, Fords and Chevys slowly baked their way toward terminal oxidation in their curbside parking spots.

People on the sidewalks stared at him as he passed. Old men in suspenders and cocked fedoras. Women in sleeveless cotton dresses and flat shoes. Younger men with oiled hair and cheap sport shirts cut with oversized collars. Some appeared curious, most seemed sullen. A cop car up here only meant trouble.

He turned left on Belle Ave. and headed west. One- and two-room houses lined the street behind brown lawns and automotive relics. Stunted trees offered scant shade to those within. He found the address a few blocks later, next to a park full of dilapidated house trailers. It was small, even by local standards, and fronted by a lawn reduced to straw stubble. A failed coat of chipped paint covered the siding. Since there was no driveway, he parked in front.

He saw the curtain part slightly as he approached the front door, and it opened before he could knock.

"Mrs. Winters, I'm Detective Stone, and I'm sorry we have to meet under these circumstances."

"Let's go." She shouldered her purse and moved past him toward the car. Stone understood. It was all she could do just to stay collected. He judged her to be an impoverished forty, whip-thin with a sprinkle of gray in her straight brown hair. She wore a dress flared at mid-calf and cinched tight on her spare waist.

He followed close behind and opened the door for her. A fat woman with a baby in arms watched them from her porch chair across the street. An oversize mutt sized up Stone from behind a chain link fence as he climbed into the car. The animal growled in a deep baritone.

Mrs. Winters kept her silence as they went back down to Chester and turned south. When they crossed back into Bakersfield and reached Highway 178, Stone knew it was time to prep her for what was coming up.

"We just need you to confirm or deny that it's your daughter. Nothing else. No paperwork. They'll wheel the body out on a gurney and just expose the face. You won't see any sign of injury. I was there when they recovered her, so I've already had a look."

"I gotta know," Mrs. Winters said.

"Of course you do."

East Bakersfield. The Kern County Coroner. Stone showed Mrs. Winters into the morgue section on the first floor. They already had the body out on a gurney. The identification was brutal and simple. An attendant pulled the cover off the face. Mrs. Winters took one look and abruptly yanked her head around in avoidance. Her mouth curled in tears but then settled in a prolonged grimace. "So that's her?" Stone asked. He had to hear it out loud.

Mrs. Winters gave the faintest of nods. "That's her."

"Okay, we're done then," Stone said.

"I ain't done," Mrs. Stone murmured. "I ain't ever gonna be done."

· · ·

She began to loosen up as they headed back north into Oildale. Stone guessed that the ID process gave her some kind of closure, however brief. She talked of her young marriage, her no-good husband, her life with Charlene. She mentioned that her sister in Kansas was a lesbian, and she seemed quite proud of it. It somehow lifted her family out of total anonymity and gave them a brand of sorts.

By the time they reached her house, Stone felt she was comfortable enough to interview. "Would you mind if I came in and asked you a few questions?"

Mrs. Winters gave a fatalistic shrug. "Sure. Why not?"

· · ·

Stone declined an offer for something to drink, and they sat in the tiny living room. A caged fan rotated and swept the room with a beam of agitated air. A small table held family pictures in plain metal frames: milestones on a modest and desperate journey.

"Let's start with last night. Can you tell me what time she left here?"

"Somewhere 'round eight. Still light out, but not much."

"And she didn't say where she was going?"

"She never said where she was going. Not no more."

"Is there anybody else who might know? Some of her friends, maybe?"

"Don't think so. Charlene didn't think much of the girls around here. She only had one real good friend. Marla Eaton. But she ain't around no more. Moved up to Fresno."

Stone chose his next words carefully. "Given the circumstances, I think we have to consider the possibility of foul play." He considered mentioning the possible strangulation, but thought the better of it. "Can you think of anyone who might've wanted to harm your daughter?"

"Well hell yeah. Bobby Simmons."

"Bobby Simmons," Stone repeated. "Who's that?" The name seemed familiar.

Mrs. Winters paused and reached for a pack of Camels. She lit one and exhaled a conical cloud of white laced with blue. "A no-good, rotten son of a bitch. That's who he is."

"So what makes him rotten?"

"He's a musician. A guitar player. He's got a whole string of women lined up. He sweet-talked Charlene, and she just couldn't get enough of it."

Stone connected the name. Simmons played in the house band at Trout's, a honky-tonk bar right here in Oildale. Didn't sing, just played, but played incredibly well. Even Joe Maphis said so, and Joe was the premier guitar player on country television in Los Angeles.

"Well, being a sweet talker and being a killer are two different things," Stone said.

"True enough. But when a man gets tossed over for another man, there ain't no tellin', now is there?"

"So what happened? Did she break it off?"

Mrs. Winters took a deep drag on her Camel. The tip went nova and glowed a brilliant orange. "She busted up with him about a month ago. In his car. Right out front. With a whole lotta screamin' and cryin'. I had the window open. I could hear the whole damn business. He lit outta here like a bat outta hell. She come runnin' in and went straight to her room. Came out a few minutes later, just like nothin' had never happened. Soon as I saw her face, I knew she was the one that pulled plug."

"So you think that he was in a jealous rage?"

"Could be wrong, but sure looked it to me. She had plans, you know. Most girls around here ain't got no plans at all, but Charlene sure did. She was doin' a waitress job out at the country club and getting ready for beauty school in the fall. Told me she was gonna open her own shop. I don't think old Bobby liked any of that. He thought the only real plan was his god almighty self."

"Was she seeing anybody else?"

"Kinda seemed like it"

"How so?"

Mrs. Winters stubbed the cigarette in a beanbag ashtray. Lipstick crowned the top end in a pink dawn. "She was out till all hours at least a couple of times a week. I'd ask her what was goin' on, but she just got mad, so I quit."

"Was there anything else? Anything unusual about what she was doing?"

"Don't think so."

"Would you mind if I took a quick look in her room?"

Mrs. Winters shrugged in a shrunken and bitter kind of way. "Go ahead. Don't make no difference now." She pointed toward the door.

"Thanks." Stone got up, opened the door and went in.

A narrow bed on an iron frame occupied the left wall. A shallow closet and chest of drawers took up the right. Several stuffed animals sat atop the dresser, the kind you won on the midway. A plain wooden table with a plastic mirror stood in back, and served as a vanity. Perfume and shampoo bottles lined its top, along with little piles of costume jewelry, makeup and a small radio done in pink plastic. A single photo was tacked to the wall behind. Bobby Simmons in glossy black and white. He held an electric guitar and wore a decorous cowboy shirt with a string bow tie.

Stone went to the dresser, opened each drawer, lifted the contents and checked the bottom, the obvious place of concealment. Nothing of interest.

He turned to the table top. The radio's tuner dial pointed to a big country station up north. He ran his finger over the perfume bottles and stopped at the last one. It was smaller, but very stylishly designed and packaged. He held it gingerly by the neck to preserve any prints and read the label: 'Worth' in an artful scrawl across the center, with 'Dans La Nuit' in simple block letters along the bottom. He pulled a notebook from his breast pocket and wrote it down.

He moved on to the makeup articles and a comb/brush set of tortoise shell plastic. Nothing of note. Next, the costume jewelry. A skein of beaded necklaces, charm bracelets and the like. He extended his index finger and idly pushed the pile across the wooden surface.

Flap! Something fell on the floor.

He knelt down and spotted a pack of matches. He picked it up carefully by the sides to save any prints on the cover. He gingerly opened it to expose a tight little formation of matches, their red tips of phosphor ready for action. All accounted for. He tucked the cover back in under the striker surface and read the bright yellow label: 'The Rancho Vista Motel' in green caps on the front, and a crude location map on the back.

He'd driven by the Rancho Vista Motel, but never stopped. It was on Highway 99 going north out of town, with a big LETS EAT sign of red neon that bellowed out into the motorized night.

Stone returned to the living room, where Mrs. Winters stared out the window through eyes steeped in sorrow. The next of wave of grief was breaking over her.

"Did your daughter smoke?" he asked.

"Sure as hell did, but not around here. I wouldn't stand for it. Not at her age."

Stone remained standing. "I think that's about it for now. As soon as we know more, I'll be in touch."

Mrs. Winter's stare remained fixed out the window, out to some impossible distance. "You do that."

"Goodbye now." Stone walked out into the gathering heat. It cast a slight film of yellow over the neighborhood. The dog across the street now curled in the shade on a porch. It no longer growled. It only panted. Stone opened his car, which had all the windows rolled up. You didn't leave them open in a place like this. A brutal blast of broiled air rolled out. He walked around and cranked down each window to let in some ventilation.

He turned on the police radio and stretched the coiled microphone cord so he could stand outside while he made a call. Dispatch put him through to records, where he asked for a quick rundown on Bobby Simmons. He took off his fedora and mopped his brow with his shirtsleeve. Maybe the old cop Brainard was right. Maybe the heat took you down in the end.

The records clerk came back on with what they had on Simmons. A couple of arrests for assault, with the charges dismissed, and a drunk driving conviction that put him on a year's probation. Stone asked for his current address and got it. Not too far away. North on Oildale Drive then left on Lincoln.

Simmons' place turned out to be a notch lower than Mrs. Winters' in terms of curb appeal. Oil spots dotted a front yard composed of packed dirt and devoid of grass. A rotting couch rested on the concrete porch, and with a rusted barbeque below the front window. A '40 Ford pickup pointed toward the street, its right front tire completely flat.

Stone knocked and waited. The porch took him out of the sun, but not out the heat. The door opened about a foot, revealing a wiry man about 25 in a sweaty tank top. "Yeah?"

Stone pulled out his badge. "Sergeant Stone. Bakersfield Police. I'm looking for Bobby Simmons."

Stone caught the flash of contempt as the man scratched his receding hairline. "Yeah, well he ain't here now."

"You know when he might be back?"

The man ignored Stone and focused on the doormat. "Hard to say."

"Where's he work?"

"Chevron."

"Chevron where?"

"Oil fields."

Stone had an inspiration. "Is he playing tonight?"

"Yeah maybe. I think he said somethin' bout The Blackboard."

"You tell him I'm a fan, okay? He's one of hell of a guitar picker."

The man looked up at Stone. "That what this is all about?"

"Pretty much." Stone smiled and tipped his hat. "You have a nice day."

"They start about nine," the man volunteered.

"Thanks."

• • •

Stone drove north out of town, then west on the China Grade Loop. Soon, he'd left behind the last traces of green and entered a scorched and barren land of rolling hills covered with oil pumps. Like a great swarm of ants, the machines spread over the ground all the way to the horizon. Insects of black, bobbing steel sucking the prehistoric life out of the earth below.

He came across a service road into Chevron, and drove north. Oncoming trucks kicked up dense dust plumes that forced him to roll up the windows and sweat. Pumps lined both sides of the road, and Stone could see how their rocker arms and counterweights pulled on cables attached to piping than ran underground. For some reason, they struck him as very patient and deliberate in their action. They were playing the long game when it came to pulling out the ancient liquid far beneath them.

He reached a tin-roofed building that served as an office. Three roustabouts in greasy denim and hardhats stared at him as he got out and approached.

"'Afternoon," he said.

"Yup," the middle one responded. It seemed that cops were no more welcome here than down in Oildale.

"I'm looking for a guy named Bobby Simmons. You know him?"

"Yup."

"Can you tell me where I might find him?"

"Up there." The middle one pitched his thumb over his shoulder, where the pumps marched up the dirt slope and over the top.

"Up there where?"

The man shrugged. "Workin' on a pump."

Stone kept his cool. "Well thanks for your time." He turned to leave.

"Always a pleasure," one of the others said in a burst of sophomoric satire.

Stone heard them snicker as he headed back to the car.

· · ·

The Wakefield represented the new post-war modality in apartment construction. It resembled a highway motel complex more than a traditional multi-family dwelling. Its narrow parking lot faced a string of one-story duplexes, each with two vented metal boxes on the roof: swamp coolers. They leveraged the blazing outdoor temperature to evaporate water and lower the temperature within. The physics of it was lost on Stone, who was simply thankful to gain some marginal relief as he sat in his unit, the one closest to the street.

He looked out through the living room window at his car, the same Chevy he'd had for five years now. It still had some life in it, which was a good thing, considering the pay cut he took after his old job at the LAPD. By comparison, justice in Bakersfield was a bargain basement proposition.

He hummed under his breath as he did the dishes and placed them in the slotted rack of wire dipped in pink rubber. A country tune, a tale of heartbreak, divorce, and bad luck without end. A story uncomfortably close to Stone's current situation.

The hell with it. He changed into some cotton slacks and donned a sport shirt.

He would mix business and pleasure. He would attempt to intercept Bobby Simmons at his gig tonight.

• • •

Dancing Six Nites A Week.

So said the lettering on the south wall of the Blackboard, which sat squat and rectangular off Chester Avenue just north of the city limits. Stone pulled his Chevy into its parking lot of packed dirt. The music was just starting but the lot was already two thirds full. The setting sun of early summer triggered a hot wind that stirred the trees in the rear.

Stone climbed out, locked the door, and looked toward the building's north wall. He knew immediately that the Blackboard was something very new and different, even if it appeared to be just another lowdown bar.

You could hear the music all the way out here in the parking lot. Even with all the doors closed, it rolled out and saturated the evening air.

He came around to the front, where two big windows of block glass cast the interior into a rippled fog. Neon beer signs occupied the center of each window, and the double doors between them sported glass portholes that afforded just a peek inside.

A Kern County sheriff's deputy stood in uniform at the entrance. Stone knew the deal. The guy was checking ID as a second job. He gave Stone a sober nod of assent as he passed. Stone was obviously not a minor.

He opened the door into a churning cloud of heat, smoke and noise. The band blasted out from a stage at the rear, and a long bar ran down the right wall. Scuffed tables and chairs surrounded a big dance floor, which was nearly full. The couples moved to the pulse of a classic country shuffle, with the snare down hard on the backbeat.

Stone moved to the bar, climbed onto a stool, and turned to face the band. The music simply refused to be ignored. In LA, country bands were mostly acoustic, with a standup bass, fiddle, guitar and drums. In a noisy bar, they nearly faded into the background behind the shouting, laughing, and hooting. Not here. The bass boomed, the guitar soared and the pedal steel moaned in a stormy crossfire behind the singer. They rode right up over the top of every other sound source in the room. Clinking bottles, guffaws, conversations, thumps and snorts were all subordinated to this musical imperative.

It was electric, both figuratively and literally.

The traditional doghouse bass and fat-bodied guitar were gone, replaced by instruments that looked they'd been cut out on a jigsaw. Their sound sprang from behind the grill cloth of amplifiers resembling suitcases with a tweed covering.

Stone turned his attention to the players themselves. In LA, you saw cowboy hats, rodeo suits and custom shirts. Not here. The band members wore plain shirts with rolled up sleeves against the ever-present heat.

The music stopped, and band leader took to the microphone for the introductions. He was Bill Woods and these were the Orange Blossom Playboys. Don Markham on sax, Johnny

Cuviello on drums, Larry Williams on piano, Truman Feathers sitting in on Fender bass, and sure enough, Bobby Simmons on guitar, sitting in for someone named Buck Owens.

"Now we're gonna play one more where we let Bobby loose, so look out," Woods declared.

He gave a quick count and they launched into an up-tempo boogie, the blues on steroids. Woods raised his fiddle close to the microphone and ripped out the lead line. That done, Bobby tore into his solo with long, utterly fluid lines. His fingers skittered over his guitar's maple fingerboard so fast that it seemed like they hardly moved at all. People at the tables quit talking and gawked. Many of the dancers stopped and stared in wonderment. He finished to a vigorous round of applause. Woods immediately steered the band into a slow waltz, a ballad about heartbreak and bad luck. Like all good showmen, he knew the value of contrast.

The noise level dropped substantially and Stone came to his senses. He turned and ordered a glass of draft beer. As he grasped the cold jacket of condensation, he pondered how to approach Bobby. It would have been a lot easier if the guy was just some low-life vermin. But Bobby was also a genius-level guitar player, which Stone greatly admired. A female voice next to him interrupted his contemplation.

"Okay buddy, we're all through here. I've had just about enough. Got it?"

He turned to a young woman on the next stool over. She was facing away from Stone, and toward a man who had crowded in close to her, his elbow leaning on the bar. He wore a sport shirt with the short sleeves rolled up to accentuate his tanned biceps. His black, wavy hair shone from a generous coat of Brylcreem. He clearly fancied himself a ladies' man. "Well hell, I think we're just gettin' started," he informed her in a tenor drawl.

The woman turned away from him and toward the bar. She reached for a cigarette she had going in an amber-colored glass ashtray.

The man grinned contemptuously and moved in even closer, inches from her ear.

She calmly turned and blew smoke in his face, a long steady cloud of it.

The grin collapsed into a snarl. He came up off the bar and cocked his right arm into a punching position.

"I think that's enough," Stone said.

The man shifted his eyes of dark almond onto Stone. He kept his arm half-cocked. The girl took a sip of her drink and ignored both of them.

"I don't think it's any of your goddam business," the man growled.

Stone had his badge in his pocket and considered playing the cop card. Then he noticed the man lurch slightly. No card necessary. Even though the guy topped him by four inches, he'd be a fraction of a second late in a fight. For Stone, that was all that was necessary. His cop career had left him well schooled in the art of personal violence.

"You don't know me and I don't know you," Stone said in a very composed tone. "And if you're smart, you're going to keep it that way."

Something about his declaration caught the girl's attention. She turned and gave him an appreciative smile.

The man swayed in drunken rumination. He'd leveraged his size and nasty attitude and it hadn't worked. His stare lost its edge and turned inward, seeking the next move. He came up empty.

"Buddy, I'll be seein' you around," he told Stone. "Yes, I will."

He pushed off the bar with a vicious shove and disappeared into the crowd.

"Sorry about that," Stone said to the girl.

"No need. He's the sorry one." The girl was blond and obviously well-kept, with stylish hair and makeup. Nothing you'd find at the five and dime in Oildale.

Stone held out his hand. "Stone. James Stone. Some people call me Jimmy."

The girl grasped his hand lightly and let go. "I like James. Let's go with James. I'm Fatalia."

"You're what?"

"Fatalia."

"What kind of name is that?"

"You'd have to ask my mother. My mother knows everything."

"She does?"

Stone definitely wanted to hear more, but they were interrupted by the approach of yet another man. Young, trim and well barbered, with a solid air about him. Like Fatalia, his clothes put him several levels above the Blackboard.

"Mr. Stone, I'd like you to meet Captain Gary Piland of the United States Air Force," she said.

"Good to meet you," Piland said as they shook hands. He moved in and put his arm around Fatalia's waist. A possessive gesture that defined the playing ground. Stone understood and didn't care. He was here in pursuit of hot music, not hot women.

"Mr. Stone needed to intervene on my behalf," Fatalia commented. "I had a gentleman caller who turned out to be not much of a gentleman at all."

Piland's sharp blue eyes wrinkled into a grin. "Damn! A guy can't even take a leak around here without some kinda trouble."

Stone did a quick sort. What kind of man would bring such an attractive date into a place like this? It was like a lit cigarette next to gasoline. Answer: Someone who lived on the edge, who not only took risks, but embraced them more than life itself.

"You a flyer?" Stone asked.

Piland nodded. "Yep. Over at Edwards."

Edwards Air Force Base. It sprawled across a broad expanse of desert eighty miles to the southeast. Fast planes, ice-blue sky, white caliche. A place of engineering alchemy, where they forged brains, balls, exotic metals and high-test fuel into machines dedicated to punching gaping holes in the stratosphere. It also served as a sudden tomb for those who went too high, too fast, too slow or were just plain out of luck.

"You got a fast bike, it's less an hour from here," Piland added.

"And you got a fast bike, right?"

"Harley Sportster. Goes like the wind."

The ballad concluded up on the stage and Woods took to the microphone. "Thank y'all. We're gonna take a little break and be back in fifteen."

Stone put down forty cents on the bar for his beer and stood up. "If you'll excuse me, I've got to take care of some business. Nice to meet you."

"Same to you," Piland said.

Stone managed to intercept Bobby Simmons, just as he climbed off the stage.

"Bobby?"

"Yeah?"

"Sergeant Stone of the Bakersfield Police. Is there somewhere we can talk?"

Simmons sighed. He clearly knew this was coming. "Yeah. Follow me."

They went through a door that took them into the rear of building. A dozen or so men hunched over two felt-covered poker tables in a thick cloud of tobacco smoke. Simmons led them to a small kitchen area off to the side. He turned to face Stone in a defiant stance.

"So let me guess. You're here about Charlene."

"You're a hell of guitar player, Bobby. I spent years in LA and you're as good as anyone I've ever seen."

The compliment blindsided Simmons and knocked him off balance, just as Stone knew it would. He pressed on before the kid had a chance to recover. "I talked to Charlene Winter's mom and she said you two had a big blowout a couple of weeks back. That true?"

"Yeah, I guess we did."

"Where were you when it happened?"

"In my car out in front of her place."

"Did you see her any time after that?"

"No sir, I did not. Nor did I want to."

"How come?"

"Because she was sneakin' around with somebody else."

"How'd you know that?"

"Because she told me. She was really pissed and she wanted to get in a good lick and she knew just how to do it. Damn! I didn't see it comin'."

"Do you have any idea at all who it might've been?"

"No sir. Because if I did, I would have run 'em down and stomped the shit out of 'em."

"Instead of her?"

Bobby shut up. His lips moved slightly. He was parsing Stone's question somewhere inside his head. He didn't like what he came up with. "No sir, I never hit her. I never hit any of 'em. That just ain't my style. I might be a liar and I might be a cheater, but I ain't no hitter. Ask around."

"I'll do that. Give me some names." Stone pulled a small notebook and pencil out of his pocket.

Simmons sighed and rattled off the names of a half dozen women. Stone closed the notebook. "Alright then, I saved the best for last. Where were you last night?"

"I was with Pork Chop."

"And just who is Pork Chop?"

"He's my bikin' buddy. Came down from Fresno. His old lady kicked him out."

"Bikes, huh? What kind of bikes?"

"That would be motorcycles. He's got a Vincent Black Night and I got a BSA Road Rocket. They're damn near dead even in a race," Bobby volunteered. "But we wouldn't be doin' that with you around."

"I'm sure you wouldn't. Has Pork Chop got a real name?"

"Yeah. Harper Lewis."

Stone opened his notebook again. "And what were you and Mr. Lewis up to last night?"

Bobby shrugged. "Just the usual. We rode around and hit a bunch of bars. Rainbow Gardens, Clover Club, Barrel House, Trout's. They're all good for a free beer 'cause I sit in a lot."

"Is Pork Chop still in town?"

"Yep."

"And where might I find him?"

"There's a bike shop out east on Niles Street. He's buddies with the owner and stays up on the second floor. He's gotta go downstairs to take a leak, but at least he's got a mattress to crash on."

"This place got a name?"

"Red Flag Repair."

Stone pocketed the notebook. "I just might want to talk to you again, so why don't you stick around town?"

Bobby shrugged. "Sure. I mean, where would I go? I always been here."

This final reply would have struck Stone as odd when he first arrived in Bakersfield, but no longer. Unless you were at the top of the heap, the place formed something close to a perfect seal. You went into the oven, baked until well done, and then came out just in time to expire.

Stone left Bobby in the back and returned to the bar. Capt. Piland was regaling Fatalia with a tale of stark terror on high. He stopped just long enough to give Stone a friendly nod and continued. "So I'm at forty-five thousand feet, and the controls are jammed. I'm going in a tight little circle. You don't want to bail out from up here. There's too much can go wrong. When it happens, they find guys out on the desert, just sitting by their chute. They look fine, but they're not fine. Zombies. Brain dead. They lost their oxygen."

Fatalia gave Stone a little sideways glance and returned her attention to Piland. He gave the couple a polite wave and headed for the door. Stone smiled to himself. He had to wonder how many women had heard that story.

Outside, he stopped to chat with the deputy, one cop to another. The guy turned out to be surprisingly articulate, and a consummate student of the Blackboard scene. Yeah, Bobby Simmons, he knew all about Bobby Simmons. The guy played his ass off but was a real prima donna. Didn't get along well the other players. Never had a full-time gig because nobody would put up with all his bullshit.

The talk turned to the body in the river, Charlene Winters. Stone told the deputy that he was the detective on the case, but didn't bring up the possible connection to Bobby Simmons. The deputy worked for Kern County, whose jurisdiction ended at the Kern River. He said the boys at the office were betting that it was some Oildale punk did it. That might pull the investigation back over the river and into their territory. He said that, for the cops, murders around here were like dog biscuits: They didn't come along very often, so you jumped and snapped if you could get one.

Stone doubted if that would bring any consolation to Charlene's mother. He said goodnight and turned the corner into the parking lot.

He walked toward the rear, where the light tapered off and the trees loomed. A hot breeze teased their leaves into a busy little rustle.

He was just about to unlock his car when he heard the voice behind him.

"Well what d'ya know. Lookee who we got here."

He immediately recognized the source. The tall guy who tried to corner Fatalia.

Stone turned to face him. He wasn't alone. Two other men flanked him. All leaned on the dented quarter panel of an old pickup about five yards away. The man in question came off the truck, his arms and legs slightly spread. The pose accentuated his height and size.

Stone had to make an immediate decision. He chose to go on the verbal offensive before the guy got off another shot. "So who are your pals? Santa's little helpers?"

"Ain't nothin' gonna help you, Buddy. Not no more." He started toward Stone. He came at a smooth and measured pace. He'd sobered up considerably.

Once again, Stone considered pulling out his badge. Once again, he decided not to. He liked the music here and wanted to come back for more. He didn't want the word out that he was a cop.

Besides, the big guy had already made his first and probably final mistake. He'd judged Stone on the basis of size, and little else. The man had four inches and maybe thirty pounds on him, and figured that this advantage trumped all others that might favor the little guy. Wrong. What he didn't know was that Stone was incredibly fast. Always had been. In high school, he was renowned for flipping a penny and catching it with his other hand before you could even see it in the air.

He also didn't know that Stone was a cop, who had long ago mastered the vocabulary of personal violence. But he was about to find out.

The man squared off a couple of feet from him. In the rear, Stone saw the two companions start slowly forward. He removed them from the current equation. One thing at a time.

"It's payback time, little buddy," the man said. "You scored one in there, now I'm gonna score one out here."

That said, he threw a vicious roundhouse right.

Stone always suspected that the world somehow appeared slower to him than to other people. Not a lot, but just enough to make a critical difference in situations like this. He ducked under the punch, which he saw as a lazy overhead arc. At the same time, he stepped forward and delivered a thunderous right to the man's midsection. He knew that in a bar brawl, nobody expects a body punch. He also knew that it's one thing to absorb a boxing glove to the abdomen, like you saw on TV, and quite another to take the impact of a hard, balled fist. The muscles caved in all the way to man's intestines. His eyes budged, his cheeks puffed, his mouth flew open.

Just for good measure, Stone repeated the same punch with his left hand.

He stepped back as the man crumbled and continued on down until he rested on his knees and elbows with his head tucked down out of sight. An almost religious pose of private agony.

Now, the other two. It was going to be problematic. One had come up with a tire iron, the other, a switchblade. They spread out as they neared him, so he couldn't engage both at the same time.

Stone was still calculating whom to engage first when he heard the unmistakable sound an automatic pistol made as it chambered a fresh round. The sibilant hiss of metal on metal. Stone and the two men all turned in the direction of the sound.

Capt. Gary Piland of the United States Air Force stood with pistol in hand and pointed skyward. "Gentlemen, what we have here is a military-issue weapon, a Colt .45 Automatic Pistol. It is part of the survival gear we take into combat to deal with unforeseen circumstances, such as crashing or bailing out behind enemy lines. As such, we are thoroughly trained in its use and proficient at distances up to thirty yards, which is somewhat greater than the dimensions of this parking lot. For this reason, I suggest that you drop your weapons, scoop up your fallen comrade and disperse. Immediately.

The men complied, silently and sullenly. They managed to get their leader part way to his feet, one holding each arm. He staggered forward in a heavy crouch and howled in torment when they tried to get him into the cab. Instead, they took him around to the rear and loaded him onto the bed. That done, they drove off down Chester in a defiant squeal of rubber.

Stone turned to Piland as the truck drove into the distance. "I thank you sir."

Piland removed the clip from the pistol, ejected the chambered round and put the weapon in his pocket. "Let me guess: That was the guy who closed in on Fatalia."

"That was him."

"Then everything's evened up. By the way, you're one fast son of a bitch. Every had your reflexes tested?"

"Not that I know of."

"You could've been a flyer."

"Yeah, maybe. But that's not the way it worked out."

Fatalia came walking out of the shadows from the far side of the parking lot. "Gary, I'm getting very bored. I don't respond well to waiting in the car, even when they're playing Sinatra. What's going on here?"

"Your boyfriend was trying to recruit me into the Air Force," Stone said. "Didn't work."

"We're going up the road to Trout's," Piland said. "Care to join us?"

"Who's playing?" Stone asked.

"That would be Tex Butler and Fuzzy Owen," Fatalia said.

"Don't know them," Stone replied.

"Well maybe you should," Fatalia responded.

"Some other time," Stone said. "I got a big day at work tomorrow, so I think I'm going to call it a night."

"Where do you work?" Piland asked.

"I'm with the Bakersfield Police Department."

"Really? Well that explains quite a bit," Piland said. An impish grin caught up with him. "You better watch for concealed weapons around here. I hear it's a real problem."

"I'll do my best," Stone promised.

Fatalia grasped Piland's arm and started to turn him. "Goodnight, officer."

"Good night."

8.

JUNE 14

CENTRAL BAKERSFIELD

"She's a dyke," Bagley argued. "I don't care how good lookin' she is. She's gotta be a dyke."

"Well maybe," Brainard said. "But I wouldn't bet all my money on it." He sat on the edge of his desk, where he could catch the breeze from a table fan.

Bagley took a deep breath, feigning patience with his fellow cop. "Look at it this way. She grows up in LA – the queer capital of the world. She goes all the way through medical school – with nothing but guys. Then she leaves town. Why? Because the word got out and nobody's going to go to a dyke doctor. Then she shows up here. No husband. No boyfriend. No nothing. How much more do you need?"

Bagley turned to Stone. "What do you think?"

Stone looked up from the report he was finishing. "Don't know. I haven't met her yet."

"Well you're gonna meet her in about half an hour," Brainard said. "So I think you should be the tie breaker on this deal. You worked LA Vice, and that makes you an expert on pervs and queers."

"I never considered that," Stone said.

"I'm not saying I like it that she's queer," Bagley chimed in. "Actually, it's a goddam shame. If she wasn't, she could be a pretty hot number."

"A lotta good that'd do you," Brainard said with a contemptuous chuckle.

"Fuck you." Bagley waved him off and went back to paperwork.

• • •

Stone couldn't believe his luck. He scored the chief's car, a brand new Chevy. The boss was out of town for a couple of days, which put his reserved car up for grabs.

A car equipped with the miracle of automotive air conditioning.

Before he did anything else, Stone set the cooling controls to maximum so the air blasted out of the vents in a beautiful sonic snow. He sighed and settled back into the seat for the trip over to the Kern County Coroner's offices.

Once out of the lot, he took Truxtun over to Mt. Vernon and headed north. He had to admit that the polemic exchange between Bagley and Brainard piqued his interest in Dr. Christine Harmon, the official forensic pathologist for the Kern County Coroner. But for now he resolved to put aside all sexual speculation and focus on the case at hand, the death of Charlene Winters. It wouldn't be foul play unless Dr. Harmon declared it was so; and if she didn't, the case slid into a whole new dimension.

Outside, the sun screamed down upon the street, the buildings, and the cars. Few people were out in the open. Most had fled into the shade somewhere. It made Stone feel slightly guilty about luxuriating within the car's cool interior.

He shrugged it off and settled back onto the case. He strongly doubted that Dr. Harmon's report would conflict with the on-scene conclusion of the deputy coroner. Lavelle was an experienced and competent professional. It was a homicide, one of only a handful per year in this small city.

And given that fact, you'd think that the local media would be all over it. But they weren't. When Stone read this morning's edition of the *Tribune*, he saw the story tucked into a single column on page seven, with no photos. It made no sense. Even in LA, the story would have made it to the front page or at least close. Since his arrival here, he'd had virtually no contact with the paper. It seemed that the DA's office served as the unofficial press contact for criminal matters, and nobody wanted to tread on their turf. He made a note to diplomatically ask the chief what was going on. In a case like this, public exposure often turned up valuable leads. So why not push for wider coverage?

"Ah, you must be Sergeant Stone." A man in golf attire strolled across the lobby, shiny bald and optimistically pink. He held out his hand and Stone shook it. "I'm Bruce Withers, and I'm the guy who runs the Coroner's Office. Sorry I can't stick around, but I've got a meeting I can't miss." He gave Stone a knowing wink. "I'm sure Christine can take care of you." He headed for the door. "Let me know how it goes."

"I'll do that," Stone said to Wither's retreating figure as the man sailed out in the parking lot.

"Our chief administrator is definitely a man of action – especially around tee time."

A female voice. Stone turned to a wry smile on the lips of a woman in her thirties wearing a white lab coat over a lace-collared blouse and pleated skirt.

"Dr. Harmon?"

She shook his hand. "That's me. And you must be Sergeant Stone."

"That's me," Stone echoed. Bagley and Brainard had it partially right. She was reasonably attractive, with hazel eyes, full lips, and broad cheeks. But her real appeal came from her supremely relaxed and confident demeanor. She cocked her head slightly as Stone shook her hand, as if she was taking him in from some fresh and mildly amusing perspective. He tried to reserve judgment, but he couldn't. He already liked her.

"Do you want to see the remains again?" she asked.

"Only if you think it's necessary. I got a good look out in the field."

They retired to a small conference room off the lobby. "The heat's a real killer," she said. "You want something to drink?"

"Not necessary. I wound up with the chief's car today, which just happens to have air conditioning."

"What a surprise!" Harmon said with a generous portion of cynicism. "We haven't met, so I assume you're relatively new."

"I've only been here a couple of months," Stone volunteered. He hoped she'd let it go at that. And she did.

"I'm still writing up the report," she said. "But I can already tell you what you need to know. I concur with the deputy coroner. She was strangled. You 've got yourself a genuine homicide."

"Anything else?"

The ligature marks suggest a braided rope, maybe a quarter inch in diameter. They were pretty faint, and we didn't retrieve any fiber strands. There were no signs of a struggle. No skin under the fingernails, no bruising." She leaned back. "That's about as much as I can give you, at least for now. We'll get back blood tests for toxicology, but that's going to take a while."

"What about the time of death?"

"All I have is an educated guess."

"And that would be?"

"Sometime around midnight the previous evening." She looked at her watch. "Oh dear. I'm afraid we need to wind this up. I've got to be at the clinic in half an hour."

"The clinic? You also work for a clinic?"

She smiled "I am the clinic. It's up in Oildale."

"I was just there. Charming place."

"Now let's not be hasty," she gently countered. "Everyone has a story, right?"

"Right," Stone admitted.

She obviously disagreed with his cynical slam but didn't descend into righteous indignation. She carried her conviction with utmost aplomb. He was beginning to understand why Bagley came up with the lesbian hypothesis. Most women came at you from funny angles. Different moods, different faces, different affectations. You never knew exactly whom you were dealing with. Dr. Harmon was a lot more male in her approach and came at you straight on. If she had hidden agendas, it was a truly masterful job of concealment. Despite this markedly male trait, she left no impression that she was a lesbian. Quite the opposite, in fact.

Dr. Harmon rose. "I'll have the report delivered to you as soon as it's done. If anything new comes along, I'll let you know."

Stone did a quick political calculation as he got up. "And how does our friend the coroner fit in?"

A wry twist crept into Dr. Harmon's smile. "Let's just say he shoots in the low eighties."

"Good for him." Stone had his answer. "Nice to meet you."

"And nice to meet you."

She left with a purposeful stride across the lobby to the stairs. Stone guessed that stride seldom left her.

• • •

Red Flag Repair. Reputed crash pad for Harper Lewis, aka Pork Chop. Stone squinted into the harsh light at the shop's front on Niles Street in East Bakersfield. One garage door, one shop door, one dirty window. All set in a wall of cinder block painted white and stained brown. A crudely rendered red flag sat above wobbly capital letters painted onto the second story wall.

Stone parked down the block to put the cop car out of sight. He walked back to the shop and circled around to the rear. Two motorcycles leaned on their kickstands inside a security fence topped with razor wire. One bore the scrolled emblem of a Vincent and most likely belonged to Pork Chop.

He went to the front and walked in. The place smelled of solvents, burnt oil and gasoline. A burly fellow looked up from a metal table holding a finned cylinder head. A mangled herd of cannibalized motorcycles surrounded him. "Yeah?"

He didn't know Stone was a cop, but saw he was wearing a suit, and that was a bad start.

"Hi," Stone said cheerfully. "I'm looking for Pork Chop." He'd learned along ago there was no gain in announcing yourself as a cop unless absolutely necessary. In fact, there was much to be lost.

"Up there." The guy pointed to some wooden stairs than ran up the wall at the rear.

"Thanks." Stone made his way around tools and dismembered machinery and climbed the wooden stairs. He reached a small landing at the top and walked down a short hall past a bathroom with a failed toilet and sink that wept tears of brown and black filth. Straight ahead was a closed door with a splintered hole near the bottom where someone had delivered a decisive kick. He stopped and knocked.

"Yo!" came a voice from inside.

Stone took it as a brusque acknowledgment and entered. Pork Chop lounged on a bare mattress near the far wall. His head rested on a soiled pillow, and he wore only boxer shorts and an undershirt to ward off the stifling heat. A cluster of girlie magazines surrounded him, all well-thumbed. He took a pull on a bottle of Hamms as he regarded Stone.

"So we finally meet," Stone said amiably "You must be Pork Chop."

"Who wants to know?" Pork Chop asked. His long black hair was shoved back over his ears, and he wore a three-day stubble. His eyes retreated to the rear of dark sockets while he took in this unexpected encounter.

"My name's Stone, Jimmy Stone." Stone glanced over to a leather jacket hung over the back of a folding metal chair. A large patch adorned the back, a human skull sprouting wings of red and yellow. "So what's the flying skull about?" he asked.

Pork Chop snorted derisively. He took another pull on his beer. Five of its siblings lay empty on the bare wood floor. "So why you askin'?"

Stone shrugged. "I like the look of it. That's all."

"Hells Angels." Pork Chop responded.

"Hells Angels? Who's that?"

Pork Chop took another pull. "Few guys around the valley. We get together and ride a little. You got a problem with that?"

"No problem."

"Well I got a problem with you," Pork Chop said. "Like who the hell are you and what are you doin' here?"

"I'm with the Bakersfield Police. I'd like to ask you a couple of questions."

"So you gonna bust me? Is that what this is all about?"

Stone raised his hand in denial. "No, no. Nothing like that. I was at the Blackboard last night and talked with a pal of yours. Bobby Simmons. You know him?"

"Maybe."

"He told me that the night before last, the two of you hung out together on your bikes. He said you hit a bunch of bars. He said you got free beers at the joints where he sits in. That right?"

Pork Chop shrugged. "Don't know."

"You don't know?"

"Never said I was with him, now did I?"

Stone knew he'd hit the wall. He also knew he'd screwed up. He should have checked to see if Fresno or Bakersfield had any outstanding arrest warrants for a Mr. Harper Lewis, aka Pork Chop. As it was, he had no leverage.

Stone also knew that there was something lurking behind Pork Chop's stonewalling. If he was clean, the easy way out was to say yeah, we rode around and had a few beers, so what?

Stone played one last angle. "Look. Your pal is in some pretty deep shit. You know that girl they found dead in the river? That's his old girlfriend and they had a big fight a while back. So we want to know where he was when she died. Simple as that. If he was with you, then he's clean. So do him a favor, okay?"

Pork Chop shook his head. "Don't remember."

"Well I'll tell you what, Mr. Harper Lewis. I'm going to remember you. Because I think you're up to something. I don't know what, but it won't take me long to find out, and then next time we meet, we can skip all the bullshit and I can get right down to kicking your ass."

Pork Chop raised his last bottle in salute. "Adios, motherfucker."

· · ·

Sunset brought on a modest dip in the heat. A momentary lapse, but a welcome one. Low pressure oozed down from the north and brought in a little moisture in the form of cloud cover, but no rain. Stone opened his wing window so the relatively cool air washed directly over his face. It felt good and validated his decision to get out and revisit the Blackboard. Woods and his electrified band fascinated him. It was country, but with distinct stripes from elsewhere, like what you might hear in a bar in Watts or some low-down joint on Central Avenue in downtown LA. Places like Zeke's Arabian Room, or The Copper Penny. He tried to visualize one of Bill Wood's guys sitting in at one of these venues, but couldn't do it.

He parked near the front and scanned the lot for the dented pickup, but didn't spot it. On his way in, the deputy said howdy in that special cop-to-cop intonation, and got the door for him. Neither mentioned anything about last night.

The band was launching into a blues shuffle as he sat down at the bar. It reaffirmed his thoughts about how Woods was pulling in influences from far afield. He remembered last night how Bill had told the audience that he was going to play their favorites in country music "with a little jazz on the side." No doubt about it.

"Check out the guitar guy when he takes a solo," someone said from next to him. "He' pretty damn good."

He turned to a man with a neatly trimmed beard and tortoise shell glasses. "I'll do that. You know these guys?"

"Just a little," the man said. He stuck out his hand. "Ron Travers."

"Jimmy Stone," Stone said as he shook hands. Travers looked about forty, and Stone sensed a sophistication about him that stood in contrast to most of Bakersfield and especially a honky-tonk like this one.

Travers looked toward the stage. "Here we go."

A young man in his early twenties took off into a guitar solo. The notes streamed out clear and bright, but somehow had a slightly dirty edge to them. The fellow had blonde hair, oiled and brushed back, and a trim build. "Who's that?" Stone asked when the solo ended.

"Buck Owens," Travers responded. "He has the drive and energy to match the talent. You watch. He's going places."

Owen's guitar struck Stone as being a little odd. A solid piece of wood with some electrical hardware on the front and a slim maple neck. No sound holes or hollow center. "Never seen a guitar like that," Stone observed. "You know what it is?"

"It's called a Telecaster. They're made by a guy down in Fullerton who's worked with a lot of cowboy bands. Leo Fender. He also makes the amplifiers. Someday this stuff will be everywhere." Travers stated it as a matter of fact.

"Sounds like you have more than a casual interest in what's going on here."

"You'd be right about that," Travers said with a grin. "I teach music at Bakersfield College."

"College? There's a college around here?"

Travers laughed and said "How about that? Right out there in the carrot patch."

"So you a professor?"

"Not quite. I'm working on my doctoral thesis. That'll put me over the top."

"Your thesis, huh? What's it about?"

Travers gestured toward the bandstand. "It's about all this. You look at these guys and what they're playing. You look at a bunch of other guys playing in rowdy little bars and clubs all over town. They're on to something. It's loud, it's slightly rude, and it's full of feeling. They're playing through amplifiers and singing songs about divorce, no job, too much booze. They're singing about themselves and the people out there in the audience. You follow country music?"

"Yes, I do."

"Then you've noticed that the stuff coming out of Nashville is becoming totally sanitized. They even have string sections behind the vocals. And you know why? Because they want to be respectable and move into the big tent where the big money is. Not so with these guys. They're a true reflection of who they are and how they live. A long time from now, it'll be recognized as a form of folk music."

Folk music. It made Stone think of somebody singing Woody Guthrie songs in a beatnik coffee house in San Francisco. "You sure about that?"

"I'm willing to bet my thesis on it."

Stone raised his beer in salute. "Then so be it. I wish you the best of luck."

"Thank you." Travers raised his beer and returned the salute.

The sound of shattered glass shot down the bar. Both Stone and Travers turned to face it. A stocky man held a broken beer bottle by its neck and prepared to lunge at another man, who grabbed a pitcher to use as a defensive weapon. Some bystanders intervened and pulled the pair apart.

Stone turned to Travers. "Is that what you mean by a true reflection of who they are?"

Up on the stage, Woods and his boys never missed a beat.

9.

JUNE 15

DOWNTOWN BAKERSFIELD

"It's your case, so it's your show," Chief Beaumont said to Stone. "I'm just here for the first round in case you need a referee."

They were halfway down the courthouse hall to the Kern County District Attorney's office. "So what's the deal with these guys?" Stone asked.

"DA's okay. He just rides with the wind, which is what you'd expect around here. He lives from one election to the next."

"What about the Head Investigator?" Stone asked.

"He's an asshole."

The chief offered no further elaboration. Not good. Before Stone could ask him to expound, they went through some double doors and into a conference room where the two men in question sat.

Stone had them pegged before he even knew who was who. Bob LaFreniere came off relaxed, friendly, engaging. Thomas Gilford came off wound tight and reluctant to play his personal hand. Lafreniere offered the broad grin. Gilford offered the civil nod.

Lafreniere, the Kern County District Attorney, the elected official. Gilford, the Head Investigator, the perpetual bureaucrat.

"Chief. Good morning," LaFreniere said as he stood to greet them. He turned to Stone. "And you must be Sergeant Stone.

Good to meet you. Thanks for making time for us." He gestured at Gilford, who remained seated at an old oak table. "I had Tom set this up so you could tell us what's going on. We don't get a lot of homicides," he said to Stone, "and when we do, they usually involve booze, broads, and barrooms. This one seems a little different, so we want to stay on top of it. Have a seat."

Stone and the chief sat down opposite the pair, and Stone placed a file folder on the table. "I wish I had more to tell you. Right now it's still pretty thin."

"I read your initial report," Gilford said. "And it seems to say that you have a potential suspect."

"You mean Bobby Simmons?" Stone asked. Asshole or not, Gilford came off as physically imposing, with broad shoulders and thickly muscled arms. But the effect dissolved as soon as he spoke in a voice pushing up into the soprano register. A fuzzy crop of red hair didn't help.

"Yes, Mr. Simmons," LaFreniere replied. He leaned back in his chair, exposing his generous belly beneath a cheerful tie. "Tell us about Mr. Simmons."

"Miss Winters was one of Simmons' girlfriends. They had a big fight a couple of weeks back. Her mother witnessed it, and Simmons confirmed it. He says that's the last time he saw her."

Gilford looked at a tablet with some scribbled notes. "So what about this Harper Lewis guy? Simmons claims they were out bar hopping until the wee hours when Winters was killed."

"That's correct. They're both motorcycle riders."

"Well good for them," Gilford said. "Let's skip the bullshit. Harper's got a record, correct?"

"Correct. All up in Fresno. Small stuff. Drunk and disorderly. Petty theft."

"Well then it would seem that Mr. Lewis would be something less than a credible witness if he was called on to testify," LaFreniere said. "Which would leave Mr. Simmons with no real alibi at all."

"I'd like to think that," Stone said. "But Simmons named about four or five different places where they stopped. If he's telling the truth, there'll be witnesses that saw them."

"Have you checked that out?" Gilford asked.

"Top of my list," Stone replied. He noted that Gilford sat with elbows on the table and hands tightly clasped.

"So what's your gut tell you?" LaFreniere asked.

"You really want to know?" Stone asked.

"I really want to know."

"He's telling the truth. There'll be people in nearly all those joints that saw them."

"Which leaves us nowhere," Gilford said. "So why are we having this meeting?"

Stone considered mentioning that Charlene was stepping out on Bobby with someone else, but thought the better of it. He hadn't put it in this first report because he was already buried trying run down all the facts on Bobby. If Bobby was cleared, then he'd include it. If he wasn't, then it didn't matter.

LaFreniere leaned forward and turned to Gilford. "Well Tom, I wouldn't quite say that we're nowhere. But it does look like it might be better to fold this hand before we start stacking all our chips behind it." He stood up and looked over to Stone. "I think your gut's probably right on the money, but let us know what you find."

"Of course," Stone said as he rose to leave.

"If we miss with Simmons, we'll hit with somebody else, "LaFreniere said optimistically. "It's just a matter of time. Right?"

"Right."

Lafreniere seemed satisfied. "Keep up the good work, Sergeant."

"I'll do that." Stone noticed that Gilford made no comment at all.

. . .

"So how do you think that went?" Stone asked the chief as they descended the courthouse steps.

"They've given you plenty of rope," Beaumont replied. "But what you do with it is up to you." He gave Stone a supportive pat on the shoulder. "Let me know if I can help."

"I may need a little extra manpower," Stone said. "Can I bring Brainard in on this?"

A faint trace of a smile came over the chief. "I don't think you heard me. I offered help, not Brainard."

"I stand corrected." He glanced over at the chief. The tiny flash of humor was already snuffed. His gloomy overcast had settled in solid.

What is it with this guy? Stone wondered, but then gave it up. Anybody who'd spent 20 years as a cop around here had plenty of reasons to tend toward a dark disposition.

. . .

By the time he left Jimmy's Bonfire in the late afternoon, Stone's gut was more or less validated. At each bar on his list, at least someone remembered Bobby Simmons coming around with that "biker guy" on the night in question. Not surprising. All these places held a tight little circle of patrons who knew each other, at least by name. Even the daytime customers knew the night crowd, and the help knew damn near everybody. The topper was that Bobby had sat in at several locations, and everybody always remembered when Bobby took the stage.

Simmons might be a snake from the ladies' point of view, but he didn't appear to be a deadly one.

On the way home, Stone pondered his meeting with the DA and his deputy. Back in LA, it would have been a whole different scene. He would have never ascended high enough up the food chain to chat with the District Attorney of Los Angeles County. And nobody in the DA's office would have been evenly mildly interested in the case until they thought they had a winner to take to court. Not so in Kern County. To be fair, LaFreniere wanted a strong case, but didn't seem to be burning with ambition to make it happen. And the Head Investigator, Gilford, was less than helpful at best.

In one sense, the meeting was a relief. No one was breathing down his neck to cough up a reasonable suspect, which gave him time to do things right. On the other hand, he didn't quite understand the rules of the game here, and that bothered him. Was Gilford simply waiting for him to fuck up? Was LaFreniere holding back so he could pounce later? No way to tell, at least not yet.

• • •

Stone plunked the Swanson TV dinner down on the folding metal tray in his living room. The dinner came in a crimped aluminum package with fried chicken, peas and carrots, and what passed for mashed potatoes. Twenty-five minutes in the oven and you circumvented the need to cook. Not a bad tradeoff, especially if you were without a wife to hold up the domestic end of things. He had the TV tuned to Herb Henson and His Trading Post Gang, which came on five days a week over KERO-TV. Not surprisingly, they called the show Cousin Herb's Trading Post, and if you were lucky, they had some big-name performer from out of town. No such luck tonight. The guest was some nervous kid named Johnny Cash.

The phone rang just after Stone finished eating. It interrupted a steel guitar number by Billy Mize and caught Stone off guard. He seldom got a call in the evening, unless it was from work. Another homicide? He hoped not. Charlene Winters was more than enough for the time being.

He lifted the hand piece off the cradle. "Stone speaking."

"Hi. It's Dr. Harmon. Do you have a minute?"

Stone stared out into his shabby kitchen/living room. "I do."

"There's something we didn't cover in our meeting, and I think you should know about it."

"What's that?"

"I'm not really comfortable discussing it on the phone. Could we meet for coffee?"

"Sure. When do you want to do it?"

"This evening. At Cy's Coffee Shop. Know where it is?"

"Yeah, it's that new place down by the San Padre Hotel."

"You got it. Could we meet in an hour?"

"Yeah, I guess we could."

"Okay then. I'll see you there. Goodbye now"

"Goodbye."

Stone cradled the hand piece. Christine Harmon, of all people. There was really no accounting for it.

On the TV, Cousin Herb echoed Stone's reflection by launching into a completely improvised commercial for a local dry-cleaner. He just made it up as he went along. Stone smiled. In the end, maybe that's what they were all doing: Just making it up as they went along.

· · ·

Cy's. Scrawled in neon on a big triangle shoved into a square cement tower atop the coffee shop proper. A redoubt of modernity in stolid downtown Bakersfield.

Stone looked at his watch. He was five minutes early, by design. You didn't keep a woman waiting alone in a public place, at least not in his book. He picked a booth by a window near the entrance so she could quickly spot him when she arrived. It was definitely the decent thing to do.

He ordered coffee from a perky young waitress, whose life had yet to step on her with any great force. Good for her, Stone thought. She could be a beacon for those in need. Was he among them? Probably so. He gazed at the booth's teal Naugahyde upholstery and soon found himself drifting between two poles of curiosity as he sipped his coffee. One centered on what Dr. Harmon couldn't tell him over the phone. The other on the woman herself. Just who was she, really?

He looked up just as Christine came in. She scanned the room before she spotted him, and there it was again. That same composed, assured stance toward the world. Just like in the coroner's office.

She smiled when she caught sight of him and started over. He slid out the booth and stood up to welcome her.

"Good evening," she said. "How are you?"

"I'm fine. Would you like some coffee?"

"I can wait. Go ahead and sip."

It didn't seem right to do that but right then the waitress intervened and she ordered. It gave Stone a chance to take her in more closely. She had light brown hair done in brisk curls, full on top and trimmed closer on the sides. Her lipstick glowed an opaque red, as was the fashion these days. Her nose was very straight, with almost no bridge, and her hazel eyes had a life all their own. She appeared to be approaching thirty, and doing so in a very pleasant way.

"I hope I didn't drag you out of the house to do this," she said.

"Not really," Stone said. "There's only me and Cousin Herb."

"You live with your cousin?"

"Sorry, that was supposed to be funny. Cousin Herb hosts a nightly TV show with live music. Mostly country stuff. I watch it during the week if I get home in time."

"You don't seem the type."

Stone shrugged. "I've got it in my blood. My family came from Oklahoma during the Dust Bowl. Okies. Lots of guitars and fiddles."

"So you're not from around here?

"You could tell?"

She gave him an amused smile. "I could tell."

"I grew up in LA, down in South Gate. Worked for the LAPD. Started as a patrolman and worked my way up to detective."

"Interesting. And what kind of things did you detect?"

"I was with the Vice Squad working out of Hollywood."

"Did you ever run into movie stars behaving badly?"

Stone laughed. She was making this easy. "I'm sure plenty of 'em behaved badly, but I never caught any."

"And what brought you to Bakersfield?"

Stone took a sip of coffee to reset. He could either cover up now and have her discover the truth later, or just get it out in the open. "It's kind of a complicated story," he said.

"It always is," she replied.

"A couple of years back, the LAPD had a big scandal. A guy in Vice killed an unarmed Mexican in a bar under very questionable circumstances. It looked like it might blow wide open and take a lot of people down inside the department."

"Including you?"

"Including me. Anyway, I had to make a bet on the outcome."

"And how did you bet?" she asked.

"I bet that if I stuck to the rules and did the right thing, I'd be exonerated if it came to trial. Never happened. They managed to put the whole thing on ice. Then they fired me."

"On what grounds?"

"On the grounds that I wasn't a team player, even when the team should have been up for manslaughter at the least."

"They can do that?"

"They're the LAPD. They can do just about anything, as long they're clever enough. And Chief Parker is a very clever chief, indeed."

"Where did that leave you?"

"It left me with no job, no wife, no house, no future. A good time to leave town, wouldn't you say?"

"A very good time. So here you are: the new cop on the block in Bakersfield, California."

"The new cop on the block," Stone repeated. "Well put."

"Then join the club," she said. "I'm not from around here, either."

"I didn't think you were. You don't come off as being a farmer's daughter, even a rich farmer's daughter," Stone observed. "And I don't think they grow doctors anywhere around here."

"No they don't. As a matter of fact, they don't grow women doctors anywhere at all. At least not as a cash crop."

"You're the first I've ever met," Stone admitted. "So what's the story?"

"Ah yes, the story," she said. A trace of sadness came over her. "Like you, I grew up in LA. In Brentwood, to be exact. I was an only child. My father was head of the chemistry department at UCLA. My mother was an editor at a textbook publishing company. I had a cousin I was very close to, a girl about the same age. She came down with brain cancer when we were twelve, and died six months later. I resolved to become a doctor, so things like that would never happen again."

"And what did your parents think about that?"

"They were wonderful. They backed me every step of the way. From pre-med in college on through medical school."

"This doesn't sound like the path to Bakersfield," Stone noted. "What happened?"

"Want to guess?"

"A man," Stone said without hesitation.

Christine smiled. "I bet you're quite the cop. Yes, a man. I met him during my first year of residency at General Hospital. He was handsome, charming, charismatic and visionary to boot. A real estate developer. He had this glorious conception of how LA would move into the future, and it made him a fortune."

"So what was the catch?" Stone asked.

"When we first met, he was very taken with the idea of me being a woman doctor. He even helped me open a clinic for charity cases down in Skid Row. An angel of mercy, right? By the time I finished my residency, we were married and the tune began to change. It seemed that the whole female physician thing was supposed be nothing more than the salad days. Now it was time to settle down, play the good little wife, have babies, and be the perfect hostess at cocktail parties."

"And you had a problem with that?"

"To be completely honest, it was tempting. A lot of women would have killed to be in my position. But the doctor in me won out. It was just too much to throw away. We lasted about a year after that, and then came the divorce."

"That's sad," Stone noted. "But not sad enough to land you in Bakersfield."

"You're right. But a funny thing happened once I was on my own and set up a practice. It seemed that even people who liked the idea of a woman doctor didn't want to actually go to a woman doctor. In the end, I had my charity cases at the downtown clinic and an empty waiting room over in Wilshire."

"Next stop, Kern County," Stone said.

"More by chance than anything else," Christine said. "I was browsing a medical journal and saw an ad in the back for a forensic pathologist here. The county doesn't have the budget for a full-time person in this position, so they were looking for someone to do it on a contract basis. I fit the bill."

"I can see where you would," Stone said. "All your patients here are dead, so none of them have a problem with you being a woman."

"That's right. Besides, it leaves me time to indulge my charitable streak. I have a small clinic up in Oildale for families who can't afford regular medical care. I can't do everything for them, but something is better than nothing."

"Very nice," Stone said. "I hope they're grateful."

Christine shrugged. "Some are. Others just take what they can get. That's the way it is when you're on the bottom looking up. Most are mothers and children. The men don't want a lady poking around. It's about what you'd expect."

"I suppose so." Stone realized that they'd strayed far from the intended purpose of this meeting. And why not? He liked looking at her, he liked listening to her, he liked the way she moved. It made him wonder why he was so comfortable with her. But he already knew the answer. She was out of reach, a well-educated professional person with a certain social standing that put her several layers above his pay grade. Since Grace, he'd had no serious entanglements. And with Dr. Harmon he didn't have to worry about any emotional flare-ups that would disturb his precarious equilibrium.

"On the phone you said you had something to tell me," Stone said.

"Yes I did. And now I'm ready to discuss it," she responded.

"You weren't before?"

"Not really. I knew you were a cop, but as you of all people know, that's no guarantee of good character."

Stone found this amusing. "And what did I do to pass the test?"

"You were straight with me. You painted a very painful picture of how you wound up here. A lot of men would have glossed the whole thing over. You didn't."

"No, I didn't. But what's it matter?"

Christine looked down and grasped the handle of her coffee cup. "Did you read the coroner's report on Charlene Winters?"

"Not with a microscope, but close enough to believe the conclusion. It's like all of you suspected. She died of strangulation with some kind of rope or cord."

"That's correct. That's what we concluded."

"Then what's the problem?"

"It's not what's in the report, she said slowly.

"And what's that?"

"Before I tell you, I need your word that you'll keep this entire conversation in absolute confidence."

"You have my word."

"Charlene Winters recently had an abortion."

"You're sure?" Stone was blindsided.

"I'm sure."

"Wow. I don't get it. How could something like that get left out?" Stone asked.

"I'm really not at liberty to say."

"Then why did you tell me?"

"Because I thought you ought to know. You're new here, so this place has yet to rub off on you, and that makes you special." She stood up abruptly to leave. "I hope you found this little chat useful. Goodnight."

By the time he got to his feet to see her off, she was halfway to the door.

. . .

Stone sat in his car outside Cy's, and stared down 18th Street. You could still see the last hint of daylight behind the Greyhound station. The heat had fallen along with the sun, dropping the temperature into the comfort zone. But he felt anything but comfortable. He'd blown it. He should have been faster on his feet when she told him. He should have come away with at least a little more useful information. Like how long ago had the abortion been done?

No matter now. His instinct told him that he'd gotten all he was going to get from her. If he pressed the issue, he'd permanently rupture their relationship, and it simply wasn't worth the damage. All he had to go on was the abortion itself, and her intimation that some kind of corruption was involved in the cover-up: 'This place has yet to rub off on you.'

He fired up his old Chevy's six-cylinder engine and turned south on H Street to head home. It was slower than Chester, but he needed the time to think. Maybe he had written Bobby Simmons off too soon. Maybe that was Bobby's baby. But then again, why kill her after the real problem was solved? And if it wasn't Bobby, then what about whoever she was sneaking out with on the side?

Which reminded him about the matchbook he'd found in Charlene's room. It was from the Rancho Vista Motel, which now became a place of more than casual interest. If she went there, he highly doubted it was with Bobby, whose budget leaned more toward the seat of his pickup, or the lawn in a park somewhere. That left the other person or persons. He had no way of knowing who or how many. All he had was the mother's suspicion about what her daughter was up to when she stepped out at night.

Back to the details. Mrs. Winters said that Charlene smoked, but none of the Rancho Vista matches had been used, which suggested that either she acquired them very recently or they had some kind of sentimental value. Either way, they pointed back toward the motel.

He pulled into his apartment, went inside and took a picture of Charlene from a file folder that was open on his kitchen table.

He hit the road again and turned left on 4th Ave. on over to Highway 99, where he headed north. It was getting late, but the hour didn't matter. Motels were a 24-hour proposition, as any vice cop could tell you.

He drove on through the big roundabout, where the city lights winked out and highway headed into the blackness toward Fresno. At the end of a long curve northward, the Rancho Vista Motel hit him with a double-barreled blast of supercharged neon. Two enormous elevated signs identified the place in radiant green and screamed LET'S EAT in pulsating red. A big yellow arrow snaked through the lettering and pointed down into the parking lot below.

Stone pulled in and stopped in front of a single-story building built of brick with a low-pitched roof to give it a little swagger. It held a big coffee shop in front, followed by a bar, and then the office.

Stone got out of his car and scanned the parking lot, the rooms, the bar and the restaurant. The cheerful neon out front was preaching a falsehood. He knew it instantly. Any veteran vice cop would have known. The place had a distinctly seedy feel. The lot was only half full and populated by vehicles not of the type driven by traveling families. Instead it held pickups, two-door sedans, a convertible, and a few sports cars. Male cars congregating in a place catering to a male market. Prostitution, drugs, homosexual hijinks, extracurricular trysts. He was sure of it.

It all added up to a big problem. Nobody in a shadow world like this was ever a witness to anything. Anonymity was the binding force, the organizing principle behind the exchange of forbidden goods and outlawed services.

That said, he still had to give it a go. If Charlene did pick up the matches here, she was definitely treading on the dark side. But with whom?

Stone walked through a swinging glass door into the office. The cool blue of the fluorescent overheads mingled with the radiant red of the VACANCY sign in the window. A clerk sat all hunched and sullen behind the reception counter. A man of middle years in precipitous decline, who looked like he hadn't slept in a week. Nevertheless, Stone opted for a positive approach.

"Good evening," he said cheerfully.

"Good evening," the man responded. His tone suggested that there was nothing good about this evening or any other in living memory.

So much for bonhomie. Stone pulled out his badge. "My name's Stone. I'm with the Bakersfield police. I'm trying to make an identification. I thought maybe you could help."

"Oh yeah?" The clerk's expression slid from boredom to outright disgust. What kind of fool thought he would volunteer information to the police?

Stone brought out the picture of Charlene. "We have reason to believe that this girl was here on at least one occasion and maybe more. Recognize her?"

"No."

"If you don't mind, I'd like to look at the register from two nights ago. Just a quick scan, that's all."

"I got a better idea," the clerk said. "How about no scan at all?"

"Look," Stone said, "if I have to, I can get a court order."

The clerk glanced down at the open register, and scratched his thinning hair. "Yeah, you could do that. But you won't."

Time to turn up the heat. "You know, maybe I could also get a search warrant so we can poke around here a little. You never know what we might find."

"Really?" the clerk said. "Well that's gonna take a little time. And by then, whatever you're looking for will be long gone."

Stalemate. Stone put away the photo. "You and I aren't through. I'll be back."

The clerk shrugged. "Your choice." His delivery suggested that it would be an utter waste of time. He was probably right.

Stone left the office and opened the door to the bar. The place held two drooping patrons on stools and a neon Hamms sign behind the bartender. Not very promising.

He continued on to the coffee shop, which was the payoff for those lured by LET'S EAT. Long glass windows lined two of the walls. A highway rig with a dense array of running lights traversed the blackness outside as it shot on into the heart of the valley.

He paused by the cash register, where a glass bowl held a tumbled heap of match packs, all the same as the one he'd found in Charlene's bedroom. After pocketing one, he took the place in. A row of booths lined the space under the windows facing the highway. They held customers of a lewd and questionable nature, the same kind he'd seen hundreds of times before in LA.

Except for the last booth, where a young girl sat facing him. Given the surroundings, she came off like an orchid discarded in a dung heap. Sixteen at the oldest, probably younger. Thick blond hair pulled into a long ponytail, full red lips, and eyes of a blueberry hue. She wore a sleeveless cotton blouse and short shorts that revealed tanned legs of perfect proportion.

She was listening intently to a young man who sat across from her. Stone couldn't see his face from this angle, but his hands moved in gestures that complemented his speech. Powerful hands at the end of arms with sinews that rippled with each gesture. The girl nodded earnestly in obvious adoration at his delivery. Teenage love. Nothing was more intense, nothing more fleeting and fragile.

But there was a hint of something hidden within the rapture. Stone couldn't see it, but he could feel it. A lunch counter with fixed stools ran along the opposite wall, and Stone took a seat at the end. He had to figure this one out. A waitress came and he ordered coffee. Between sips, he discretely stole sideways glances at the couple. The decidedly sleazy venue aside, what was wrong with this picture? The answer came abruptly when the object of girl's affection got up to leave. As he turned, Stone caught his face full on.

Gary Willert.

The one that got away. Stone wouldn't have remembered except for the circumstances. They had him dead to rights for hustling in the park in North Hollywood, and they would have carted him off, but then they got the call to hightail it to the Showboat. For Sergeant James Stone, LAPD, it was the beginning of the end, and this prick bore witness to it. Stone turned away, stared into his coffee, and struggled with the urge to extract some latent justice, to kick the son of a bitch in the small of the back, to step on his head once he fell, to put the cuffs on a couple of clicks too tight.

He closed his eyes and took a few deep breaths. When he opened them, Willert was gone. In the booth, the girl sipped her Coke through a plastic straw and floated in a fog both romantic and toxic. She knew. Stone was now sure of it. She knew who Willert was and what Willert did. It was no accident that he was at the Rancho Vista. He was hustling the queer action, just like in LA. Probably even had a room here. His moves with the girl also confirmed Stone's earlier suspicion that Willert wasn't really gay. It was only business, easy business if you had a trim body and fetching face.

Stone spooned a little sugar into his coffee and played with idea of intervening. He could go sit down with the girl and identify himself as a police officer, albeit a concerned one. He could ask her if she really understood what she was getting into with someone like Willert.

He sighed and got up to leave. It wouldn't work. He'd come off as some kind of father figure, full of righteous conviction and dictating the terms of her life with a certainty that bordered on stupidity. He could deal with her in a police context, but from any other perspective he felt pretty much lost. While women were ultimately a mystery to all men, they were doubly so for him. He'd grown up with no sisters, only a brother, and his dad was the dominant parent in his life. He'd had a smattering of flirtations in high school and then married Grace. Thereafter, police work had immersed him a heavily male culture. In sum, it left him with a very narrow window into the vast spectrum of female behavior.

As always, he'd just have to work with what he had. He left a quarter for a tip and headed for the parking lot.

10.

Stone's job seldom took him into an exclusively female domain, but this morning was an exception. Balencia's dedicated itself to women of means with a refined sense of fashion. In Bakersfield, this focus narrowed the market dramatically, which made for an establishment of modest size yet prodigious price tags. For everyone else J.C. Penney's was just a few blocks away.

Stone walked past several racks of dresses and mirrors. The textures of the materials, the flow of the lines, the subtext of the colors and all else lay somewhere far beyond him. It didn't matter. It was the perfume counter that counted. An attractive young woman stood behind the glass. She wore a conservative but elegant skirt and jacket, and smiled at his approach.

"Good morning. Can I help you, sir?" Her voice had that creamy sweetness found only in women of her particular age.

"Well I hope so," Stone said as he pulled his notebook out. "I take it that you're familiar with a lot of perfumes?"

"I try to be," she said modestly.

Stone flipped the notebook's pages until he came to the one where he'd recorded the name of the perfume bottle in Charlene Winter's room. "You're going to have to pardon my accent. It's called 'Worth', and I think it's made by somebody called 'Dans La Nuit'. You ever heard of it?"

"No sir, I'm afraid we don't…"

"She's being quite kind, officer." Stone turned to the voice as it approached the counter. Fatalia, the date of the flyboy at the Blackboard, he of the Colt .45. "For starters, you've got it backward. The perfume's called Dans La Nuit, which means 'In the Night' in French. And Worth is the company that makes it."

Stone had to smile. "I stand corrected. Anything else you'd care to share?"

"As she was about to tell you, they don't carry it here."

"And where might I find some?"

"Your best bet would be a trip to Paris, but there just might be a few bottles floating around New York."

"I assume then that it's not exactly cheap."

"I'm not at liberty to discuss the price. That's what would be cheap."

Stone raised a hand in capitulation. "Forgive me."

"Only if you'll buy coffee for us at the place around the corner."

"Done."

. . .

Tiny's Waffle Shop and Fatalia presented an odd couple, but Stone took it in stride. They sat at a table by a window that looked out onto Chester Avenue where the traffic surged to the beat of an overhead stoplight. Dishes clattered in the back, and an expletive or two drifted out of the kitchen, along with a steady stream of pancakes, waffles, eggs and bacon.

"And how is Captain Gary Piland of the United States Air Force?" Stone asked.

"Captain Piland is flying higher, faster and harder than any man that's gone before him. They have yet to make a great silver bird that he can't ride," said Fatalia.

Stone raised his coffee cup in salute. "Well give him my regards."

"I'll do that," Fatalia promised. "Fancy meeting you in Balencia's. Is there another side to you? A secret, sensitive man?"

"Not that I know of. The perfume's part of a case that I'm working on."

"Shoplifting?"

"Homicide."

"Oh." At last, she seemed shy of a comeback. "I'm sorry. If I'd known that, I wouldn't have been so damn cute."

"It's okay. It does tend to bring people down once they know."

"Can you talk about it?" she asked. "The case, I mean."

"I'd rather not. I'm starting to find just how small this town really is. The less said, the better at this point."

"I get your drift," she remarked. "And you're definitely drifting in the right direction. Look around here and you'll find three kinds of citizens: If you start at the bottom, you've got the people who go to the Blackboard, and there's a whole lot of 'em. In the middle, you've got the people who own the Blackboard, and there's a whole lot less of 'em. Then you've got the people who own everything else, and there's almost none of 'em."

"But not quite," Stone suggested.

Fatalia smiled. "But not quite."

"And just where might you fit into a scheme like this?" Stone asked.

"Want to guess?"

"I'd guess that you're almost none of them." Stone liked the clever ambiguity of his answer, even though it was accidental. In its own way it captured her perfectly. She lived somewhere outside the scheme she'd just described. She obviously came from wealth and position, but she also liked slumming around the local honky-tonks.

"Name three things that go on the back of a tractor," she demanded.

"I don't think I'd get much farther than a plow and a hay trailer," Stone admitted.

"My father could name you a hundred. At least at one time he could. Now he'd have to confine himself to the cocktail menu on the Queen Mary. What I'm trying to tell you in my own tangled way is that about the same time they first watered the desert out there, my family got into the farm implements. Their timing was impeccable. At least, up until they had me. I was supposed to be a boy, and I was supposed to know a lot about things like milling machines. As you can see, it didn't quite work out that way."

"Obviously not," Stone observed. "I don't think you've ever mentioned your last name."

"Castle. It has a nice ring to it, especially if you've got enough money to actually own one."

"Do you?"

"No. But it's always an option. Right now, I'll have to settle for room and board at mommy and daddy's place. It's not so bad, really. They're off to Europe for the summer, so I've got it to myself so I can practice what it'll be like when they're dead and gone."

"You planning on sticking around that long?"

"Not really. I'm sort of on probation with them."

"Oh yeah? What were you convicted of?"

"Until a few months ago, I was at Vassar. Senior year. Almost had it made. But then I had a little trouble conforming to their policies about proper behavior with male guests."

"They kicked you out?"

"That's a very crude interpretation. Let's just say that we mutually agreed to part ways."

"I see," Stone said. "Speaking of parting ways, I've got to get back to work."

Fatalia reacted with a wry smile. "That's what men always say."

"And most of the time, it's really true," Stone responded as he picked up the check.

"We're not quite done," she declared and pulled a card and ballpoint pen from her purse. "Here's my number in case you need more details on Dans La Nuit." She wrote down the number and pushed it across to him. "You never know."

"You never do," Stone agreed as he picked up the card.

· · ·

Stone found himself embedded in the frantic clacking of dozens of typewriters, all laboring to meet the next deadline in a string of deadlines went on forever. The newsroom of the Bakersfield Tribune took in several rows of metal desks manned by those doing the typing. All men, mostly middle-aged or more, wearing white short-sleeved shirts with opened ties.

Stone sat outside the only private office on the floor, a glassed-in room belonging to William Flannigan, the managing editor. He was on the phone and gesturing emphatically with his free hand.

Flannigan knew he was here but failed to acknowledge his presence. Twenty minutes had ticked by since the reception desk notified him that Stone was coming up. Stone knew it was intentional. It sent a silent but clear message about whose time was more valuable. The editor obviously wanted to define his sphere of power before talking.

Stone shrugged it off and used the time to mull over the Winters murder. The fact that the perfume was rare and valuable presented an interesting twist. Almost certainly, Charlene had not bought it herself, and neither had Bobby Simmons or anyone else of his ilk. Once again it pointed toward a third party, and now that party was beginning to take shape. It appeared to be someone with a lot of disposable income, someone whose life was not limited to the cultural confines of Bakersfield. New York and Paris were a long way off.

Now the big catch. He had two items of interest, the motel matches and the perfume, but were they linked? At this point, he had no way to tell. He simply didn't have enough information. And that's why he was now cooling his heels outside the office of this minor league martinet of a journalist. The police needed help from the media. And in Bakersfield, that meant the *Tribune*.

"You Stone?"

Stone looked up to Flannigan standing in the open door to his office. "That's me."

Flannigan waved him in without shaking hands or introducing himself. "I've only got a couple of minutes. I'm on a deadline."

Stone took a seat on the far side of the desk, which was littered with news copy. "I'm the one who's in charge of investigating the Charlene Winters murder. I'm here to ask for some help."

"What kind of help?"

Stone chose his words carefully. "We need the case to get a little more public exposure. Right now, we're very short on information, and it might bring in some leads."

Flannigan leaned back in his chair and clasped his hands. "So, you're not happy with the way we've reported the case."

Stone didn't take the bait. "If we were further along and had a credible suspect, it probably wouldn't matter. But quite frankly, we're at a standstill. That's why I'm here."

"Does Tom Gilford know about this?"

"No. I didn't think that was necessary."

"Well you thought wrong. Head Investigator Gilford is the official press officer for the DA's office, and I deal with him, and him only."

"I wasn't aware of that."

"And now you are. Good day, sergeant." Flannigan picked up a copy sheet and started to read.

Stone briefly considered firing a parting shot, but held back. Better to contain the damage than lash out. "Thanks for your time."

. . .

The trouble started the moment Stone returned to the station. It would not end for a very long time.

Mrs. Crenshaw looked up just as he reached her desk. "Chief Beaumont wants to see you," she announced. Her tone suggested that she was very pleased to make this announcement, as if she operated from some higher moral platform.

"Did he say when?"

"He said right now."

Chief William Beaumont stared out his office window down onto Truxton Street where an old Plymouth rolled by. "I'm going to give you the benefit of the doubt," he said to Stone. "I'm going to assume that you didn't know that all the press stuff goes through Gilford over at the DA's. You're new here, and this is your first major fuck-up. And I sincerely hope it's your last."

"So do I," Stone said. "Nobody told me. It doesn't seem to be written down anywhere."

Beaumont gave his head a quick twist toward Stone, which revealed wide-set eyes under bushy brows. "It doesn't have to be," he hissed, and then paused to temper his exasperation. "Now you know. Don't let it happen again."

"I won't," Stone promised. "I was just trying to get a little help on the Winters case. An appeal to the public. Maybe you could step in with Gilford and see what we can do."

Beaumont's icy stare bored in deep. "I didn't make up the game. I just play it. Understand?"

"Yes sir."

"Good. Now go find me a suspect that we can put in front of LaFreniere."

Mrs. Crenshaw gave Stone a sanctimonious smile as he passed her on his way back to his desk. Now that he was gelded she seemed to see him in a different light.

His phone rang before he could even sit down. "Stone," he answered in that flat, cryptic tone that all cops seemed to instinctively adopt.

"Dispatch," the voice on the other end said. "We got a call from two units over on Elm Street. Apparent homicide. They need somebody from your division to respond."

Stone thought it ridiculous to refer to himself and Brainard as a "division" but didn't bother to comment. "Have you checked with Brainard yet?" he asked.

"He's out today. Something about his back," the dispatcher said.

"Yeah, right. His back," Stone said with all cynicism he could muster. "Okay, I'm on my way."

11.

JUNE 17
WEST BAKERSFIELD

Stone saw two parked squad cars from down the block when he arrived on the stretch of Elm Street that snaked along the river. Neighbors gawked from the safety of their porches. Kids cruised by on the bikes. Dogs barked their bestial warning. The June sun descended on all and baked them without discretion.

A roof of terra cotta tile topped the house in question, a low-slung dwelling only recently built. The coroner's van sat in the driveway. Stone parked behind it and went up the walkway past a neatly clipped and well-watered lawn. Two patrolmen stood on the porch, telling each other jokes. As Stone neared, they gave him a perfunctory nod and went back to their banter.

The front door was open and he entered a living room that took him back to his days in Hollywood with the LAPD. The décor was ultra-swank, the kind of thing you'd see in a bachelor pad in that new rag called *Playboy,* the one with the naked babes in the middle. A bricked fireplace ran floor to ceiling. Minimalist furniture of chartreuse and turquoise sat on metal legs poking into wall-to-wall carpet. Polished wooden sculptures portrayed African deities and abstract art lined the walls.

The body lay face up at the far end of the living room. A big pool of dark blood crept out over the green carpet. A male in his forties, slightly overweight. Dressed in khaki pants, loafers and a pricey-looking sport shirt. The face drained of color, the eyes and mouth open wide in eternal alarm.

Lavelle, the deputy coroner, popped his head out of the master bedroom just off the living room. "Sorry," he told Stone. "No pretty girls in blue dresses this time." A flashbulb popped from down a short hallway. A lab tech was documenting the scene. Hopefully, he was good at it.

Stone moved closer to the corpse. The blood-soaked shirtfront told him it was probably a stabbing. Bullet holes seldom bled in this manner. They left pink cones of destruction within.

"So who was this guy?" Stone asked.

"He was one Richard Fancher up until a few hours ago. Now he's just another dead guy. In the end, we're pretty much all the same."

Stone passed on the philosophy and took in the rest of the room. Party time. Beer bottles, wine bottles, overflowing ashtrays. The coffee table caught his eye, and he gave it a closer look. Most of the stubbed cigarettes bore rings of lipstick in an assortment of shades. One of the ashtrays held a partially smoked reefer – and an open pack of matches from none other than the Rancho Vista Motel.

"In the master bedroom you'll also find a tortoiseshell hand mirror with a razor blade parked on top," Lavelle remarked "Plus a neatly folded little packet of white powder of unknown origin."

"I see. Anything else?"

"A spent condom floating in the toilet in the bathroom down the hall. But I guess that's not illegal, is it?"

"Depends on what you do with it. Any sign of a weapon?"

"Not yet. We're looking at a single knife wound to the chest. My guess is that the killer got lucky and punched one through into the heart."

As soon as Stone entered the master bedroom he saw real trouble coming. The room had been ransacked, like in a burglary. Every drawer stood open, with clothes and shoes strewn on the floor. Gabardine suits and crocodile loafers. The mattress on the unmade bed rested at an odd angle.

Stone walked down the hall and found the two remaining bedrooms in the same state. In the bathroom, the medicine chest was wide open, with pill bottles littering the tile floor.

A murder, a dope party, and a burglary. All wadded up into one big, ugly mess. Whatever happened here was far from simple.

He went back to the corpse in the living room, where Lavelle was gingerly picking at the bloody shirt with a tweezers. "Richard Fancher, huh?" Stone queried. "You ever hear of him?"

"Oh hell yes. He's a big-time real estate guy. Owns properties all over town."

"Married?"

"Don't think so. Sort of a playboy. Or at least as close as you can get to that in Bakersfield."

Stone chuckled to himself. It wasn't close at all. Hollywood would have chewed this guy up and spit him out in single chomp. But as Stone was rapidly learning, it was all a question of scale, a matter of matching pigs and puddles. He crossed to the other side of the house, which held the kitchen, the dining room, and what the realtors were now touting as a "party room." The dining room appeared unused, but a motley assortment of beer bottles and glasses and the remains of snack food covered the kitchen counters and the sink. Apparently, none of the women had volunteered to clean up. Why bother when you're high on narcotics?

Stone grimaced as he surveyed all the glass. He guessed there'd been maybe half a dozen people here, each with ten digits, all handling bottles and glasses. It would be a huge job to sort and organize all the fingerprints.

A poker table stood at the center of party room. A bottle of bonded scotch and three tumblers sat regally on the green felt, along with a casual spew of chips and cards. Probably best to start lifting prints here, which narrowed the field.

The two cops on the porch had come in and were staring at the scotch bottle. "I bet that booze would cost me a month's pay," one of them remarked.

"So who reported this in the first place?" Stone asked them. He was used to this. You seldom got the facts in a linear fashion at a crime scene.

"No one," the other patrolman said. "We got a call from dispatch to come over here and inform the owner about the recovery of a stolen vehicle. What you see is what we found."

The guy from the crime lab came into the kitchen, evidence kit in one hand and flash camera in the other. He stopped to survey all the glassware, and scowled." "Jesus."

"I know," Stone sympathized. "But everything has to be dusted and lifted. Same thing in all the bedrooms. And see if you can lift some hair samples off the pillows. Get some guys over the from the county if you need help."

"Can I tell 'em you said so?"

"Goddam right. Let's get going."

He went back to Lavelle, who was packing up in the living room. "You got a time of death?"

"Early this morning. Maybe two or three," Lavelle reported.

"Swell," Stone commented. It meant there was little chance that any of the neighbors were going to be much help. He turned to the patrolmen. "I want you guys to check with the houses on either side and across the street to see if anyone saw or heard anything. Maybe we'll get lucky."

"Got it." As the pair departed, yet another patrolman came in through the front door. "You're Sergeant Stone, right?"

"That's me."

"I just got a radio call. They want you to contact dispatch."

"Did they say why?"

"They think they've got your killer in custody."

12.

Lincoln Jefferson's name gave a strong hint that the officer was a Negro but didn't prepare Stone for the scale of the man. He was enormous. Better yet, he was a motorcycle cop, a giant black motorcycle cop. Upon meeting Jefferson in the squad room, Stone had this amusing vision of some white Ku Klux Klan guy speeding on his way to a meeting and getting pulled over by Jefferson. Stone was sure that the look on the guy's face when he rolled down his window would be justice enough.

Jefferson came in wearing his full patrol uniform. Goggles pushed up around an 8-point cap, black leather jacket, holstered automatic, jodhpurs and carefully polished knee-high boots. The color of his skin only magnified the effect. "Sergeant Stone, this just might be your lucky day," he declared in a deep baritone.

"That's what I understand," Stone said. "Tell me about it."

Jefferson put down a blue nylon gym bag he was carrying. "I'm out on the Rosedale Highway around nine this morning, right on the edge of town. I'm looking to bag a speeder or two, so I park on the far side of this substation. Sure enough, a big black Lincoln convertible comes by doing about 80. The top's down and I can see the driver. White male in his early 20s. I take off after him, with lights and siren. The guy hits the gas and tries to outrun me. Never gonna happen. After a couple of miles, he sways over onto the shoulder and loses control. The car skids off into a plowed field and tips on its side. The guy gets tossed out. He's banged up, but not dead, so I radio for an ambulance. I check him for ID, but he doesn't have any.

"By now, I'm pretty sure we're looking at a stolen vehicle, so I check the registration. It belongs to a Richard Fancher, who lives in town on Elm Street. Dispatch says they'll send someone over to tell him about it. Anyway, a little later, I hear a call on the radio that Fancher's dead and it looks like homicide. I come back and tell them they better put a guard on the driver guy at the hospital."

Stone looks at the nylon bag on the table. "What's this?"

"I found it in the back seat of the Lincoln," Jefferson said. "You can judge for yourself, but it sure looks like booty from a burglary." He unzipped the bag to reveal the contents. "Cash, watches, jewelry, silver pieces. The usual stuff."

"Yep," Stone agreed as he peered in. "The usual stuff." He looked up at Jefferson. "What kind of shape is the driver in?"

"He was conscious when they took him off, but he was definitely busted up. I don't think he'll be going anywhere soon."

Stone took the bag. "I'm taking this to the lab so they can dust for prints. I'm going to start a chain of evidence form, and I'll need you to sign off as the officer who picked it up at the scene of the crash."

"No problem," Jefferson said. He understood the drill. It was critical that they created paperwork that showed an unbroken chain of possession from one person to the next as the evidence flowed through the system. Without the chain it might be thrown out in court, because the defense could claim tampering.

"One more favor," Stone said. "Would you take a quick look through some mug shots and see if you can ID this guy. I'd sort it by burglaries in the past five years."

Jefferson shrugged. "I can give it an hour."

"Thanks." Stone held out his hand. "Officer Jefferson, it's a pleasure to meet you. Have fun out there on that bike."

Jefferson shook Stone's hand, which seemed to be about twice the size of his own. "Hope it all works out for you," Jefferson said as he left.

. . .

Stone sat in a small room across the hall from the crime lab. He wore rubber gloves to keep the evidence uncontaminated as he tagged each item in the bag and recorded it on the chain of evidence form. A Rolex wristwatch, a Cartier wristwatch, three pairs of gold cufflinks, a silver serving dish, a silver soup tureen, fourteen $20 bills, five $100 dollar bills, and a diamond ring. And of course, the bag itself.

Once done, he took the bag and its contents to the lab, and signed them over to a lab technician named Hoffner. Stone wanted everything dusted and the prints lifted, which was done by applying a strip of tape to capture and preserve them. The lab didn't inspire a lot of confidence compared to what Stone was used to in Los Angeles. A pair of benches full of jars, beakers, scales, and test tubes. Still, it would have to do.

. . .

Bakersfield Memorial Hospital. The window at the end of the hall looked out over a desiccated neighborhood to the east of Union Ave. No one stood guard outside the suspect's room, which annoyed Stone. He put it aside to collect himself for the confrontation. They'd gotten lucky and Jefferson identified the suspect from a shoplifting case a few months back. Gary Willert. The same guy he and Murphy arrested in Hollywood. The same guy he saw with the girl at the Rancho Vista. His pattern of offenses in the state of California characterized him as a vicious drifter. Numerous assault charges, drug possessions, and petty larcenies along with the hustling stuff. All the way from Crescent City to San Diego. It would seem that Gary got around.

Upon entering the room Stone saw why a guard wasn't necessary. Willert's leg was suspended in a cast that went halfway up
his thigh. He had a handsome face cast in a nasty smirk at Stone's
arrival. Deep tan, blue eyes, wavy black hair.

"How are you doing, Mr. Willert?" Stone asked cheerfully as
he took a seat at the end of the bed. "Long time, no see."

Willert gave Stone a suspicious squint. "You're a cop, aren't
you?"

"Hey, pretty good," Stone said brightly. "Detective Sergeant
James Stone of the Bakersfield Police. How'd you guess?"

"Hollywood. You busted me and let me go. I don't forget stuff
like that."

"Well I'm afraid I can't do that this time," Stone said apologetically. "You know, Gary, you're in just about as much trouble
as a guy can get into right now."

Willert feigned a puzzled look. "And just how's that?"

"There's quite a bit to it," Stone explained. "So let me just hit
the highlights. You're driving a stolen vehicle belonging to one
Richard Fancher. In that vehicle, we find a bag full of items from
his house. We go there and find him stabbed to death. Now it's
going to take a little work to connect all the dots, but we will. I'd
bet your life on it."

Stone's last remark downgraded Willert's smirk to a concerned scowl.

"What it comes down to is that you have very few options
open to you," Stone continued.

"Like what options?"

"Well option one is that you clam up and take your chances
in court. But given the evidence, that's probably not going work.
When it's all over, you can only hold your breath for so long
when you're sitting in the gas chamber."

"So what's option two?"

"You give me an honest and detailed account of what happened. I take it to the DA, and tell him how remorseful and

cooperative you were. A plea bargain's worked out that lets you keep breathing indefinitely."

"And what's option three?"

"There isn't any option three. Sorry."

Willert put on a façade of puzzlement. "I don't get it. All I did was borrow this car I found. I was going to..."

The door flew open and cut Willert off in mid-sentence. Ironically, the man that entered resembled a middle-aged version of Willert. Attractive, athletic, black hair silver-streaked and wavy. His tailored suit gave him an amplified air of authority.

"My name's Samuel Delfort," he announced to Stone. "I'm an attorney and I'm representing this young man." Delfort looked over to Willert, whose mouth hung open in a state of non-cognition. "Don't say another word. I'll take it from here." Delfort turned back to Stone. "I think that'll do it for you, officer. Good day."

"How do you know I'm a cop?" Stone had to at least get one jab in.

Delfort looked him up and down. "Suit from Sears. Bargain basement shoes. Timex watch. You're a cop, alright. Goodbye now."

• • •

Stone sat as his desk and entertained cruel, vindictive thoughts about Mrs. Crenshaw, who was typing a form in triplicate. He hoped she would make a mistake on the last line and have to type the entire thing over again. He wasn't pleased with these thoughts, but knew that they were a reflection of his current mood, and not a permanent affliction.

Willert's attorney, this Samuel Delfort character, was an asshole of the highest order. Stone had asked around the office and discovered that he was the managing partner of Delfort, Holmes, & Chalmers. Very prestigious. Extremely well connected. Highly profitable. He was sure Fatalia knew all about them.

A formidable opponent by any measure. So why was Delfort defending a low-life pseudo-queer drifter with an ugly resume? It seemed that for the good of community relations, the firm occasionally took on pro bono clients that were slated for the public defender. It demonstrated what generous, compassionate souls they were in their heart of hearts.

Stone had to admit that at least a small bunch of these sour grapes were part of his internal ferment. He'd had Willert on the defensive when Delfort barged in and ruined his play.

As long as he was this far down, Stone thought, he might as well dive all the way to the bottom. Delfort's remarks about his clothes really hurt. In a different context, he could have shrugged them off. He would've dismissed them as coming from a jerk with no redeeming value, and let it go at that. But after two years of domestic, financial, and professional disaster, his moral armor was paper thin. He wished it wasn't so, but it was so. All he could do was grope around in the dark for the bottom rung to start back up.

The phone rang and cut his brooding short. He picked it up and said "Stone" in his best cop mono-drone.

"Hi, it's Christine Harmon," the voice said.

It took Stone a moment to absorb the message. If she'd said Doctor Harmon he would have processed it immediately. But she'd omitted her official title and it threw him for a brief loop.

"Yes, Dr. Harmon," he answered. "What can I do for you?"

"I understand that you're assigned to the Richard Fancher case."

"For better or worse, yes."

"Let's hope it's for the better. I wanted to tell you that the post-mortem is scheduled for tomorrow and I should have some preliminary results the day after. Of course, the full report will have to wait for toxicology."

"Understood," Stone said. "You know, I got a good look at the victim at the scene, and I doubt that he died of a stroke."

"As do I. But before we all jump to conclusions, we need to go through the process, right?"

"Right."

"Are you married?" she asked in a dead level kind of way.

"No, I'm not." Her query knocked him off balance. Where was this going?

"I didn't think so. I have a favor to ask of you," she continued.

"A favor?" Stone couldn't imagine any way he could possibly contribute to this woman's life, either personally or professionally.

"What are you doing this evening?"

"I, uh, really hadn't thought about it."

"I need an escort to a social function tonight. All the usual suspects are unavailable," she explained.

"What kind of social function?" Stone asked cautiously.

"It's a party, a big one," she told him.

"Is it a formal kind of thing?" He felt a residual twinge from the attorney Delfort's nasty comment about his cheap suit.

"No, no," she said in a soothing kind of way, as if she knew what was bothering him. "It's an Hawaiian-style luau. Just wear a sports shirt and some shorts and sandals. You'll be fine."

Stone felt a flood of relief. That much he could manage. "All right," he heard himself saying. "What time does it start?"

"It starts at seven, so I'll pick you up about a quarter to. That'll give us plenty of time."

"You'll pick me up?" Stone asked in wonderment. He was standing on the edge of some vast unexplored plain, with no behavioral landmarks anywhere it sight.

"About a quarter to seven," she repeated. "Let me have your address."

Stone gave it to her and they said goodbye. He looked up at the familiar buzz of the cops at their desks, the phones ringing, the typewriters clacking. All of it had shifted a few degrees to some unknown heading. Not bad, not good. Just different.

• • •

"I'm tired of calling you Sergeant," Dr. Harmon told Stone as she guided her 1953 Buick Roadmaster convertible onto Oleander Street just south of downtown. "Could we go with James, or Jim, or something like that?"

"When I was growing up, they called me Jimmy," Stone volunteered.

"Jimmy won't do," she declared. "You've outgrown it. Let's go with James."

"Well then James it is," he said. He'd met her out on the street in front of his apartment so she wouldn't see what a dump it was. But something changed within him when she pulled up in this gorgeous car of sea foam green with its wheels sporting chrome wire spokes. This woman, this car, this social engagement had slipped somewhere beyond reason and into the realm of absurdity. He stepped out of himself and became a witness to events in a world not his own. And as he crossed over, he left behind any residual sense of shame or self-doubt.

The party announced itself a block before they arrived at the house. Cadillacs, Lincolns, Packards, and new Ford Thunderbirds lined both sides of the street. A little tribe of valets scurried to park them and return for more.

"So who's throwing this thing?" Stone inquired.

"Oh. I should have said. It's Jonathan Blitz. He publishes the *Bakersfield Tribune*, among other things." Christine pulled into the driveway of a property shielded from the street by dense shrubbery and trees. Cars filled a long turnaround next to an elegant house done in a style more suited to Long Island than Bakersfield. A lawn of luscious green stretched out from a colonnade at the front.

Several taxis were interspersed in the car line. Stone surmised that they were ferrying guests from out of town. He pictured a line of DC-3s parked on the tarmac out at Meadows Field. Their pilots like limo drivers, leaning against the fuselages and smoking while their employers indulged themselves in the most elevated ways imaginable.

Stone and Christine joined a stream of guests heading toward the rear as a valet whisked their cars away. Live music immediately caught Stone's ear. Hawaiian music done in the modern style on electric instruments. He liked what he heard. It was a close relative to country swing.

They arrived at a large covered area housing the core of the party. The guests had all dressed themselves in the spirit of the occasion. Sports shirts and shorts for the men, gaily colored sundresses for the women. People of privilege. People who had actually been to Honolulu and strolled along Waikiki Beach at sunset.

A long serving table presented cuisine done in classic luau style. Salmon, squid, Kalua pork, long rice, sweet potatoes, tropical fruits. But the first order of business was alcohol, and people clustered at the bar where the bartenders stayed true to the theme with loud sports shirts and white cotton pants.

A man of medium proportion and maximum tan glided up to Christine with arms extended as they approached the bar. "If it isn't my favorite lady doctor!" he exclaimed with perfunctory kiss on her cheek.

"It's also the only lady doctor you've ever met," Christine countered with a smile. "James, I'd like you to meet our gracious host, Jonathan Blitz."

Hearing himself called James caught Stone off balance. It would take some getting used to. "James Stone," he said as he shook Blitz's hand.

"Mr. Stone, welcome." Blitz touched Christine's arm. "Sorry sweetheart, I've got to be the proper host. Talk to you later."

Stone fought an impulse to corner the publisher and ask why the paper had such anemic coverage of the Winters murder. But the current context seemed all wrong. Besides, he didn't want to embarrass Christine.

He recognized a face in the growing crowd. "I may be mistaken," he said to Christine, "but I think that's Ava Gardner over there."

"No mistake," Christine replied. "Just remember whose date you are, okay?"

He liked the way she said it. He didn't bother to mention that he also noticed Peter Lorre standing over by a nearby Tiki torch. It didn't seem nearly as important.

Just as they got their drinks, an older woman elegantly done up approached Christine. "Darling, in case you didn't know, I'm Hedda Hopper. Jonathan just told me about you. A woman doctor! Congratulations. Could I speak to you for a moment?"

She glanced at Stone as she said it, and he got the hint. "Ladies, if you'll excuse me, I'm going to check out the music."

Stone made his way to the far end of the covered space where the band played. Four musicians, all native Hawaiian. Pedal steel, bass, drums, guitar. It definitely had the same swing feel you might hear in one of the local honky-tonks, and basically the same instrumentation. The vocalist was singing in some Polynesian language unknown to Stone. He wondered if the lyrics had to do with cheating wives and jail time. Ron Travers might know. Too bad he wasn't here.

"Excuse me. Haven't we met?"

Stone turned to Cary Grant. Of course they'd met. Stone had waved him through the gate at Paramount maybe a hundred times. "Probably at Paramount," he said without elaborating.

"Really?" Grant looked genuinely puzzled.

"Cary!"

A big, imposing man with a pugnacious face and hair retreating into baldness lurched up to them, drink in hand. Stone recognized him from the papers. William Knowland, U.S. Senator from the great state of California. "I've got a fund raiser coming up in Beverly Hills. You could be a big help. You know that, don't you?"

"Well yes, maybe I could." Grant seemed less than enthused.

"Good! I'll be in town for a couple of weeks. I'll give you a call. Oh, and I loved you in that Hitchcock thing. Great job!"

"Thank you," Grant said with a genuine streak of modesty.

Knowland left with a big wink and went in search of his next target.

"Did he mean *To Catch a Thief*?" Stone asked.

Grant shook his head. "I have no idea." He offered his hand to Stone. "Sorry about the intrusion. Have fun."

Grant wandered off and Stone looked out on the lawn at the long rows of folding chairs and tables, which were starting to fill with diners attacking their luau pork and pineapple slices. The thick canopy of trees and shrubs warded off the summer sun and cast an opulent shadow over the scene. It all seemed much closer to the emerald topography of Bel Air than the flat dirt and grit of Bakersfield. But then again, that was the whole idea, wasn't it?

Christine appeared and took his arm. "Done so soon?" he asked.

"She cooled right down when I told her about treating Okie families up in Oildale. It would have gone a lot better if I was a heart surgeon in Manhattan."

"But you're not," Stone said. "So let's eat."

They passed through the buffet and seated themselves at one of the long tables. Stone sat to Christine's right and Hal Powers to her left. The lieutenant governor was taking a big interest in her, which was understandable, except that he was married. She seemed amused and clearly had the upper hand as the man persisted in making a pompous fool of himself.

A small snatch of conversation poked through from his right. Something about Okies. Three couples sat next to him facing three more on the other side of the table. The man in the middle on the far side clearly commanded the group's attention. He broadcast Alpha on all channels to the male sycophants in the group, who cocked their heads to take in every word while their deferential wives stared modestly at the tablecloth.

Stone did a quick take on the man, a cop take. Tall, trim, slightly gray, with a tan face aligned in perfect symmetry. Large ring on his right hand. High-end watch on the other. He spoke in a powerful, yet relaxed tenor.

"We've had twenty years of Okies around here and they're still bottom feeders. White trash. No will to succeed. Do you see any Okie lawyers? What about doctors? Or teachers? Not happening."

What about cops? Stone thought. Ask me about cops.

"The minute you hear that twang, it says it all," the man continued. "It's unfortunate, but that's the way it is. We just have to accept it and work with what we've got."

Stone was very close to injecting himself into the conversation when Christine touched his arm. "I don't know about you, but I'm almost ready to go."

Stone exhaled deeply. "Yeah."

"Are you okay?"

"Do you know the tall guy across the table?"

"That's Walter Sumner."

"And what does Mr. Sumner do for a living?" Stone asked.

"He sells the hardware that irrigates half the valley."

"I don't like him."

"You're probably not alone in that sentiment," Christine said. "Shall we go?"

"I don't want you to leave on my account," Stone said.

"I wouldn't even consider it. Now let's get out of here."

They went out into the warm night, where one of the valets fetched Christine's car. "I'd say goodbye to Jonathan, but it would take an hour to find him in all this," Christine said.

"At least," Stone agreed. He tipped the valet a dollar, which was a lot, but he didn't have any change.

"Let's go have a drink at the Padre," Christine said as they pulled out onto the street. She was referring to the bar in the Padre Hotel, whose new owners promised an innovative air of sophistication. Stone wasn't sure that was possible in downtown Bakersfield, but was willing to give it a try.

• • •

Twenty minutes later, they were seated at a little table in the bar at the Padre. Christine sipped a Daiquiri and Stone nursed a whiskey on the rocks. They had the place mostly to themselves.

"I'm resisting the temptation to talk about work," Stone admitted. Christine's post-mortem on Fancher was scheduled for the morning and he was intensely curious about her impressions going in.

"As well you should," Christine remarked. "So forget about it and tell me about your ex-wife."

Stone shrugged. "I'm not sure where to start. What do you want to know?"

"Was she attractive?"

"I suppose she was, especially at the beginning. But that wears off after a while. Know what I mean?"

"Yes, I do. Did she like being a housewife?"

"Yeah, she was fine with that. Most women are."

A wry smile from Christine. "You're right. Most women are."

"But not you."

"Not me," Christine said, and then quickly hid behind another query. "You haven't mentioned any children."

"We tried. It didn't work."

"Did you seek medical help?"

"Oh yes. We sought medical help. Over and over. Didn't work."

"Someday it will," Christine said. "And your participation will make some tiny contribution to that."

"I suppose you're right. I thought never thought about it like that."

"Was the baby problem what finally did you in?"

"It was part of it, but not all of it. She had some very specific expectations. We were going to live in a certain kind of house and have a certain kind of life, a very normal kind. Truth is, I was okay with that. I was a cop and got more than enough excitement at work. But then I lost my job, and it all went up in smoke. She tried to roll with it, but she couldn't. She never recovered."

"And what about you? Have you recovered?"

"No."

Plates rattled in a distant kitchen. A thin laugh drifted in from the lobby. A piano tinkled over a remote speaker. An awkward void opened, the first of the evening.

Christine brought them out of it. "You know why you're here tonight?" she asked him. "Here with me?"

"I have no idea," he admitted.

"Because most men would be scared. They wouldn't admit it, but I'd know it right away. But you're not. I don't know exactly why, but you're not. I like that."

Stone recalled the moment when she pulled that big convertible up to the curb, the moment when he shifted into some unknown gear. She was right. He wasn't scared. He suspected that if he dwelled on it, he might very well become scared, so he let it go. "I'll take that as a compliment."

"Good." She looked at her watch. "We should probably be going. As you well know, I have a busy day tomorrow."

"Same here."

"Besides, there's probably a curfew around here for expatriates."

"Expatriates?" He'd heard the word but wasn't sure what it meant.

"People living far from home in a strange land," she explained. "We both fit the definition quite nicely."

"Yes, we do."

He tried to think of something else they had in common, but he couldn't. And it didn't seem to matter.

Stone was still adjusting to the social scale of this place compared to Los Angeles, where anonymity carried the day. Here you were never more than five minutes away from someone you knew. Ron Travers confirmed this by showing up just as Stone and Christine stepped out onto H Street in front of the hotel. He was strolling down the sidewalk with a man that was new to Stone. Travers gave them a friendly wave and stopped to exchange pleasantries.

"The Padre, huh?" he said to Stone. "Does this mean no more slumming at the Blackboard?"

"Definitely not," Stone said.

After a round of introductions, Travers gave Christine a quizzical squint. "You look familiar. Have I seen you over at the college?"

"Maybe. I've done some guest lectures for the biology department. Great fun. I liked the kids a lot."

"Kids," Travers reflected wistfully. "You're right. And they look a little younger every year."

"I'm sure they do," Christine agreed.

Stone half listened to the banter, but something else had grabbed his attention as he looked at Travers and his companion. They were homosexuals. For most of the populace, homosexuality was a secret world, one kept carefully out of view. But not if you worked as a vice cop in Los Angeles. You had a more or less continual exposure to this hidden subculture and came to recognize it on very short notice. And in some inexplicable way, you also came to tolerate it to a certain degree. He'd heard all the rants about the perversion of it, the baseness of it. They started with your local pastor and went on up to the director of the FBI, one J. Edgar Hoover, who came off a little queer himself. But when all the raving was done, what was left? Stone wasn't sure, and at some point he'd put the whole matter on permanent hold.

"I've got an eight o'clock class, so I think we'll be off," Travers was saying to Christine. "Nice meeting you."

"My pleasure," Christine said.

Travers turned to Stone. "Until next time at Trout's or the Blackboard."

"You got it." Stone watched the pair walk off down the sidewalk. He was tempted to show off his observational powers to Christine and tell her that they were queer. But he held back. Travers seemed like a decent guy, so why cast him in a nasty light? Stone didn't like the idea of puffing himself up at someone else's expense. Besides, after being immersed in the Fancher case, he'd just as soon dwell on some other subject entirely, like how to juggle two homicide cases without dropping either one.

13.

"So what have you got for me?" Stone asked Hoffner, the lab technician.

"Quite a bit," replied Hoffner, who was seated on a tall stool next to his lab bench. He reached into a file folder and extracted several pages of fingerprint images and documentation. "First of all, the prints on the stolen items from the Fancher place match the prints we took from Willert at the hospital. There were also several prints from Fancher on the stuff, which is to be expected."

"Anyone else's prints?"

"Not on that stuff, but plenty more from the party scene. With all those bottles and glasses it looked like it was going to be a real mess, but we got a real break from what we found in the bedrooms."

Stone hadn't been there when they went through bedrooms. He'd left to respond to Lincoln Jefferson's story.

"We were looking at three bedrooms total. All of them had bottles, glasses and ashtrays with cigarette butts. It gave a pretty easy way to sort it out."

"How's that?"

"First of all, we found Willert's prints in all three, probably from when he tossed the place looking for loot. But when we examined the bottles and glasses, each room had prints from only two other individuals." He showed Stone a page from the report. "Here's Fancher's thumbprint, which we took at the morgue. Here it is again off a glass on a nightstand in the master bedroom. Now in here's a second thumbprint, a smaller one, from a second person. Probably female. When people hold bottles and glasses, they tend to use only their dominant hand. So we wound up with five prints from the second person."

"What about the other bedrooms?"

"Same idea. We wound up with a single hand's worth of prints that appear to be male, and a second set from a woman. We got the same pattern from some hair samples we found on the pillows. Two different types in each of the three bedrooms."

"Anything else?"

"Yeah. The cigarette butts. Based on color, we came up with three different shades of lipstick, one per room."

"What about the ashtrays out on the coffee table in the living room?"

"We found all three shades out there. Plus it looks like all the shades show up on the reefer. They must have been passing it around."

"That it?" Stone asked.

"That's it for now."

It was plenty. Stone now saw a pattern evolving. A prominent citizen and two of his pals have a poker night that goes way beyond a couple of rounds of five card stud. They import a trio of whores from downtown, along with all the narcotics necessary to keep them entertained while the card game plays out. Then they pair off and copulate their way into the wee hours. Fancher's compadres leave with the women and sometime after that the robbery goes down. Did Fancher catch the Willert in the act? If so, it would explain the stabbing.

"I've got to get all this stuff boxed up and stored in Evidence," Hoffner was saying as Stone emerged from his speculation. "Good work," he told the lab technician. "Keep me posted."

"Will do."

. . .

Stone interrupted Detective Sergeant Bagley, who was stretching rubber bands over a pencil tip and shooting them into his wastebasket. "Got a question for you."

"Yeah?" Bagley didn't bother to look up as he loaded a new rubber band.

"You worked Vice for a while, didn't you?"

"Yeah." Bagley launched the rubber band, which sailed over the wastebasket in a ragged arc and skittered across the linoleum floor. He looked up. "You made me miss."

"You're sure about that?" Stone challenged.

Bagley shrugged. "So you want to know where to get a blowjob on Saturday night? Go out east on Edison past Oswell."

"I need to get an idea of how many different hookers you bust every year around here."

Bagley smiled cynically. "Well you got to understand it's nothing like the circus you guys must've run in LA."

"Didn't think so. So how many?"

"A few dozen. Same faces over and over."

Stone nodded. It squared with the size of the community. "Thanks."

"Don't mention it."

Stone moved on and plunked down behind his desk. He had prints from the three women, who might or might not be whores. He was sure there were enough loose women up in Oildale to give the pros a real run for their money. And that was the problem. It was going to be a big time sink to check the prints against those he'd find in the arrest records. He'd have to do it by hand, fingerprint by fingerprint. And what if he came up empty? It just wasn't worth the gamble, at least not yet. They already had a very strong circumstantial case against Willert, even without the murder weapon.

So now what? He stood up and grabbed his fedora. Time to switch trains and hop back on the Winters case.

· · ·

The drive east out Highway 178 was hot, flat and straight. Stone didn't notice. He was focused on a single piece of evidence from the Fancher crime scene, the pack of matches on the coffee table. They came from the same place as the pack he'd found in Charlene Winters' bedroom: The Rancho Vista Motel. It presented the intriguing possibility that Charlene was somehow linked to someone at Fancher's fatal party. Her mother and Bobby Simmons both said she'd been stepping out with some unknown party. Maybe Fancher or one of his buddies? It seemed an indulgent speculation, but maybe not. When he worked in LA he was connecting the dots inside a population of four million people. But this was Bakersfield, population fifty thousand. He needed to adjust his thinking to the size of the jurisdiction where he was now working. The dots were much closer together.

The Bakersfield Country Club stood in lavish dignity against the afternoon sun as Stone pulled into its covered entrance. Two stories of stucco topped by a roof of terra cotta tile. Manicured palms, green velvet lawns and pools of water where there should have been none.

Stone exercised the standard police privilege and left his car parked on the far side of the entrance. He pushed through double doors of carved wood into an air-conditioned interior and stopped to sigh at the wonderful coolness of it all. No wonder people paid outrageous fees to be here.

He scanned the lobby looking for administrative offices, but saw none. Nor was there a reception desk. Of course not. You either belonged here or you didn't. No need to find your way around. He picked a likely looking corridor and followed it toward the sound of clinking glasses and a pleasant trickle of conversation. Soon he came upon the Grill Room, which overlooked the golf course and the Tehachapi Mountains beyond.

The bar opened up to an outdoor patio that was now in shade, with a few people lounging at tables with wicker chairs. And among those people, he spotted Fatalia Castle. White shorts high on the thigh and cotton blouse low on the cleavage. No surprise. A male of military bearing sat opposite her in khaki shorts, a flowery sport shirt and aviator sunglasses. Undoubtedly another resident of Edwards.

Stone considered moving on, but if Fatalia was a member, she might be useful a source of information. He headed toward the patio.

"Excuse me, sir. Are you a member?" An old bulldog of a bartender peered at him from below bushy brows.

Stone put on his best statesman's smile, and pointed toward the patio. "I'm a guest of Miss Castle." He kept on walking all the while. Never play the cop card if you don't have to. The bartender glared but didn't respond.

Fatalia looked up at his approach. If she was surprised, she didn't show it. "Officer Stone," she said with a lazy smile. "Good to see you." She pointed toward her male escort. "Meet Lieutenant Ronnie Grisfield, one of Edward's finest."

Grisfield swung his hand out, all loose and cool and cocky, and Stone shook it. Another flyboy for sure.

Fatalia raised a glass full of gin. "You caught me on a bad day. I'll let Ronnie explain. Have a seat."

"Truth is, I'm here on business," Stone said. "So I should probably be off."

"Have a seat," Fatalia insisted. "I guarantee Ronnie will make it worth your while." She was at least a little drunk.

"You know Captain Piland?" Grisfield asked.

Stone immediately recalled the incident in the parking lot at the Blackboard, and the drawn .45. "A little," he replied.

"Well this morning he found himself doing the sabre dance," Grisfield said.

"Doing the what?"

"Here's how it works," Grisfield explained. "You're in one of the new F-100 Sabre jets and you're on approach to land." He stiffened his right hand to imitate a plane and brought it down toward the table. "You've got to come in fast because if you don't, you're going to lose your lift and stall." His hand continued toward the table. "And once you stall, the nose tilts up." He angled his palm up while his hand continued down. "And once the nose is up, she starts to twist and turn at the same time." He rotated his hand at odd angles. "Now you got yourself a sabre dance. Your only chance is to gun it and hope for the best." He let his hand fall to the table and looked up at Stone. "Didn't work. He crashed and burned."

"Wow," Stone said. "What happened then?"

"The emergency crews were all over him in just a couple of minutes," Grisfield said. "They doused the cockpit and pulled him free. I talked to the docs just before I left, and they say he's probably going to make it."

Stone noticed that Grisfield didn't appear very hopeful. "That's got to be good news, right?"

Grisfield shrugged. "Depends on what you call good news. He's got burns over seventy-five percent of his body."

Cop or not, Stone found this almost too gruesome to contemplate. A dead playboy with a punctured chest was pretty bad, but a good-natured pilot turned into a living barbeque was a step beyond. "I'm sorry. He seemed like a great guy. He didn't deserve it. I don't know what else to say."

Grisfield settled back in his chair and took a generous sip of his drink. "Goes with the job."

Stone turned to Fatalia. "Sorry I bothered you."

She waved off his apology and changed the subject. "You said you're here on business. Can you tell us what it is, or is it secret police stuff?"

"No secrets. I'm looking for the personnel manager."

Fatalia pointed to the bar inside. "Back down the hall to the lobby. Up the stairs and to the right."

"Thanks." Stone got up to leave. "Let me know how he's doing, okay? I owe him one."

Fatalia and Grisfield each managed a weak wave at his departure.

. . .

The management offices were right where Fatalia described them. This time Stone had no choice but to play the cop card. He pulled out his badge and showed it to a young secretary facing the entrance. "Hi, I'm James Stone from the Bakersfield Police. I need to talk with whoever your personnel manager is."

The young woman perked up. Sgt. James Stone had just juiced up a very boring day behind the typewriter. "That would be Mr. Nelson. I'll go get him."

She returned with a man in his late fifties wearing a severely trimmed mustache and rimless glasses. He had that anxious look common to all bureaucrats when they feel their boat start to rock. "I'm Fred Nelson," the man said. What can I do for you?"

Stone looked over at the secretary, who was devouring every detail. "I need to sit down with you for a couple of minutes," he told Nelson. "It shouldn't take long."

"Let's step back into my office," Nelson reluctantly offered.

Once in the office, Stone took the lead. "In case you haven't guessed, I'm here about Charlene Winters."

"Yes, it's very sad," Nelson offered. "We were all shocked."

"She was a good employee," he added stiffly.

Stone imagined that Nelson was exceptionally good at firing people without any remorse. "What did she do here?"

"She was a waitress in the dining room."

"What shift was she on?"

"The day shift."

"Did she have any friends on the staff? Anyone she was close to?"

"Not that I know of." Nelson shook his head. "Sorry."

Stone nodded. It was obvious if anyone had any friends around here Mr. Nelson would be the last to know. He pulled out a card and pushed it across the desk. "If you think of anything, give me a call." He stood up to leave and Nelson started to rise also. "Don't bother. I'll show myself out."

Instead of showing himself out, Stone showed himself down to the main dining room, which had yet another spectacular view over the course to the mountains. Not an oil pump or beet field anywhere in sight. Lunch was long gone and dinner still on the horizon, so the staff was pretty much idle. Perfect. People would have time to talk. He spotted two young women in waitress uniforms standing by the doors into the kitchen.

"Good afternoon," he greeted the pair. "Sorry to bother you. I'm Sgt. Stone from the Bakersfield Police and I'm working on the Charlene Winters case."

The pair's expressions sank from curious to fearful. Both appeared to be about Charlene's age.

"Did either of you know her?" he asked.

"Yeah, kind of," the first one said. The second nodded in agreement.

"Was there anybody here that she was good friends with?"

The pair looked at each in silent consultation. "That would be Denise," the second offered.

"Is she here now?"

"She's in the kitchen," the first said. "Want me to get her?"

"I'd appreciate that," Stone replied.

She left and the second girl said, "Can you tell us what happened? They don't say much about it in the paper."

"I've noticed that," Stone commented dryly. "I wish I could tell you more, but it's an ongoing investigation and that kind of limits me. I'm sure it'll all come out in the end."

"I sure hope so," the girl said and looked away to hide misted eyes.

The first girl returned with Denise, a willowy girl with chestnut hair and a long face and prominent nose. Stone needed a tactful way to separate her from the other two girls.

"Denise, I'm Sergeant Stone and I understand that you were friends with Charlene."

Denise gave a solemn nod. "If you don't mind, I'd like to chat with you for a couple of minutes," he told her, then immediately turned to the original pair. "Ladies, I'd like to thank you for your help. If I need any more from you, I'll be in touch." He put his hand on Denise's shoulder and guided her out into the dining area, where two busboys were setting tables. He picked a table that was still bare and they sat down.

"I know this isn't easy," Stone said. "But it might be very helpful to us."

"She had a lot of dreams," Denise volunteered. "A lot more than most of us."

Stone knew the drill. Some people provide better information if you just follow the thread and steer very gently. "What kind of dreams?" he asked.

"She was gonna have her own beauty shop. Then she was gonna save up a bunch of money and move to San Francisco. Then she was gonna do the same thing there, only bigger. Then she was gonna be rich." Denise paused. "Personally, I don't think it was ever going to happen."

"Why not?"

"Truth is, she was kind of lazy. She was slow picking up her orders from the kitchen and always behind on her tables. But she was a talker and she was beautiful, so she got away with it. People liked her."

"Did she ever talk to you about boyfriends and things like that?"

Denise smiled wistfully. "All the time. She had a thing for that guitar player guy, but then they busted up. She said he kept shooting himself in the foot, so he wasn't ever going to be a big star, and that was important to her."

"How did she feel about them splitting up? Was she sad, or mad or disgusted?"

"Not really. She said it didn't matter because she was ready to move up to higher things."

"Higher things?"

"Yeah, you know: Some guy with a car and a nice house and some money. Somebody that might help her to get her business rolling."

"Did she mention any names?"

"Nope. Never did. But she did say she had somebody picked out"

"She did?"

"Yeah, it was kind of funny how she told me."

"How's that?"

"We were standing pretty close to where we are right now. I asked where this new guy lived and she just pointed out the window and smiled. Then she clammed up. That was all I got."

Stone looked out the window at the golf course and the mountains. "What do you think she meant by that?"

"I think she meant it was somebody out there playing golf."

Stone saw a sliver of light. "Do you think it was a member?"

"I dunno. Could have been a guest but probably not. Most of the time it's members out there."

Time to change direction. "What was Charlene like when she was waiting tables?"

"Real friendly. Kinda on the flirty side."

"Did she flirt with some more than others?"

"Not really. She spread it all around. Got better tips that way."

"Let's go back to when she pointed out the window," Stone said. "Do you remember when it was?"

"You mean the date?"

"The date, the day of the week. Anything you can remember."

"Well I'm not sure about that. I..." Denise paused and looked down in concentration. "It had to be a Tuesday."

"A Tuesday?"

"Yeah, a Tuesday."

"How's that?"

"Because there's a group of lady golfers that has breakfast every other Tuesday. I always remember because I don't like 'em. They're real picky and they don't tip for beans. That was the day she told me."

Stone gave Denise his card and left the dining room. He descended a flight of stairs to ground level, where a little fleet of golf carts stood ready to serve the membership. He spotted man with a polo shirt and clipboard. Stone guessed he was the starter, and walked over.

"Hi," Stone greeted him. "Could you tell me how to reserve a tee time?"

The man had a blond flattop haircut that spread a greased tree line across his upper forehead. "You a member?" he asked with a nasty inflection.

Stone responded in kind by pulling out his badge. "No. I'm member of the Bakersfield Police Department."

The man's face fell. "Oh," he mumbled, and pointed to a sheltered outcrop of the main building. "You need to talk to our resident pro. He's over there."

"Thanks." Stone walked across a concrete apron to where the resident pro stood behind a wooden counter. He wore an open white shirt that accented his tanned arms and green eyes. No doubt he was a favorite with the lady golfers. He looked up at Stone's approach in a most condescending manner. Who was this guy in a cheap suit intruding on paradise?

Stone put it aside. "Hi. I understand that you're the golf pro here."

"That's right," the pro said.

"And so that makes you the one who keeps all the tee times, right?"

"That's right," the pro repeated, and volunteered no more.

"So you could tell me who was playing on a certain day?"

The cool green eyes held steady on Stone. Not a trace of flicker. "I could. But I won't."

Badge time. Stone pulled out his identification. "Even if I'm a police officer?"

The pro calmly leaned close enough that he could read Stone's ID. "Sgt. James Stone of the Bakersfield Police. Do I have that right?"

"Yes you do."

"Would you excuse me a moment?" the pro asked with a caustic smile.

"Certainly," Stone reciprocated.

The pro walked back into the main building. Stone leaned on the counter and looked out over the course. Green and beautiful. A large pond stood in front of the first hole. A trout-sized fish leapt from its water to devour a passing insect. Stone could do nothing but marvel.

He turned to the sound of approaching footsteps. He wished he hadn't. Right behind the pro was none other than Samuel Delfort, the attorney from hell, the lawyer who so brutally put him in his place in front of the vicious Willert kid in the hospital. Same guy, only this time dressed in upscale golf attire that would have cost Stone a month's salary.

"Ah yes, Sergeant Stone," Delfort said by way of verification. "On the job as always." He joined the pro on the far side of the counter and casually leaned forward on his elbows. "I understand that you want to look at certain records that are kept here. Care to tell me why you want to do that?"

"No, I don't." Stone answered.

"Is it something you could explain to a judge? Something that might get you a search warrant?"

"At this point, probably not."

"Well maybe I can help," Delfort said in feigned sympathy. "I know just about everyone on the bench here in Kern County. It's not a big place, you know. It's not like LA."

Stone got the message. In fact, he got a double-barreled blast. Delfort was making it clear that if Stone tried to get a warrant, the attorney had the political clout to block it. Second, he pegged Stone as a transplant from LA, which Stone hadn't mentioned to him. It might very well be that Delfort was sizing him up for the professional kill.

"I appreciate the offer," Stone shot back. "But I think I can manage all by myself."

"All by yourself," Delfort reflected. "That sums it up very nicely. Good day, sergeant."

· · ·

It wasn't quite a haystack, but it definitely leaned in that direction. On the way out Stone chatted up a couple of women in the lobby and learned that the club had nearly four hundred members, and about a hundred were active golfers. Without knowing who had regular tee times on Tuesday mornings, he had no way to narrow the field to a manageable number. To compound the issue he couldn't be sure about Denise's assumption that a member was the object of Charlene Winter's desire. It was simply a guess.

A lot of what he did as a cop was to bet his time against the odds that a particular lead would pay off. Did he want to bet checking out over a hundred people against the assumption that Charlene's gesture out the window meant that she was chasing a member? Not really.

But maybe there was another way. A more interesting way.

· · ·

"Want to guess what he died from?" Dr. Harmon asked Stone in a deft touch of black humor.

They stood beside a gurney containing the supine corpse of the late Richard Fancher. Once wealthy, once respectable, now dead. A towel covered his lower half, which was not pertinent right now.

Stone played along with Christine's remark. "A heart attack maybe?"

"In a way, you're right," Christine answered. "See the chest wound?"

An open slit of dark red interrupted the deathly pallor that covered the rest of the torso. Pretty hard to miss, even after Dr. Harmon had taken Mr. Fancher apart and put him back together with some crude stitches up the center.

"Your killer got lucky. One stab did the job. Usually, we see multiple wounds and have to sort out which ones did the real damage. In this case, a single thrust penetrated deep enough to sever the left anterior ascending artery. That'll do you in every time."

"I guess so," Stone said. "So what's it tell you about the knife?"

"Most likely a switchblade, a stiletto. The entrance wound is too narrow in the horizontal for most kitchen knives or a hunting knife. The blade penetrated about six inches, which means the ricasso went in up to the guard and left the kind of entry shape you'd expect from this kind of kind of weapon. Also, if you want to take a closer look, you'll see a subtle deformation along one side of the wound."

"I'll take your word for it," Stone said.

Christine smiled in amusement. "That's what they all say. Anyway, that little blip came from the blade lock, which clicks in once the spring has put the blade in place."

"Very astute of you," Stone said.

"Thank you. We also got some dried semen off the bed sheets in the master bedroom, but it doesn't do us much good because there's no way to match it to anybody."

"Too bad," Stone commented.

"Yes, it is. But eventually, we'll able to."

"How? Don't all sperms cells look pretty much the same?"

"Think about it this way," Christine said. "Semen is the juice that carries the sperm cells. And down inside those sperm are the chromosomes that carry the genes that make the babies. We can't see the genes themselves, but we know that they contain the instructions to help make new little people. Someday we'll be able to read those instructions and tell you exactly who they came from. Just like a fingerprint."

"Pretty far out," Stone commented.

"Not as far as you think," Christine predicted.

"Next week would be fine with me," Stone said. "Are we missing anything here?"

"Not right now."

"Well, I'm off then. Keep me posted." Stone felt a sudden impulse to ask her out for a drink after work, but shrugged it off. He had plenty to deal with right now besides a woman he couldn't match in brains, money or social standing.

"I'll do that," Christine replied. "You take care now."

He couldn't help but like the way she said it.

· · ·

Stone pulled up in front of the Castle residence on a prosperous stretch of Kane Way in the southeast part of the city. He left his suit coat and hat in the car before he got out. A little less formality would get him a lot closer to what he needed from Fatalia.

Like many other upscale residences around town, it beguiled you when viewed from the street. Its true dimensions and styling hid behind strategically placed plants and fencing. It wasn't until he reached the front door that he realized the true extent of the house and landscaping. It spilled out down three long wings, and he could see through to a large swimming pool out back.

Fatalia answered the door in a white bathrobe open to a two-piece swimsuit cut as low as public decency might allow. "That didn't take long," she said.

"I was nearby," he explained.

She showed him in. Air conditioning rushed through hidden vents. Sleek furniture sprawled over floors of polished wood. Oriental carpets covered all the right vacancies.

She took him by the arm toward the pool area. "You said you had a favor to ask. I'm sorry, but I can't talk about favors without us having a drink."

"Okay by me," Stone said.

She slipped behind a bar with long stools and a top of polished stone. "What'll it be?" she asked, with an affected flip of her hair.

"It's hot," he said. "A beer would work."

"Then so be it." She fetched a bottle of Heidelberg from a refrigerator behind the bar and made a screwdriver for herself.

"Isn't there something that says you can't drink while you're on duty?" she asked while she mixed the orange juice and vodka.

"Could be, but I haven't gotten around to reading it yet."

"I'd say that gives you temporary immunity."

She brought the drinks around and handed him his beer. He'd have to play this carefully. He could have a drink and get away with it during working hours – but he couldn't have her. Too much risk, no matter how tempting. Time to pour just a little water on the fire.

"How's Captain Piland?" he asked.

She shrugged. "They took him to some kind of burn center in Maryland. I haven't heard much since."

"If you do hear from him, give him my best."

"I'll do that." She sipped her drink. "You caught me in the middle of tanning time when you phoned. Let's talk out by the pool."

They passed through a sliding door of tinted glass into a sunlit blast of pale cement and pool water turned dazzling blue. She doffed her robe and lay stomach down on a chaise lounge. A magnificent display of curved surfaces done in a perfect shade of brown. She turned her head to face him. "So you need a favor, right?"

"Right."

"Well so do I. Why don't you pull up a chair?"

He pulled a blue chair of molded plastic up to the chaise lounge while she opened a bottle of tanning oil and lay back down. With no pretense, she unfastened her swimsuit top. It fell limp to the sides, exposing a crescent of breast. "I hate tan lines. I need some oil, and there it is."

"That's the favor?"

"That's it."

He put some oil on his palm at applied it to her back. The sun had already made her skin warm to the touch. He rotated his hand up and down the length of her exposed flesh. It glistened in a wet sheen under the travel of his motion.

"My turn," Stone said.

"Go ahead," she murmured.

"I assume you know the golf pro out at the country club."

"That would be Ronnie," she answered. "Everybody knows Ronnie."

"But some better than others, right?"

"Right."

"Do you know him well enough that he might share regular tee times for certain members?"

"I might."

"Would you give it a go?"

"Maybe," she said. But what if he clams up? What then?"

"Then we're even. As long as you try."

"Deal."

Stone let his hand linger for a while longer on her back. It seemed only prudent.

. . .

"Mr. Hoffner wants to see you over at the lab," Mrs. Crenshaw announced as Stone walked past her desk. She said it in a most irritated manner, as if relaying a spoken request was far beyond her range of responsibilities.

"Did he say what it was about?"

"No, he did not." She went back to typing. End of conversation.

Stone surrendered to a small surge of hope as he crossed the parking area to the lab. Maybe Hoffner had uncovered something new that would move the Fancher case forward.

One look at Hoffner's face when he entered the lab told him otherwise. The technician appeared pale and stricken.

"You haven't heard?" Hoffner asked.

"Heard what?"

"It's gone."

"What's gone?" Stone saw a calamity coming and couldn't even begin to estimate its dimensions.

"The evidence in the Fancher case."

"Gone? What do you mean: gone?" Stone allowed himself to sink into a warm bath of denial. Some idiot had misplaced the stuff, and it would show up after a little searching.

"I mean gone. I went to the evidence locker to fetch some of it, and the whole box was gone. I had Francine look at the log, and nobody checked it out. We've asked all around, but nobody's seen it."

Stone got out of the bath and shivered in the cold. He fought off panic and went over the process for handling evidence. Once evidence was tagged in the field, it was brought back here and stored in the evidence locker. In reality, the "locker" was simply a spare room full of shelves and a refrigerator. It was presided over by the "evidence officer," who in this case was Francine, a clerk with a desk near the door to the locker. She kept both the key to the room and a log of who put stuff in and took stuff out. If you wanted to put something in, you signed the log as such and Francine unlocked the door for you and locked it back up when you departed. Same thing if you took stuff out. Thus the chain of evidence was preserved.

So what in God's name had gone wrong?

· · ·

The band started early at the Rainbow Gardens, but Stone had decided to get drunk before they even reached the stage. He'd do it slow and steady. And if in the end, he was too far gone to drive, he'd have a patrol car take him home. He sat on a stool at the bar and ordered a beer to ease into the process.

He was two drinks in when Lefty Frizzell and his boys fired up.

He was on his third when Ron Travers sat down next to him.

Neither spoke and both listened as Lefty belted out "I'm An Old, Old Man." The tune ended and Travers turned to Stone. "So, you've got me pegged," he declared.

"What do you mean?" Stone asked, even though he knew precisely what Travers meant. He preferred to have the whole issue slide off gently into oblivion, along with his sobriety.

"In front of the Padre. You took one look at Jim and me, and you knew what the deal was. I don't know what kind of cop you are, but clearly you've dealt with this kind of thing before."

"As a matter of fact, I have," Stone admitted.

"So are you going to arrest me?"

"What for?"

"For being a homo, for being a pervert."

"Yeah, I could do that," Stone said. "But I just don't see much point in it."

"Why not?"

"I'm in the middle of two homicide cases. One's stalled, and the other's in really big trouble. It makes you seem hardly worth it. Sorry."

"Good," Travers said, and smiled. "Shall we get back to the music?"

Stone raised his glass in a mildly tipsy salute. "Back to the music."

Travers pointed toward the stage. "Roy Nichols is backing Lefty on guitar tonight. You know about Roy Nichols?"

"Can't say I do."

"He gets this steel guitar sound by bending the strings sideways. He's got it down cold. A lot of other guys have picked up on it, but nobody can do it like he can. Take a listen."

Lefty and the band obliged by starting their next tune. Halfway through, Nichols took a turn on lead, and started pushing strings around, just as Travers predicted. And sure enough, it came off as some kind of hybrid between steel and straight guitar.

Stone turned to Travers as the tune ended. "I like it."

"Thought you would."

And then Stone realized that for about three minutes, the space of the song, he'd forgotten all about nasty people at golf courses and ransacked evidence rooms. He celebrated by ordering a whiskey on the rocks.

And on the way home in the patrol car, he entertained the two officers by singing his very own versions of Lefty Frizzell's songs.

14.

"First and foremost," Bob LaFrieniere declared, "We've got to keep this thing contained. Anybody disagree?"

The district attorney looked around the table for a dissenter. Chief Beaumont stared at the table. Head Investigator Gilford clasped his hands tightly. Lab tech Hoffner nodded in humble acquiescence. Police clerk Francine Waters held back tears.

Detective Sergeant James Stone gazed out at the morning light that streamed into the conference room on the top floor of the courthouse building. He had a very dull edge after last night's indulgence at the Rainbow Gardens. His only consolation was that one of the patrolmen who drove him home kind of liked his singing and thought maybe he should give it a go for real.

"Alright then," LaFrieniere went on. "We've gone over the paperwork, and that's getting us nowhere. Everybody signed everything, just like they're supposed to, but somehow all the evidence is gone. Correct?"

"Correct," Beaumont answered.

"What about the key?" LaFrieniere asked. "The key to the room. Who keeps tabs on it?"

The DA's question caught Stone's attention and pulled his focus back into the room.

"I guess that would be me," Francine volunteered.

"So how do you account for it?" LaFrieniere asked.

"I keep it in my purse right beside my chair. If somebody wants in, I take it out and unlock the door, then I lock it after they leave and put the key back in my purse."

"Do you take it home in your purse at night?"

"Oh no," Francine said. "I wouldn't do that. It's police property." She now had the full attention of the entire table.

"Well then where does it go when you leave?" LaFrieniere asked.

"I take it over and give it to the duty officer at the front desk. It goes on the key rack behind him, along with my log. That way, if anybody's working late, they can go through the duty officer to get in or out."

"Okay, so now we have the key out in the open," LaFrieniere observed. "On a peg in a rack with a lot of other keys. That right?"

"That's right," Beaumont answered.

Stone noticed that now that there was trouble Head Investigator Gilford receded far into the background and out of the line of fire. Beaumont had called the beefy redhead an asshole. Apparently, he was also a weasel.

"So let me ask this," LaFrieniere went on. "What's to stop someone from simply walking up and removing the key?"

"The desk sergeant's responsible for the security of the key rack," Beaumont said. "That would be Ernie Wheeler this week."

"Can you guarantee that Sgt. Wheeler had his eye on the keys every minute of his shift?"

"No," Beaumont answered. "I cannot."

"Jesus!" LaFrieniere exclaimed. The room fell silent, except for the big rotating fan in the corner. It paid no heed and buzzed on into the still air.

The DA surveyed the faces at the table. "Let me repeat myself: None of this leaves this room."

An interesting corollary occurred to Stone, but the fog in his head was too thick to get it out. If indeed somebody had subverted the process to use the key, it had to be someone who thoroughly understood the process itself.

The DA turned to the chief. "I think you better have a talk with Sergeant Wheeler."

Gilford finally spoke up. "Forget about Wheeler. He's not the real problem. It's the case itself. We're as good as dead. When we reach discovery, Willert's lawyer will find out we don't have a leg to stand on. Everything that ties him to the inside of the house is gone. All the loot, all the prints, everything. The only thing left is the car. We caught him in Fancher's car. That's it. I can just hear it now: Willert will say he found the car in some parking lot with the keys in it and took off. We'll be lucky if we can even nail him for car theft."

Stone spoke up. "Let's not forget we figure there were five other people at the scene. Were they there when the murder happened? Doesn't look it, but we don't know that for sure. We may have some witnesses out there. In any case, they could tell what was going on before the killing went down."

Silence fell as everyone at the table absorbed Stone's contribution.

Gilford pounced. "You also found a bunch of dope on the scene. You think anyone is going to voluntarily come forward? No way."

"Maybe someone saw them entering the premises," Stone countered. "Maybe we can track them down."

Gilford gave a derisive snort. "Good luck with that. You don't even have their prints, so where you going to start?"

LaFrieniere rose, indicating the meeting was over. "I think that'll do it for now. Anybody gets a break, let me know."

Thanks for the vote of confidence, Stone thought.

· · ·

Stone stood on the sidewalk across the street from the home of the late Richard Fancher. A large insect whizzed uncomfortably close to his ear and he batted it away. He suspected that it was driven mad by the incessant heat and wanted to tunnel into his ear seeking shade.

His Timex watch read 1:30, which meant it would only get hotter as the afternoon trudged toward sundown. It left him looking forward to his next stop at the Rancho Vista Motel, which had air conditioning in the restaurant. With all the physical evidence up in smoke, he had to work out on the far periphery of the case. When the cops had canvassed the neighborhood here the morning after the murder, they didn't come up with any leads. But now he wanted to find out for himself.

It didn't take long.

An elderly woman came onto the porch behind him. She wore a cotton dress and crocheted shawl, which Stone found incredible given the temperature was now above 90. "You look like you're lost," she observed. "Can I help you?"

"Yes ma'am," Stone said respectfully. "I'm with the police, and I'm working on the case across the street."

"Oh, that would be Mr. Fancher's house. It's very shocking to have that happen so close to home."

"I'm sure it is," Stone agreed.

"He was always so nice," she went on. "He even let his gardener come over a few times and mow my lawn.

"He had a gardener?"

"Yes he did. A Negro. An elderly gentleman. It was so nice of Mr. Fancher to give him the work."

"Do you remember his name?"

"No, I don't. I never spoke with him."

Stone made a note to check it out; it was a long shot at best. Better to go for something more immediate. "Ma'am, do you recall anything out of the ordinary that went on over there?"

The woman turned thoughtful. "Not really. Except for the cars."

"The cars?"

"Every couple of weeks, there would be these big, beautiful cars parked out front in the evening."

"Do you remember how many?"

"Oh, just three or four. It never created any trouble."

"Well that's good," Stone remarked. "Do you recall anything else?"

"Yes, as matter of fact, I do," she said wistfully. "Mr. Fancher had the most beautiful brown, wavy hair." Her expression collapsed into regret. "I never had hair like that, even when I was his age. It just doesn't seem fair."

"Life seldom is," Stone commented.

"And that's why we go to church, right?"

"Right." Stone tipped his hat. "Thanks for your help."

"Do you go to church on a regular basis?" she asked.

"As often as I can." Which was almost never.

"I attend every week," she said. "You know what our pastor told us from the pulpit last Sunday?"

"No, I don't."

"He said we should pray for the deliverance of Senator Joe McCarthy. He said the Communists are conspiring to bring this good man low and undo all his good work."

"I wouldn't know about that," Stone said.

The lady broke into a triumphant smile. "That's because you don't attend church every week."

"You're probably right." He declined to mention that those conspiring against McCarthy now included the entire United States Army.

He thanked the woman for her help and headed back to his car.

15.

The drive north on 99 gave Stone time to mull over one of the more intriguing aspects of the Fancher case. While the Charlene Winters murder rated page seven, the Fancher killing received no newspaper coverage of any kind.

In checking on Fancher's background, Stone had discovered that he was a person of some consequence in Bakersfield business and political circles. But the only mention of his demise was an obituary notice that conveniently failed to mention the cause of death.

The only way to make sense of the omission was to factor in all the smarmy trappings at the crime scene. Drugs, loose women, and bad behavior by those who should have known better. The upper social stratum of Bakersfield was small and tight-knit, as Stone had learned on his visit to the country club and his conversations with Fatalia. Even though Fancher and friends had crossed the line, he was one of their own, which was sufficient motivation to close ranks around him. No matter what the situation, you always stayed true to your tribe. Even in a sordid affair like this one, where the victim was engaging in highly questionable antics just before being savagely dispatched.

The parking lot at the Rancho Vista Motel held only a handful of cars that sat baking in afternoon heat. No surprise. The real commerce here didn't begin until the sun was long gone and the true trade emerged from the shadows. Stone locked his coat and hat in the car and made straight for the air-conditioned Valhalla offered by the restaurant. It was last place he'd seen Willert prior to the murder and the first place he'd try to track his movements. Most likely, he had a room here, a base for his hustling operation. The same might be true for any or all of the three women at Fancher's party, as indicated by the matches on the coffee table. He pushed through the glass door, which felt mercifully cool to the touch.

The girl fell immediately into his line of site. The same one who'd sat in adoration across from Gary Willert just two days ago. She wore the same shorts, the same sandals. A lit cigarette was her only company. Its smoke rose in twin strands of blue from a beanbag ashtray on the Formica tabletop. A partially consumed sandwich sat in front of her, and she idly rotated a plastic straw in a glass of Coke. Her gaze tracked the bubbles, as if their motion held some hidden meaning.

As Stone approached the booth, he revised his estimate of her age from their last encounter. She was just barely in full female bloom, perhaps thirteen or fourteen, the remnants of childhood only recently shed.

She sensed his approach and looked up suspiciously as he slid into the booth opposite her. "What are you doing?" she asked.

Stone intuitively parsed her delivery. This wasn't the first time she'd dealt with strange men. The melancholy fled her eyes, replaced by a hardened glaze.

"My name's James Stone, and I'm with the Bakersfield police. I saw you here two days ago with a guy named Gary Willert. You know who I mean?"

Her face collapsed. The glaze melted and the fear inside burst naked into the open. "Yeah, I know who you mean."

"Are you aware of what's happened to him?"

"I didn't have anything to do with it," she blurted. Her eyes left Stone's and sought asylum somewhere deep within the bubbles in the Coke.

"Nobody said you did." Stone stifled the elation rising within him. At last, a big break, possibly a home run. He needed to proceed carefully, deliberately. "All I'm trying to do is sort this thing out and get to the truth. The more you help me, the more I can help you. That's the way it works."

"It was all his idea. He told you that, right? "

"Not exactly, but pretty close. Why don't you walk me through it, and we'll see where we wind up?"

The tears started. Parallel tracks flowing over flawless skin. "How could I have been so stupid? I really loved him. I really did."

"We all make those kinds of mistakes. Sooner or later. Nobody blames you." Stone gave her a sad smile laced with wisdom. He reached over and extracted a napkin from a chrome dispenser and offered it to her. "Here."

She dabbed her cheeks and sniffled. It wasn't an act. Stone had seen plenty of acts, and this wasn't one of them. "How old are you?" he asked.

"Fourteen."

"You're a juvenile," Stone explained. "Gary's an adult. Whatever happened, he's the one that's going down. That's the way the law is going to look at it."

"We were going to go away," she said softly. "Together."

"Did you have some kind of plan?"

"Not really. We used to sit here and talk. For hours. He's the only one who ever listened to me."

"Where did you meet him?"

"Right here. He has a room."

I'm sure he does, thought Stone. Was he sleeping with her? It didn't seem appropriate to ask right now. "What's your name?"

"Rhonda. Rhonda Savage."

"So Rhonda, do you have parents? A family?"

"No." She said it with an immediacy and conviction that took Stone by surprise.

"Do you live around here?" he asked.

"I live in LA," she replied with obvious condescension. A sophisticate amongst the savages in the land of alfalfa and crude oil.

"So what brings you here, to the Rancho Vista?"

"The parties."

Once again, Stone struggled to keep his professional equilibrium. "The parties?"

"Yeah. We come over a couple of times a month. For the rich guys. We're hostesses."

Hostesses. A euphemism of stupendous proportions. "So where were the parties? Were they here?"

"They were at this real cool house."

"Richard Fancher's house?"

"I don't know. They never said their last names."

"What about their first names? Was one of them called Dick?"

Stone could feel her wince inside and watched it flicker across her face before she caught herself. "Maybe. I don't know."

Time to back off a notch. "Look, nobody's holding you responsible for what happened. You already told me it was Gary's idea. I believe you. And if you're straight with me, you'll be okay. So let's start again, back at the beginning. What happened on the day of the party?"

"Nothing happened until night. We all had our own rooms, but I always went over to Gary's room and stayed there." She smiled wistfully. "He had it fixed up kind of like an apartment. Pretty cool."

"So there were other girls besides you?"

"Yeah, two other girls. Jane and Diane."

"Are they the same age as you?"

"Jane is, but Diane's a liar. She says she's fourteen, but I think she's really thirteen." Rhonda turned scornful. "She lies about everything, all the time."

"So how did you get to the party? Did someone pick you up?"

"Yeah, the guy named Johnny. He has a really neat car. Like the kind you see in Bel Air."

"How many people were at the party?"

Rhonda shrugged. To her, it was apparently all routine. "Same as usual. Three guys, three of us."

"Can you tell me what went on at the party?"

Rhonda paused, retrieved her cigarette, took a big drag, and exhaled. It put another couple of years on her. "The guys played poker in the other room. We watched TV. Dinah Shore was on. She's kind of old, but she's okay I guess. Then Bob Hope. He's really not very funny, at least not to me."

"So what happened after the poker game?"

She took another drag and locked her eyes onto his. "What do you think?"

The depth of her cynicism demolished what remained of Stone's sensibility. It tunneled on through and detonated somewhere close to dead center. This beautiful young girl, dead on arrival in adulthood.

"Okay then," he said. "What happened when the party was over?"

"The guy named Johnny brought us back here. Just like always."

"You said you came from LA. How do you get back there?"

"Brenda picks us up the next day."

'Brenda' represented an interesting tangent, but Stone needed to keep focus. "Alright, so the party's over and you're back here. Is this where Gary comes in?"

She parked the cigarette and stirred her Coke with the straw. "Yeah, this is where Gary comes in. I went to his room. He was drinking beer. He wanted to know about the party. He always wanted to know about the parties."

"He did?"

"He was kind of jealous. He used to say that those rich fucks get all the breaks. But this night it was different. He said it was payback time."

"Payback time?"

"Yeah. He asked me if there was a lot of cool stuff at the party house. I said yeah, and he wanted to go back there and boost it. He figured it would never get reported because of the Cradle Club."

"The Cradle Club?"

She nodded. "That's what the guys at the parties called themselves. Gary said they'd be in deep shit if it ever got out."

"So you took him back there?"

"If you're walking, it's only about half an hour from here. When we got there, he found a window open and crawled in. Then he came around and let me in through the front door." She paused. "I don't know if I should be telling you all this."

"He's the one that broke in, not you." Stone failed to mention that she was an accomplice.

"I waited in the living room while he went around looking for stuff to swipe. He must have screwed up when he went into the bathroom. There was a crash, like bottles hitting the floor. Then the living room light came on and there was Dick, the guy who owned the house. He asked me what the hell I was doing. Before I could answer, Gary came down the hall and they stood there staring at each other."

"And what happened then?"

"I don't know."

"You don't know?"

"I took off. I knew it was going to be bad. I ran out the front door and walked back to here. I went to Gary's room and waited for him. I waited all night. He never showed up." She sighed. "I guess he just didn't care."

Stone had to marvel at her twisted sentiments. If she was telling the truth, she'd fled on the brink of a potentially violent confrontation. But now, she expressed no concern about the outcome. Instead, she was focused on being dumped by her boyfriend.

"I kept waiting for him in the morning, so I missed my ride back to LA," she continued. "I kept on hoping that he really wanted me, that he'd come back for me. But it didn't happen."

"You're assuming that he got the best of this Dick guy at the house," Stone commented. What if he didn't?"

"He was real fast and strong, a lot more than any of those guys. But that's not it. He was all through with me. That's the truth of it." She looked up at Stone. "So can I go see him in jail? He's in jail, right?"

"Oh yeah, he's in jail. He's a suspect in the murder of the guy you call Dick." Stone declined to mention that all the evidence was gone.

Her expression imploded into horror. "Gary killed him?"

"That's what it looks like. Then he stole his car and lit out with the loot. He got caught speeding and we brought him in. He's in the hospital."

Her face fell. "In the hospital?"

"Yeah, in the hospital. He crashed the car."

Her eyes went wet. "Will he be okay?"

"Yeah, he'll be okay. At least for now." Love dies hard, Stone thought, especially at fourteen. "Look, I'm going to have to take you into custody. You understand that?"

She nodded in solemn resignation. "Can I finish my drink?"

"Sure." Stone watched her perfect young lips enclose the straw. Hostesses. Rich guys. The Cradle Club. Imports from LA. Narcotics. All with a tasty little crust of burglary and murder baked on top.

No wonder this hadn't made the paper.

. . .

"Maybe he was coming back for me when he crashed," Rhonda speculated from the back seat of Stone's police car as he turned off 24th onto Elm.

"Yeah, maybe so," Stone said. Not likely. Willert was headed full tilt west out of town on Rosedale when Jefferson bagged him for speeding. Better to let her float in her hopeful little bubble until it popped of its own volition.

He turned onto Fancher's street. "I need you to show me exactly which house the party was at."

"But you already know that."

"Yeah but you're the only witness, so I need you to corroborate for me."

Rhonda's face contracted in puzzlement. "What's corroborate mean?"

"It means to help me confirm something." In fact, he didn't need her help at all. What he did need was to eliminate the outside chance that she was fabricating all or part of her story.

"That's it," Rhonda said as she pointed to Fancher's house up ahead.

The crime scene tape on the front door came into view as Stone pulled into the driveway and stopped. Rhonda knew precisely which house it was, which confirmed her story. And it also meant she had a working knowledge of went on there. He needed every scrap she could give him, and he had one obvious lever to get at it. "You know, there's always the possibility that we got the wrong guy," he started. "Maybe Gary didn't do it. Maybe Rick had some kind of beef with one of his party pals and they showed up later and had it out with him."

Rhonda perked up. "You think so?"

Stone shrugged and turned back toward Rhonda. "It's definitely possible, and if it's true I need all the information I can get. Is there anything inside here that might help identify the people involved?"

"There's pictures. A whole bunch of 'em."

"Pictures?"

"Yeah. Rick had one of those new cameras. The kind that makes the picture right in the camera. Sometimes he'd get it out and take some shots."

Rhonda now had Stone's full attention. She was referring to a camera made by a company called Polaroid. It had some of kind of fancy film that developed itself. If you wanted to take pictures that no one at a photo lab would ever see, it was the perfect choice.

"We didn't find anything like that when we went through the house," Stone countered.

"He hid them really good, but I saw him get them out once to show to one of his friends."

"So you know where they are right now?"

"They're inside the furnace."

"Oh yeah? What's to keep them from burning up?"

"Don't know. But that's where they are. On the side at the bottom. You slide the metal open and there's a box with the camera and pictures."

Stone cranked the front windows halfway down to let fresh air flow into the locked section in the back where Rhonda sat. "I'm going to check it out. Stay put."

He noticed that the lawn was already going brown as he mounted the porch. In the living room, he passed by the crusted pool of blood that had once dwelled comfortably within the confines of Richard Fancher. Upon reaching the kitchen he flipped on the light at the top of the stairs and descended to the cement floor below. An oil-burning furnace stood in the corner, a metal octopus that poked a tangle of ductwork up into the ceiling. It was difficult in June to imagine the need for it, but temperatures sometimes dipped close to freezing during the winter. If you could afford it, you had forced air heat; if you couldn't, you had a blanket.

One duct was much bigger than the others and went all the way down to a metal enclosure at the base. Stone now understood. It was the cold air return, and you could put something inside without it being damaged by the heat from the burner. He squatted and peered at its mottled surface of galvanized steel. In the shadows it appeared seamless, so he got up and checked a nearby workbench where he found a flashlight.

When he trained its beam on the box, he saw a small gap in corner. He tried to pry on it with his finger, to no avail. He took a quarter from his pocket, inserted it, and rocked to gain leverage. The entire side of the box quickly came loose and fell to the floor with a loud clang.

And there was the box. Just like Rhonda said.

Stone always kept a pair of cotton gloves in his pocket for occasions like this. He put them on to prevent contamination, and slid the box out to where he could get a better look. The box was cardboard, with flaps shut and crisscrossed to keep out the dust from the vent above. He gingerly picked it up and placed it on the workbench, where he opened it.

What appeared to be a camera casing rested atop a pile of unsorted photographs. The casing had a brown crinkled surface that was rounded at either end. Stone spotted a latch and popped the case open to expose a lens and bellows. He closed it and put the camera aside.

The black and white photos were all the same size, about three by four inches, and placed face up. Stone gingerly sorted through the ones on the top of the pile.

Three girls. Rhonda, Diane and Jane. Rhonda sodomized on the couch. Diane buggered on the ottoman. Jane trussed up tightly on the bed. Rhonda's backside striped with belt marks. Diane getting it from both ends. Jane gagging on a phallic thrust. Rhonda choking on a rope while buggered.

Whatever was depicted here wasn't just a little hanky panky on boys' night out. It delved into a far deeper and darker place, where the light of day gave way to an awful molten glow.

Stone stopped to steady himself. He had to look past the savagery, the depredation, the bestiality of it. He needed to find evidence. Faces, furnishings, background objects.

A pattern emerged. The participants engaging the girls changed from shot to shot. The differences in anatomy were fairly obvious. Each photo was framed to exclude the male's face but still capture the action. It appeared that Fancher was always the picture taker and not the one in the picture. It made sense. With the Polaroid, Fancher could snap the picture, show it to the other party to assure him he couldn't be identified, and then add it to the collection.

The one picture, the photo that explained so much, sat nearly at the bottom of the pile. It was the only one where no girl was visible. Two men sat on the couch, both fully clothed and holding a drink. They were grinning and leering at something outside the frame of the picture. A painting was visible on the wall behind them. Stone remembered it from upstairs in the living room.

Samuel Delfort sat on the left. Partner in the prestigious firm of Delfort, Holmes, & Chalmers. Esteemed member of the legal community. And now defense attorney for Gary Willert.

Jonathan Blitz sat to his right. Publisher and owner of the *Bakersfield Tribune*, the biggest newspaper between Los Angeles and San Francisco.

Stone's mind raced down tracks previously untraveled. How did this picture even make it into Fancher's collection? Two possibilities. First, there was nothing incriminating in its content, so it didn't matter. Second, the pair had been drinking and weren't even aware that the picture was being taken.

Stone had to put the brakes on and get grounded. He also had to resist the temptation to seek instant revenge on Delfort for the verbal beating he'd received at the hospital.

At first glance there was nothing in the pictures that proved that either man had molested one of the girls. So far, they weren't guilty of anything but having a drink at Fancher's house. But even if this picture wasn't a legal calamity, it could be a social disaster if it leaked out into the community at large.

No wonder Delfort jumped so eagerly to Willert's defense. He had to build a case where Willert didn't testify and bring Rhonda into it.

No wonder the *Bakersfield Tribune* managed to go completely dark on Fancher's murder. Blitz wanted to make it simply disappear from public view.

Even more disturbing was the missing evidence against Willert. It was almost certainly an inside job. Delfort wasn't acting alone to scoot Willert through the justice system as quickly and quietly as possible. He had help in high places.

Stone put the pictures and the camera back in the box and closed it up. For the time being, they were his and his alone.

• • •

Rhonda sat quietly in the back seat as Stone got into the car and plunked down the box.

Stone stared out at the garage door for a full minute before he turned to Rhonda. "You're in really big trouble."

"I kind of figured that," Rhonda said.

"It's not the kind of trouble you think."

"Then what kind is it?"

"You know way too much about way too many people."

Rhonda watched a cat cross the lawn. She didn't respond until it slunk off under a hedge on the far side. "What's going to happen to me?"

Stone sighed. "I'm working on that." He reached over to the box on the seat beside him, took out the picture of Delfort and Blitz, and showed it to Rhonda. "You recognize either of these guys?"

Rhonda squinted at the Polaroid. "Yeah, it's Sam and Johnny. They called each other Mr. D and Mr. B sometimes. Everything was sort of a joke with those guys, even when they got really nasty."

Sadly, the photos gave Stone a very good idea of what 'really nasty' meant. "Can you tell me anything else about them?" he asked.

"I used to see Johnny sometimes at parties in LA. He was friends with Ray."

"Who's Ray?"

"He's this guy I met at a hamburger place on Santa Monica. The owner was really teed off because I didn't have enough money for my fries. So Ray came over and paid my bill. He was real nice and kind of cute, so I started going out with him."

"How old was he?"

"I don't know. Maybe forty."

"And what did your parents think about that?"

Rhonda went rigid. "I already told you, I don't have any parents."

"Sorry, I forgot. Did you move in with him?"

"No. But he got me a really cool apartment in Westwood. And we went shopping for clothes on Rodeo Drive. When he came over, he'd send out for Chinese food. I could order anything I wanted."

"Did he ever tell you what he did or where lived?"

"He did something in the movies. He used to tell me about all these famous people he knew, but I never got to see them."

"Were the parties like the ones here?"

"Yeah. Pretty much."

"And so Ray was friends with Johnny from here in Bakersfield, right?"

"Yeah. That's how we started coming here."

Stone flashed on the luau, on the genial and charming Mr. Blitz, the perfect host, the intimate of movie stars, journalists and politicians. Who would have guessed what was festering behind that grinning mask? His wife? His editors?

"You said somebody named Brenda drove you over here from LA. Do you know anything else about her?"

"Not really. She always picked me up last. When we got here, she told the clerk that she was our aunt when we registered."

"Were there any other girls at the parties besides you three?"

"Sometimes, but not very often."

"What about the men? Were there other men?"

"Yeah, they came and went."

"How many?"

"Maybe about six or so. I don't remember. Most of the time, I was pretty loaded."

Stone nodded. The dope buffered a brutal reality, softened it, made it pliable and manageable. "I'm going to need the name of your apartment and your apartment number back in LA."

"It's the Sunset Terrace, number twelve. What's going to happen to me?"

"You're going to need to do exactly what I tell you," Stone said.

Her chin elevated into a pose of defiance. "I've heard that before. So why should I?"

"Because if you don't, there's a good chance you'll wind up face down in a bean field with some crows having you for lunch," Stone explained. "And it won't even make the paper. Want to know why? Because Johnny boy, Mr. B, owns the paper. And his pal, Mr. D, is at the top of the heap in the legal trade around here. Somebody inside the cops is in on it, too. And none of them want to hear about big boys having parties with little girls. Get it?"

Rhonda's chin came back down. "Yeah, I guess I do."

Part Three

BAKERSFIELD AND OILDALE
JUNE 18 TO NOVEMBER 2, 1954

16.

JUNE 18

EAST BAKERSFIELD

"So tell me one more time: What's your last name?" Stone asked Rhonda as they pulled into the rear parking lot of the Kern County Juvenile Hall in East Bakersfield.

"Wentworth," Rhonda answered. "Linda Wentworth."

"And where did you come from?"

"Sacramento."

Stone switched off the engine and turned to Rhonda in the back seat. "Your best move while you're here is to keep your mouth shut. Got that?"

Rhonda nodded. "Got it."

Stone climbed out and opened the back door. "Okay, let's go." He took Rhonda's arm and turned them toward the entrance to a drab one-story building fronted by dead shrubs in a bed of gravel.

"How long will I be here?" Rhonda asked.

"Can't say. I have to work some things out."

"What kind of things?"

"I'm not sure," Stone said. "That's the problem."

They ascended a short set of concrete steps to a gray metal door. Stone rang a buzzer and picked up a phone mounted in the wall.

"State your business," the phone commanded after the third ring.

"Detective James Stone, Bakersfield Police. I have a minor in custody and need to book her."

A relay clicked. The door opened. A beefy guard looked out at them. Blue uniform. Pink face. He motioned with his thumb to a reception counter backed by file cabinets where a second guard stood.

"I'll need to see your badge and ID," the second guard said. "Don't think we've met."

Stone showed him his credentials, and the guard copied them onto some kind of booking form. Stone stood by Rhonda while the guard wrote. The man put down his pen as he finished and looked over at the girl. "So, what have we here?"

"Name's Linda Wentworth, or so she says," Stone replied. "No ID. Claims she's fourteen and that looks about right. Picked her up downtown at Sears for shoplifting. I want her held while we sort it out with the store. Just a temporary thing."

"Hope so," the guard said. "We're damn near full up. Lots of stray dogs out there."

"Shouldn't take long," Stone said. "She's down from Sacramento. I'll see if I can round up any family and we'll take it from there."

"Good luck," the guard offered. He picked up the phone and called for the matron.

Stone turned to Rhonda. "Behave yourself, okay?"

"Yes sir."

"Now that's a real good start," the first guard said.

On his way out Stone looked over at the detention area, where a pair of two-story barracks stretched across a shriveled lawn. A troubled pipeline on the way to nowhere. Stone could only hope that Rhonda's street smarts would give her at least a little edge. While there was some risk, her internment was the right move. Stone had to hedge against the possibility that she was actively involved in the killing and would disappear the moment she was cut loose. It didn't seem likely, but the downside was just too big and ugly to ignore.

Did she have a motive? Of course she did. Despite the loose locker room talk about "young stuff," the reality of it was quite another matter. As they grew older, most men came to realize that it was pretty much a fantasy rooted in their teenage past. And by the time they reached their middle years and had teenage daughters, the notion withered away entirely.

For most men. For a few, it burned on, a flame of jet black, impervious to extinguishment. Some visited their lust upon their own offspring. Others stalked the world at large to feed the beast within. And a few people of privilege, like Fancher and friends, willfully exercised their prerogatives to sustain the hunt indefinitely. To Stone, this added a special touch of monstrosity to their deeds.

· · ·

Stone got home just in time for Cousin Herb's Trading Post on KERO TV. He fished some leftover macaroni and cheese out of the refrigerator and plopped it into a small pot along with a splash of water. He stirred the contents while the burner came up to speed and the TV belted out a new tune by local hero Billy Mize. A few small wisps of steam eventually told him it was ready. He'd heard there was now an oven that would heat stuff almost instantly using something called microwaves. All you needed was a grand or so to buy the thing. What a deal.

He loaded the macaroni onto a stone blue Melmac dinner plate and fetched a beer to go along with it. Jelly Saunders was cranking out an up-tempo fiddle piece, but Stone couldn't stay locked into it. The enormity of what he'd set in motion was starting to assume a tangible and dismal shape. By stowing Fancher's lurid photos, he'd withheld evidence in a capital murder case. Worse yet, he'd failed to book a potential suspect in the form of Rhonda, who at the very least was a possible witness. He was no

longer risking just his career, he was putting himself in some serious legal jeopardy.

Worst of all, he sensed a replay of what happened to him with
the LAPD. Forces far beyond his control were once again creat-
ing a murky and treacherous miasma, where predictable certain-
ties gave way to shifting probabilities.

He teetered on the edge. He could still back out. He could
book Rhonda on suspicion of homicide, and turn in the pictures
as evidence from the murder scene.

He couldn't do it.

He'd like to think it was because he was protecting Rhonda,
who would be instantly turned into a disposal liability. He wished
that it centered on favoring the lives of a few abused kids over the
comfort and privilege of some very nasty and powerful adults.

But he knew better.

It was all about the cheap suit.

He could clearly visualize Samuel Delfort in the hospital room
with himself and Willert. He could still feel the man's brazen arrogance as he delivered the acid remark about Stone's clothes and
watch. If his life had been on an ascendant trajectory, he could
have deftly shrugged it off. Maybe even delivered a counterpunch.

But he'd lost too many rounds over the past few years to take
the hit and fight back.

It cut to the core and shamed him deeply.

But now he had the pictures.

He just had to figure out how to play them.

Stone finished his dinner and turned off the TV. Cousin Herb
would have to wait. He got out the box with the pictures and
spread them out on the kitchen table. After repeated viewings, the
shock value was essentially gone. He could focus on details, on
evidence, on patterns. But this time through, he picked up nothing new. In all, there were maybe two dozen pictures, plus one
unused piece of film that was stilled sealed up. Maybe it awaited

the unholy resurrection of Richard Fancher and his continued documentation of the dark side, the blackest side of all.

The phone rang. It sat on the far side of the table. When Stone picked up the receiver, its coiled cord raked across the photos and returned them to a disordered state. He reached out clumsily to keep the top ones from falling on the floor. "Stone," he answered in his best minimalist intonation.

"My god, you sound like you died last week."

Stone had to smile. Fatalia's voice and attitude were both unmistakable. "I've seen better days," he said. "But I'm still here."

"Good. Because I've got what you asked for."

"The tee times?"

"Yes, silly. The tee times."

Stone perked up. He'd considered his request for the Tuesday tee times to be a long shot at best. Now here they were. "Good job," he said. "Why don't I come by and get them?"

"I've got a better idea. I let you see mine, now I want to see yours."

Stone scanned the conceptual horizon and grabbed the first thing he spotted. "You mean my house?"

"Yes, I mean your house."

Stone took in the shabby tableau in front of him. "I'm not exactly set up for visitors."

"Somehow I'm not surprised. So let's do it like this: You give me your address. I come by and knock on the door. You open it and I peek inside. If I'm shocked and revolted by your male primitivism, I hand you the list and flee."

"And if you're not?"

"We step into an entirely different world."

"And what goes on there?"

"Nobody knows. Nobody's ever been there."

"So that's it?"

"That's it. Were you expecting an essay or something?"

"No, I guess not," Stone admitted. He gave her his address. She told him it would be about an hour. He scooped up the photos, but them back in the box and stowed it in the closet.

He went to clean the place up and realized that there was really nothing to clean up. He opened another beer and turned the TV back on. A quiz show appeared, with a genial host and anxious contestants. It seemed that sixty-four thousand dollars were at stake. One of the competitors stood fidgeting in a cylindrical booth that added a touch of claustrophobia to the affair. The drama of it was lost on Stone. He had plenty of drama of his own right now. He finished his beer and dozed.

The doorbell snapped him out of it. He shook off a somnolent buzz and opened the door to a sly smile from Fatalia. She wore tight fitting toreador pants, high heels and a sleeveless blouse. Her lipstick glowed with a radiance to match only the deepest of sunsets.

"I've come to collect my peek," she informed him.

"So you have," he said, and moved slightly aside so she could see in.

"Spare, neat, orderly," she observed. "Very police-like. I have to admit, it does have a certain appeal."

"Would you like to come in?"

"As a matter of fact, I would." She moved past him and took one of the chairs at the kitchen table, where she placed a clutch purse.

"I'd offer you something to drink, but all I have is beer."

"That will do just fine."

Stone took two cans of Hamms from the refrigerator and two glasses from an open shelf. The beer took on an amber fizz as he poured it. "So what about the list?" he asked.

"Just like that? You don't want a detailed account of how I got it? What kind of cop are you?" she teased.

"A very busy one."

"Very well then." She opened her purse, took out a folded piece of tablet paper, flattened it out, and held it up to him.

She dangled it just far enough away that he couldn't make out the hand-written contents. "So near, so far."

"At this point I'd really appreciate a little cooperation."

She refolded the paper and tucked it into the bosom of her blouse. "And so would I."

· · ·

Later, Stone watched her car pull out into the languid warmth of early morning. Its taillights glowed like dragon's eyes on the deserted street. Blood red on dirty black.

She'd never be back. She'd gotten what she wanted. She'd made a cop.

He really didn't care. She wasn't any good in bed, she just lay there, waiting to be entertained. In the end, she came out on the deal because he was carrying a great load of pent-up demand. Afterwards he couldn't help but think about Christine Harmon. To quote Fatalia, so near so far.

Her car rounded the corner and disappeared. He walked back through to the bedroom with its crumpled sheets and spent condom – she'd just happened to have one in her purse. He picked up the list from the country club off the night stand and took it the kitchen table, where he opened it.

The names were neatly written in pencil in clusters of four, each with a time assigned to it. Stone got it. They launched a new foursome every twenty minutes. That way, they wouldn't run over each other out on the course. In total, twelve foursomes were slated between eight o'clock and noon.

But Stone quickly spotted the only one that really counted. It went out at ten o'clock every Tuesday, at least until recently. Because one member was now dead. The late Richard Fancher.

Accompanied on course by Jonathan Blitz, the publisher. Samuel Delfort, the attorney. And Walter Sumner, the industrialist.

Stone carefully folded the list back up and tucked it in his wallet. He fetched a beer to celebrate. The pump in the overhead swamp cooler woke up and chugged its way into the nocturnal silence. He leaned back in his chair and stared out the open door into the night. Or was it the heart of darkness? He wasn't sure anymore.

Walter Sumner, he who held sycophantic court at the luau. An industrial Moses, who supplied the machinery that watered the valley. An arrogant jerk that belittled the Okies and their agonizing journey.

Was he the one fatally entangled with Charlene? Or was it one of the others? Or none of them? And was Sumner a member of the Cradle Club, as well the country club?

Mr. Sumner, he who sat atop the local heap, deserved a closer look, a much closer look.

17.

JUNE 19
OILDALE

NO NIGGERS!

That's what the sign said. In clumsy capital letters scrawled with black paint on an uphill slope. Along with a ragged 'KKK' carved into the home's front door. A raw wound of naked wood etched into the red paint.

Stone took in the grim signage as he came up the short cement walkway to Christine Harmon's clinic in north Oildale. It occupied a small residence fronted by a minimal yard of bare earth.

Christine opened the door at his knock. "Welcome to the neighborhood," she said in the driest of tones, and stepped aside to let him in.

"So when did all this happen?"

"Some time last night." She wore a white lab coat and stethoscope, the universal symbols of her profession. They knew no gender.

Stone looked around. An old couch and coffee table served as a waiting area, with a wooden desk and file cabinet opposite. The open kitchen housed medical supplies.

"Did you call the cops?" Stone asked.

"The county sheriff? You've got to be kidding. Half the deputies probably moonlight as Klansmen."

"This ever happened before?"

"Nope."

"What do you think set it off?"

"The Jones family."

"Are they Negroes?"

"Yes, they're Negroes. They live down in Cottonwood. They have two little girls, one with chronic asthma. The mother heard about us and brought the child here. I worked out a treatment plan."

"Did it include the new sign out front?"

Christine shrugged. "One of the neighbors must have seen her come or go. Word gets around."

Stone nodded. "Yes it does."

"You know, the funny thing is that the white people around here aren't any better off than the black people in Cottonwood," Christine observed. "They just think they are."

"Makes them feel better," Stone said.

"And there you have it," Christine concluded.

"Do you want me to look into this?"

"Absolutely not. I like you just the way you are. I don't want someone to rearrange you over a dumb act of vandalism."

Stone savored her concern. "You think the deck's stacked that bad around here?"

"You know it is. Don't pretend you don't."

"Which is why I came over to see you," Stone explained. "You got time to talk?"

Christine looked at her watch. "I've got about an hour, then I've got to be back at the coroner's office."

"That's more than enough."

"We can sit out back. You want something to drink? I've got ice water or Coke. That's about it."

"I'm fine."

Christine led them down a short hall and gestured to a single bedroom on the left. "That's the examination room. Now you've seen it all."

She opened the back door to a small patio of cracked cement with weeds sprouting from the fissures. They sat in a pair of metal deck chairs with a little wooden table between them. The house put them in the shade and fended off the worst of the heat.

"You've got the floor," she said. Stone noticed that her exceptional composure had settled in once more. The Klan and a little black paint weren't going to slow her down.

"When we met for coffee and you told me about the abortion, you gave me your trust," Stone said. "That's something I don't take lightly."

"Nor should you. Was I wrong to do so?"

"No you weren't. Because I gave you my word that it was all in confidence. And no matter what else I am, I'm always true to my word."

"I'm glad to hear that. I'm not surprised."

"Good. Because now I'm going to ask the same of you."

She smiled softly. "You didn't have to, but since you did, you have my word."

"Have you kept up on where we are with the Fancher murder?"

"I heard from some of the county people that you caught somebody who fits the bill quite nicely."

"We arrested a young guy named Gary Willert. A real nasty piece of work. He had a bunch of stolen stuff from Fancher's house, plus he was driving Fancher's car when we caught him."

"Sounds pretty open and shut to me," Christine said.

"It was until all the proof disappeared from the evidence room down at the station. I bet nobody told you that part of the tale."

"As a matter of fact they didn't. So what do you think?" Christine asked. "Is it Keystone Cops or something a little more involved?"

"A lot more involved. I ran into Gary Willert at the Rancho Vista Motel a few days before the murder. You know the place?"

"Not personally, but our public health officer tells me it's real petri dish for sexually transmitted diseases."

"I'd have to agree. Anyway, Willert wasn't alone. He was in the restaurant talking to a teenage girl, a very young one, maybe fourteen or so."

Christine shrugged. "Sleazy, but not illegal."

"Not yet. After the murder, I go back there looking for the girl and she tells me this incredible tale. Her name's Rhonda Savage, and it seems that she and a couple of other very young things were imported from LA to party with Fancher and friends. On a regular basis. She had a big crush on Gary and they went to rob Fancher after the party was over on Tuesday. Fancher woke up and there was a confrontation with Willert. It spooked her and she took off back to the motel."

"Do you believe her?" Christine asked.

"I would've had my doubts, but then she told me about the pictures Fancher took at the parties. You know about Polaroids?"

"You mean that new instant film?"

"Yeah. She told me where to look and I found a couple of dozen pictures. Really ugly stuff. The kind that would get you jail time if introduced in court. Lots of jail time."

"But Fancher's dead, so where's that leave you?"

"A lot of the pictures show Rhonda and friends in various sex acts with people that are always out of the frame. But one shows none other than Samuel Delfort and Jonathan Blitz sitting together in Fancher's living room. Very clearly and unmistakably."

"Oh dear." Christine leaned back into her chair. A sparrow landed on the gutter above them and flittered off.

"I used to hear rumors about this kind of thing when I was in LA," Christine mused. "Rich men buying whatever they wanted. I never thought I'd have to move to Bakersfield to find it for real."

"I showed the picture of Delfort and Blitz to the girl. She remembers both of them. They were regular attendees at Fancher's. It all adds up in a slimy kind of way. Fancher was a bachelor and these other guys were married. That's why they made his house the party pad."

"And what about the girl, this Rhonda?" Christine asked. "Where is she now?"

"I just booked her at the juvenile hall under an alias. She's better off there than out on the street or at the county jail. At least for the time being."

"I should take a look at her," Christine said, "and make sure she's okay." Stone could hear the nurture and maternal concern in her voice. He liked that.

"Right now, it's safety first," Stone declared. "A lot of people don't want the Willert case ever to come to trial. If it does, the girl would be a key witness and blow the lid off the whole business. You know what they call themselves?"

"What?"

"The Cradle Club."

A wave of revulsion broke over Christine, who sagged in her chair. "That's awful."

"It's also worth a minimum of ten years in the state pen, if it can be made to stick," Stone added.

Christine slumped even lower. "It'll never stick. Not around here. They'll never let it happen. None of it." Fear invaded her eyes. "You've got to be very, very careful."

"That's not the end of it," Stone added.

"Really? Where else could it possibly go?"

"To the Charlene Winters murder. She worked at the country club so I went out there looking for leads. The management was none too happy to see me, but a waitress friend suggested that she might have been carrying on with one of the members."

"That includes a lot of people," Christine noted.

"Yes, it does. But I managed to narrow the potential list down to a set of foursomes that go out on Tuesday mornings. And one of those just happens to include the late Richard Fancher, Samuel Delfort, Jonathan Blitz, and for an added bonus, the venerable Walter Sumner, water boy to the entire valley."

"So do you think Sumner is a member of the club?" she asked.

"Could be. In any case, he's more than just a person of interest. If he's the one Charlene was chasing, he has a lot of explaining to do, both to the cops and to his wife."

Christine stared down at the cement, where a solitary beetle made its way across the pebbled surface. "There's something you should know. And it's definitely not going to make things any simpler."

"What's that?"

"I'm the one who performed the abortion on Charlene Winters."

"You what?"

"I performed the abortion. Ethically, I don't have any problem with what I did. It was in the first trimester. She was a young woman with no husband, no education and a really dismal future, both for herself and the baby. If she'd gone out on the street to have it done, she would've put herself in real danger. There's maybe a half dozen places within a mile of here where you could get it done in the back of an old trailer or something worse. You risk hemorrhage, infection, you name it. Anyway, the procedure's not the problem. It's the circumstances."

"What circumstances?"

"The whole thing was arranged and paid for through Samuel Delfort, esquire. In case you're wondering, I put all the proceeds back into funding the clinic."

"I'm sure you did. Keep going." Stone had been here before in other times. She needed a little prompting to remain in the confessional.

"When Delfort set the thing up, he wouldn't identify whoever was paying for it," Christine continued. "He just said he was acting on behalf of a third party. Anyway, when Charlene turned up dead, it was pretty obvious that the abortion and the murder might be linked. I contacted Delfort and demanded to know who was behind it."

Stone could see what was coming, but held back. "And what did he tell you?"

"He said that the arrangement was a matter of attorney-client privilege, so he didn't have to reveal it to anyone under any circumstances. Then he reminded me that the abortion was clearly illegal under California state law. The mother's life was definitely not in danger, so what I did was technically a criminal act. If the authorities found out about it, I could be prosecuted. At the very least, I would lose my license to practice medicine."

"So what you're saying is that he blackmailed you into silence."

"Not exactly silence. I came to you and told you about the abortion. I just left out certain details." She paused and sighed. "I did what I could."

"Yes, you did."

"Anyway, there it is. For whatever it's worth. I'm glad I told you, but you're not much better off than you were before. You can't go to Delfort because he'll exercise his right to confidentiality. That doesn't leave you much to go on."

"Maybe. Maybe not."

"How's that?"

"Two things. First, Delfort as much as told you that the person behind the abortion is one of his clients. Second, given the pedigree of his clientele, it's someone who's pretty well off."

"Which takes you back to the country club," Christine suggested.

"Which takes me back to the fabulous foursome," Stone added. "Fancher made big money in real estate, Blitz owns a publishing company, and Sumner is the main faucet all the way to Sacramento. I wouldn't be surprised if they're all major clients of Delfort's law firm. It doesn't give me all the answers but it narrows the field considerably."

Christine nodded slowly. "Makes sense." She looked up at him. "Congratulations. You're now in triple jeopardy. You know that, don't you? They're going to close ranks and do whatever it takes to stop you."

Stone managed a wry grin. "I guess you could look at it that way."

"Oh well," Christine said with a resigned shrug. "When all this is over, I just hope I'm still a doctor."

Stone understood. A battle was shaping up. A really nasty one. And as it played out, Delfort always had the option to inform the authorities about the abortion and Christine's role in it.

"You'll still be a doctor," he promised. "No matter what happens."

Stone felt a pang of regret the moment he said it. He'd just added another complication to a very convoluted situation. But he couldn't help it. He couldn't let her down. In some inexplicable way, if he pulled this off and delivered some form of justice, he would achieve a kind of parity with her.

"So where do you go from here?" she asked him.

He stood to leave. "I'll tell you when I get there."

• • •

Stone wound up the long driveway through a luscious mix of green and brown landscaping. Walter Sumner's place reminded him of something you might see back in LA, but not out here on the bare edge of things. The drive ended in an enormous house. Thousands of cubic yards of stucco topped by about an acre of red tile roof.

Stone parked on a generous expanse of concrete out front, and noticed that the property abutted one of the golf holes at the country club. Perfect. Walter could step over some immaculately tended shrubs and practice his short game right on the spot.

He got out and felt the hot cement giving up its store of late morning sun in radiant waves. A Negro maid answered the door, a slim attractive woman with an intelligent face. "Yes?"

Stone removed his hat as a sign of courtesy. "Hello, I'm Sergeant James Stone with the Bakersfield Police. Is Mr. Sumner home by any chance?"

The maid's eye's narrowed. "Do you have some kind of identification?"

"Yes, I do." Stone presented his badge and ID.

The maid gave it a careful examination and looked up. "Sorry, but we do have rules. Would you wait here, please?"

"Of course."

The maid shut the door behind her when she retreated into the house. Stone was sure it remained locked. An annoying interval passed and the door opened once more.

"Would you follow me please," the maid requested. They passed through a stupefying display of opulence. Custom furniture covered in sumptuous fabrics. Rugs of exotic design and weave. And of course, the art. Stone knew little about painting, but his intuition told him it could easily hang in a museum somewhere in LA.

"I take it that Mrs. Sumner is a patron of the arts," Stone suggested.

"Oh my, yes," the maid responded. The implication was that if Stone had any acculturation at all, he would have already known.

They came to a windowed wall of glass that emptied onto a deck. Walter Sumner sat at a bluish metal table, reading the morning paper. He fit Stone's recollection from the luau: tall, trim, tan. He wore a tropical sport shirt, white cotton pants and leather sandals. He looked up and smiled at their arrival, exposing large, immaculate teeth. Stone found his expression disturbing. It had a carnivorous cast to it.

"Sergeant Stone." He gestured to a seat at the table as the maid left them. "What can I do for you?"

Stone already understood that he could only travel on the far periphery of the matter at hand. He wasn't searching for hard information so much as Sumner's reaction. "Mr. Sumner, thanks for seeing me on such short notice. I know you're probably very busy, so I won't take up much of your time. I've been assigned to the Charlene Winters case. I assume that you're aware of it."

Sumner smiled. "Of course I'm aware of it." He gestured toward the golf links. "She worked right over here at the club. You know that, don't you?"

"Yes, I do. Did you ever meet her?"

"How could I not meet her? She worked in the dining room. Everybody knew her. It was a real shock to all of us."

"Can you recall what she talked about when she waited on you? Anything unusual?"

Sumner became reflective and scratched his forehead. "Not really. She had big dreams, more so than most of the others. Wanted to start her own business. Very admirable."

"Do you recall what kind of business?"

"No. Can't say that I do. But I admire that kind of competitive spirit. It's what keeps this country on top." Sumner pointed to a Negro man out tending the shrubbery. "See that man. That's Thomas. Right now he's just a weed puller. But you know what he really wants to do?"

"What's that?"

"He wants to learn how to repair lawn mowers. Maybe even open a little shop someday. And you know what? He just might do it. I like that, Sergeant. I like that kind of thinking."

"Did Charlene ever mention any boyfriends?" Stone asked.

"Not that I recall." Sumner toned his smile down to the avuncular level. "But she was a pretty girl, so I'm sure they came a courtin'."

"I'm sure they did." Stone couldn't resist a little jab. He looked around, then back at Sumner. "Nice house. What line of work are you in?"

Sumner remained impervious. "Very simple. I make things wet. I think you'd find the details pretty boring. Now I'm curious: You're talking to other members at the club about this case. Right?"

Stone's brain took a step backward. Sumner's perfectly timed counterpunch had just blindsided him. He should've seen it coming. You didn't live in a place like this by being the slowest guy around, or even the second fastest. "I've got a number of people on my list," he said evasively.

Sumner delivered the knockout. "Well I hope it doesn't include my old golfing buddy, Dick Fancher. I'm sure you know all about that. A real tragedy."

"Yeah, a real tragedy," Stone mumbled. He had no clever moves left. The veranda had become a chessboard, and he'd just been checkmated.

Sumner leaned back in his chair. "Now if you'll excuse me, I've got a phone call coming up."

Stone stood to leave. "Of course. Thanks for your time."

Sumner didn't even bother to lean forward in his seat. "Can you find your way out?"

"I'll be fine."

It wasn't true. Not even close.

· · ·

President Dwight D. Eisenhower stared down at Stone from the picture on the wall in the visitor's room at the juvenile hall. Why Eisenhower? Stone wondered. A father figure for troubled youth? A guarantor of public safety? A symbol of order and authority? Who knew? Probably no one.

He was still flagellating himself over his disastrous encounter with Walter Sumner. In truth, it had been impulsive and uncalled for. He'd hoped that Sumner would stumble and make some revelatory remark or at least broadcast a little paranoia. Very dumb. Sumner had the upper hand going in and still had it going out. Worse, he now knew that Stone considered him a person of interest.

He shrugged it off and pulled out a picture of Walter Sumner that he'd clipped from the weekly society section of the *Bakersfield Tribune*. It was one of many photos documenting the recent luau at the home of Jonathan Blitz. And quite naturally, one of the photos depicted Walter Sumner and his wife. His leering grin displayed dental perfection amplified by a sportsman's tan.

Hopefully, the photo would help resolve one of several key questions about the real Walter Sumner. Stone knew that Sumner and Delfort were linked through the lawyer's legal practice and the golf course, but were they also linked through Fancher's parties?

The door opened. Rhonda stood in front of a matron, a stout woman who towered over her. The girl wore a T-shirt, dungarees and tennis shoes. She also wore a veil of arrogance and disgust, a princess from the big city rudely sequestered in a rural hovel.

"Rhonda," Stone said. "Have a seat." He looked to the guard. "We're fine." The guard nodded and closed the door as she left.

"How are you doing?" Stone asked.

"Fine," Rhonda said flatly.

"I'm close to getting you out of here," Stone announced. "But not quite yet."

"When?"

"A few days, a week. I'm not quite sure. But soon." Stone took out the Sumner picture and passed it to Rhonda. "I want you to take a good look at this guy. Was he ever at any of Fancher's parties?"

Rhonda leaned forward to scrutinize the picture. "No." She shook her head. "Never saw him."

"You're sure."

"I'm sure."

Stone took back the picture and stood up. "Like I said, I'll get you loose as soon as I can." He moved to the door to summon the guard. He felt tired. He'd come all the way out here just for another dead end. It felt like he was several laps behind the competition, and slipping further all the time.

"He was at the Rancho Vista," Rhonda said to Stone's back. "That's where I saw him. Not at the parties."

Stone slowly turned around and returned to his seat. "The Rancho Vista?"

"Yeah. He was in the room next door to me."

"When was this?" Stone asked.

"I don't know. A while back. It was night. I was waiting to go to one of the parties. Then I hear all this noise coming through the wall. Two people yelling at each other, a guy and a girl. After a while, it stops and there's a knock on my door. It's a girl in a negligee, a real cool one, a pink baby doll."

"Do you remember what she looked like?" Stone held his breath waiting for the answer.

"She had blond hair and blue eyes and was really loaded."

"How old was she?"

"I don't know, maybe like just out of high school, something like that. That's all I remember. I was a little loaded myself."

Charlene? Stone struggled to stay in a professional prospective. "So did you let her in?"

"Not really, but she came in anyway and sat down. She started bawling that this guy named Walt didn't really love her. He was never going to leave his wife. He was going to string her along forever and ever. Her makeup was a real mess. And then this Walt guy showed up."

"The guy in the picture I showed you?"

"Yeah, that guy. He had on a bathrobe and was really pissed. He grabbed her and pulled her out the door. That was the last I saw of them."

"Did you tell anybody about this?"

"No. Why would I?"

"I don't know," Stone said absently. Walt, as in Walter Sumner. Blonde as in Charlene Winters. All tangled up in a tale that defied the bounds of time and place, one that stretched back to very limits of mortal memory. Husband takes mistress, promises to dump wife but never does. Mistress lashes out and threatens to tell all to wife. Husband resolves the matter by permanently extinguishing mistress. Marital equilibrium is restored. Time washes the matter clean, leaving only a vaguely troubled dream that slowly slides beyond recall.

Stone took a deep breath. "You've done well, Rhonda. Better than you could possibly imagine." He stood up to go. "I just need you to sit tight a little bit longer."

"Sure." Rhonda didn't believe it.

Stone wasn't sure that he did, either.

• • •

The evening sky had gone to a burnt ochre as Stone cruised slowly down the block toward Fancher's house. The futile hiss of a lawn sprinkler and fading birdsong pushed in through his car's open window. The sidewalks and yards were deserted. The residents had retreated to their patios out back for a final stand against the oppressive heat.

By now he'd completed a working hypothesis of the Charlene Winters murder. In its own twisted way, the Rancho Vista was the perfect choice to provide deep cover for a tryst like the one Sumner had engineered. You'd never run into your friends and neighbors there, unless they were of highly questionable sexuality; and in that case, they'd be very committed to total anonymity. At some point in the affair, Sumner had impregnated Charlene and arranged for the abortion via Delfort, who obviously had plenty of secrets of his own. The pair was bound through a lot more than just golf.

In the end, Charlene had played the blackmail card and Sumner set up one final encounter at the Rancho Vista, where he strangled her in their little love nest. All very private. No screaming. No noise. The larynx clamped shut, the vocal cords rendered useless. He then packed the body over to the Kern River and pitched her into its depleted waters. A dead girl adrift in a dying river.

The green MG yanked him out of his rumination. It was parked at the curb in front of Fancher's. A small, blockish British sports car with its canvas top down. Stone knew the car from LA but had never seen one here in Bakersfield. It seemed an almost alien presence among the local pickups and sedans.

Stone got out and headed toward the house. He checked his holster for his .38 revolver. The car out front validated his trip over here. The house was still officially a crime scene, but apparently someone was willing to violate it, looking for scraps, just like he was.

With Fancher dead, the yard had gone to hell in a hurry. Brown grass, shriveled shrubs, wilted blossoms. Stone opened the front door, ducked under the crime scene tape and entered. He paused and listened intently. Nothing. He drew his weapon and walked through the stylish décor and fashionable furniture. He moved quietly and methodically from room to room. Still nothing.

That left the basement. He reached the stairs, turned on the lights and descended the wooden steps. At the bottom the furnace and its tangled ductwork came into view.

Suspicion confirmed. The cover for the cold air return rested on the floor, torn loose from the duct that once held the Polaroids. Crude pry marks covered its edges.

Someone was here looking for the photos. Someone who understood their ruinous potential and wanted to take them out of contention.

Stone barely felt the blow from behind. It crashed down on the crown of his skull and knocked him cold before any real pain could register.

When he came to, he lay face down on the cement, his head turned to the left, facing his dented hat. His skull bobbed atop throbbing waves of pain. He rose to his knees and looked around.

His pistol lay on the floor near the cold air duct, where the metal cover had been replaced.

He felt the back of his shirt collar. No blood. Must have been a blunt instrument of some kind. He retrieved his pistol and slowly climbed the stairs. Up in the living room he steadied himself against the couch to collect his wits.

He must have surprised the intruder with his arrival, which caused him to lay in wait and exercise the element of surprise. He got up carefully, walked to the door and looked out. The MG was gone.

· · ·

"You feel dizzy at all?" Dr. Christine Harmon asked as she shined the penlight in Stone's eyes.

"No, not really."

"Any ringing in your ears?"

"Don't think so."

"Nausea?"

"Nope."

"Confusion?"

"Yeah, plenty of confusion," Stone said from where he sat on her examination table. "But I don't think it has anything to do with a hit on the head."

She pocketed the penlight and stepped back. "You've got a nasty bruise, but otherwise you'll survive just fine."

"Glad to hear it. You know anyone around here that drives an MG?"

"What's that?"

"A British sports car. Kind of antique looking."

"Can't say as I do. Does it belong to your assailant?"

"Most likely."

"So why would somebody want to smack you on the head in an empty house?"

"They were after the pictures, the ones of Rhonda and friends in all the lewd poses. I never turned them in as evidence, so they thought that they were still there. I surprised them in the act. They didn't want to be identified and the rest is history. So now you know half the story."

"Only half?"

"The rest of it's going to take a drink or two." He motioned toward the door.

. . .

They had the bar at the KC Steakhouse almost to themselves. The exception was an elderly man wearing a Stetson cowboy hat. He complained bitterly to the bartender about the goddam Communists and how they were spreading out of LA and into the valley like some kind of hideous plague.

"This isn't what I normally recommend after suffering a concussion," Christine said as she looked around.

"There isn't anything normal about any of this," Stone explained. "We start with four wealthy golfing buddies. Three of them threw jailbait parties with a pipeline to LA for fresh meat. Bad stuff, but not the worst stuff of all. It appears that that honor goes to the fourth member, Walter Sumner."

"Charlene Winters?" Christine guessed.

"Charlene Winters," Stone confirmed. "I'm still filling in some of the blanks, but it's a pretty solid case, and the girl is right smack in the middle of it."

"The girl from Fancher's parties?"

"The very same. She always stayed at the Rancho Vista when they brought her into town. One night she saw Sumner and Charlene there together. Better yet, she actually talked to Charlene, who was skunk drunk and told her Sumner didn't love her anymore and would never leave his wife."

"So in cop language, you've got a material witness and a motive all wrapped in one," Christine observed.

"Looks like it." Stone took a sip of his bourbon on the rocks. "Sumner thought he'd found a place to mess around where nobody would ever notice. He was almost right."

"Walter Sumner, "Christine said. "Wow." She stopped and took another sip of her highball, a generous sip. "What are you going to do about it?"

"I'm going to take your advice to heart," Stone said. "There's no way this thing will ever come to trial, or anything close. At least, under normal circumstances."

"And what about abnormal circumstances?" she asked.

"They'd have to be a very special. They'd have to let you keep your medical license and me my job."

"Do you think such a thing is possible?"

"I don't know yet. I'm working on it."

"And what should we do in the meantime?"

Stone smiled. "Easy. We have another drink."

• • •

Stone carefully tapped the ashes on his Chesterfield into a bean-bag ashtray on his kitchen table. He noticed that the little metal waves on its holder bar were stained brown. Was the same true of his lungs? Probably not. Lots of doctors smoked and didn't seem worried. Besides, if you really cared, you could switch to one of those new brands that had a filter tip.

He left the cigarette in place and watched the heat lift its vertical trail of smoke in a thin blue column toward the ceiling. The buzz from a couple of cocktails with Christine was fading. A bat whizzed by the porch light out the open door. The light cast its feeble radiance on his aging Chevy, which badly needed a wash. But he had no hose, no bucket, no sponge. It wasn't going to happen.

Much more pressing was the bizarre entanglement of his two murder cases. He stretched in his chair and extended his arms as if to gather in the essence of the situation. Four golf buddies, three borderline pedophiles and one killer. All linked through a very young girl. Under normal circumstances Rhonda's timely encounter with Sumner and Charlene would be good news. It would point toward prosecution and justice.

Except for the pictures.

If either Sumner or Willert went to trial for murder, the girl would be called to testify, and the defense would immediately try to paint her as an unreliable witness. A street kid from the big city, with all kinds of ugly baggage. Alcohol, drugs, promiscuity. But the pictures, if introduced, would tell a different story altogether. They'd present a lurid portrait of bad men doing evil things in stark black and white to victims barely out of childhood. Rhonda's testimony would become very credible indeed, and an ugly stain would creep across Bakersfield's top-tier citizenry.

Stone picked the Chesterfield up, inhaled and expelled the smoke in a pensive column. Christine was right. In a direct confrontation sans the pictures, he would lose. No arrests, no convictions, no nothing. His job gone, Christine's medical career destroyed.

But the photos gave him other options. He could play dirty. Really dirty. They wouldn't be expecting that. They'd assume that he'd plod through the justice system in the timeless manner of the faithful foot soldier. If he did otherwise, he'd most likely gain the element of surprise.

The pictures. Stone pushed back his chair and stood up. His course of action was hiding somewhere in the pictures. He was sure of that.

He fetched the box and started through the photos. Patiently and methodically. About a dozen pictures in, he stopped and smiled. He'd found what he was looking for.

18.

JUNE 20

DOWNTOWN BAKERSFIELD

Stone stood on a downtown sidewalk outside Wickersham's Jewelers, which he'd just visited. The edge of a big dust storm out in the valley had kissed the town sometime before dawn. It left wispy islands of powdered grit on the pavement to writhe in the midmorning heat.

The proprietor inside had been both patient and helpful. All Stone could show him was a drawing he'd made of the watch in question. The real thing was in the Polaroids, and he had no way to copy and isolate it without a photo lab coming into play.

The man was in his late sixties and impeccably dressed, as befitted a jewelry store of this caliber. He'd nodded thoughtfully as Stone explained the nuances that the drawing failed to capture. When Stone finished, the man held up his index finger with an enlightened, wordless smile. He walked to a file cabinet and returned with a folder holding several slim catalogs. He silently thumbed through one of them until his finger stabbed a picture of a particular watch. He rotated it on the counter to give Stone a good view. It was, indeed, the watch in question.

With no prompting from the text, the man delivered a detailed explanation of the watch's provenance and construction. From Stone's standpoint, it couldn't have been better

• • •

"You have three phone messages," Mrs. Crenshaw informed Stone when he arrived at the office. She said it as though each was a count in some kind of indictment. The three pink notes sat in an orderly stack by her ink blotter. She was supposed to deliver them to his desk, but had conveniently forgotten.

Stone picked them up and smiled. All were from Samuel Delfort.

Once settled in, he phoned the law offices of Delfort, Holmes and Griffin and asked to speak to Mr. Delfort, who came on in no time at all.

"Ah yes, Sergeant Stone," he said. "You do have a way about you."

"A way of what?" Stone asked.

"A way of inserting yourself where no such action is really appropriate."

"So what did I do this time?"

"You showed up at the home of one my clients, a Mr. Walter Sumner."

"Oh, him," Stone said in mock innocence. "Yeah, I remember. The rich guy with the big house."

"You implied that he might have some connection to murder of Charlene Winters."

"I did? You know, I don't remember anything even close to that. Funny how people read things into what you say."

"It's not funny, sergeant. Not in any way, shape or form."

"You just might have a point," Stone admitted. "You know, it's very public here at my desk. Maybe I could drop by and we could discuss this in person so other folks don't get the drift of it. It would seem I've already done enough damage."

"I have an opening for fifteen minutes in half an hour. That's the best I can do."

"See you then." Stone hung up.

• • •

Three blocks and four stories later, he sat down in the reception area of Delfort, Holmes & Griffin after checking in. He placed the manila envelope with the photos on his lap. Without a doubt, Delfort would keep him waiting. So the game was played. He reached over and picked up a copy of *Time* magazine, which had a photo of Humphrey Bogart on the cover. He was starring in a new movie called *The Caine Mutiny*, where he played Captain Queeg, an oddball naval officer who becomes unhinged in the middle of a hurricane. The *Time* editors loved it, and said so at some length. He'd just finished the review when Delfort's secretary came out and showed him back to the senior partner's corner office.

Delfort stood up from his desk when Stone entered and gestured to a chair opposite. His eyes went right to the manila envelope. Like all good weasels, he had a highly developed sense of smell when it came to snares of any kind.

"Detective," he said. "Have a seat."

The office was done in dark hardwoods with a thick green carpet. Out the windows, Bakersfield sprawled into the irrigated mist of the valley. The remaining walls trumpeted the everlasting glory of the man himself. Law degrees, awards, pictures with politicians, athletes and movie stars.

All lost on Stone. Only the watch counted. And there it was, darting in and out of a French cuff under Delfort's perfectly tailored shirt.

"So shall we continue?" Delfort said.

"Sorry," Stone apologized as he pointed toward Delfort's left hand. "But I couldn't help but notice your watch. Beautiful."

"Yes, I'd have to agree," Delfort said smugly. "It's a Patek Philippe. I picked it up in Paris a couple of years ago."

"Paris, huh?" Stone said. "So where would I go if I wanted to get one around here?"

Delfort leaned back and crossed his arms behind his head. He smiled a lurid smile drenched in condescension. "For someone in your position, that would be a rather significant investment."

"Well let's say my uncle died and I picked up a little cash. What then?"

Stone unfolded his arms and leaned forward. "If you were really lucky, you might find one in Los Angeles, but probably not. Same thing in New York. Europe's your best bet. Paris, London or Rome."

"Well I guess that makes me really lucky," Stone said as he brought the manila envelope up onto the desk.

Delfort went dark all over. He sensed a trap, but knew it was too late. "What do you mean?" he asked.

"I didn't have to go anywhere." Stone opened the lid on the envelope. "I found one right here." He pulled out a Polaroid, a close-up of Rhonda's head being held in place to perform an oral act. The hand doing the holding had the Patek Philippe on its wrist.

Delfort's mouth opened slightly in silent exclamation. His eyes flashed alarm. But he quickly recovered his professional demeanor. "What are you trying to do? That could be anybody. What's it prove?"

"You're right," Stone admitted. "It could be anybody. Except for this." He reached into the envelope and pulled out the photo of Delfort and Blitz on the couch. The watch was clearly visible on Delfort's wrist. "And it could be anywhere," he continued. "Except for that painting in the background. Recognize it?"

"Why would I?"

"It's hanging on the wall in the living room of the late Richard Fancher. One of your best buddies." Stone brought out a handful of photos depicting the girls in various compromising positions. "You guys were very busy boys."

Delfort suddenly relaxed and settled back in his chair, utterly composed. He now understood the subtext of this encounter.

"So I have to ask myself, why are you doing this?" Delfort said. "Why didn't you just take all this to the DA?"

"Because I've learned that that's not the way things are done around here," Stone said.

"And just how are they done?" Delfort asked with a thin smile.

Stone shrugged. "You're the expert. I'm just a cop."

"I see," Delfort said. "Well I tell you what. Let's pretend otherwise. Let's say you wanted to make a deal of some kind. Just what might that deal be?"

"It would start with your premier client, Walter Sumner. I've good reason to believe he killed Charlene Winters. I intend to arrest him and have him charged with homicide."

Delfort managed a cynical chuckle. "That's utterly absurd. What makes you think the DA will buy into anything so ridiculous?"

"I have a witness that places him with Charlene in a seedy little room out at the Rancho Vista. Ever heard of the place? I bet you have."

"If something like this ever went to trial, you'd have to tell me who the witness was. So why don't you just go ahead and tell me right now."

"I'd be more than happy to. It's one of your favorite party girls. Or should I say party children? They're at that tender age where I tend to get confused. Your good buddy Jonathan Blitz put her up out at the Rancho and she just happened to land right next to Mr. Sumner and Miss Winters, who were having quite a row. Oh well, I guess they eventually resolved it, didn't they?"

Delfort stared at his desktop and pursed his lips.

"It's not so surprising if you stop and think about it," Stone continued. "In a town this size, dirty little secrets tend to get all tangled up."

Delfort looked up. "The deal. We haven't gotten to the deal, the quid pro quo."

"We've already covered the quid," Stone responded. "That's Sumner on a murder charge. The quo is this: we forget about your parties. You and your pals walk. That's the deal. The king loses his head and the princes live on. Only from now on, they confine themselves to golf because they know someone's watching."

"As always, detective, the devil's in the details. If this girl took the stand in a case against Mr. Sumner, she might want to talk about things that are best left alone. Wouldn't you agree?"

"I understand that Walter Sumner was never part of the Cradle Club. Am I right?"

One of Delfort's eyelids twitched at the mention of the club. He knew how truly awful it would sound in open court. "Let's assume that's the case," he told Stone.

"Then let's keep it that way. He never has to know that the girl was anything more than a teenage runaway who was holed up in a sleaze pit at the same time he was there with Charlene. That's the way you can play it. Now I'm not an ace defense attorney, but it sure seems like you might want to work with the DA's office and enter some kind of plea that spares Mr. Sumner the inconvenience of the gas chamber. Which also means that you never have to confront the girl in a public courtroom, which might be just a little embarrassing for everyone involved."

Delfort's hands assumed a position of prayer and he tucked them under his chin. "I see. And what about Mr. Willert? How do you suggest that we handle his case?"

"Easy. You have him plead guilty to simple car theft. Given the lack of any other evidence, that's the end of it and the girl never has to testify about what went on at Fancher's. I'm sure that given all your excellent relationships within the local justice system that all his can be easily worked out."

Delfort pointed to the manila envelope. "The photos. What about the photos?"

"When all is said and done, we can have a little barbeque at your place and put them on the grill. What do you think?"

"Let's assume for a moment that this was a real deal," Delfort suggested. "What guarantee might I have that you'd keep up your end of it?"

"Because we've both got our hands dirty, and they'll stay that way as long as the pictures are around. I've withheld evidence in a capital murder case. If that got out, I'd be fired and maybe even prosecuted for obstruction of justice. Better for me that the pictures go up in smoke, and the sooner the better."

"Up in smoke," Delfort repeated. "I assume you haven't brought any of this up with DA's office yet."

"You assume correctly. I thought it best that we work it out from this end first."

"I see," Delfort said. "You've obviously given this quite a bit of thought. I'll have to do the same."

"But not for long," Stone said as he rose with the manila envelope in hand. "I'm going to need an answer before three 'o clock."

"Why three?"

Stone turned away from Delfort and headed for the door. "Because I've set up a meeting with LaFrieniere for then." He opened the door and turned back toward Delfort with an approving nod. "Nice suit."

. . .

Twin stone eagles guarded the entrance to the Bank of America from their granite perches that flanked the entrance on Chester Avenue. Stone hoped that they excelled at their job as he sat in in the bank's office section. He brooded over the compromise he'd made to pursue Sumner. Ultimately, it was a matter of letting the little devils go in order to bring down the big one. In the end, murder trumped borderline sexual practices. Delfort and company would sidestep prosecution while Sumner went down in flames. Hopefully, their party circuit had died along with Fancher and they'd lead more circumspect lives going forward. At the very least, they'd likely limit themselves to women who were comfortably past the age of consent.

"All right Mr. Stone, I think we're all set."

Stone looked up as the assistant manager returned, a middle-aged fellow named Farnsworth. Stone didn't know why, but it seemed like an ideal name for a banker. Familiar and dependable. The man had a graying mustache and round spectacles. He handed Stone a small envelope.

"Here's the key. It has the box number right on it. Just sign in with the clerk any time you want to take something in or out."

"Thanks for your help," Stone said. He got up, crossed the lobby, signed in with the clerk and entered the vault. It reminded him that he was slightly claustrophobic. He put the manila envelope with the pictures on a marble-topped counter in the center. The back wall held a matrix of metal squares, and he traced the key number to his box location. It required only a single key, unlike newer versions. He unlocked his box, slid it out, placed it on the counter and opened the top.

He looked up to make sure no one was watching as he transferred the obscene photos from the envelope to the box. Given the current circumstances, it was definitely the prudent thing to do. They needed 24-hour protection until this whole business was resolved. He closed the lid, returned the box to its slot, and locked it in place.

He turned back once on his way out to the wall full of boxes. It reminded him of a mausoleum, where each slot held the eternal secrets of those long dead. All lost in darkness.

But the secrets in Stone's box were still very much alive and still longed to see the light of day.

. . .

The motorized hum of the big floor fan partially masked Brainard's bitching about his back. He sat one desk over from Stone and reached around to point to a particular locus of agony on his spinal column. Bagley, the recipient of the carping, didn't even bother to look up from his paperwork.

Stone glanced over at the big wall clock with its numbers done in some utilitarian type font that delivered unadorned information. Two o'clock and a little change. It was going to be tight, if it happened at all. He didn't want to cancel with LaFrieniere at three, but he would if he had to.

His phone rang. It was Delfort. "Okay, we have a deal. But you best take great care in how you proceed. Understand?"

"Understand."

Delfort hung up. Stone leaned back. So far so good. He rose and went up front to Mrs. Crenshaw. "I need to see the chief for a few minutes."

"I don't know if that's going be possible," she said.

"It's not routine. It needs to happen now," Stone countered.

"There are other considerations," she retorted.

"Well consider this," Stone said. "I wouldn't take up his time if it wasn't important. And if I'm unable to do so and something bad happens, you'll be called upon to explain why I couldn't see him. How does that sound?"

Mrs. Crenshaw rose in a silent grimace and headed down the hall, where she disappeared into the chief's office. She emerged with her grimace still intact, returned to her desk, gathered her dress and settled into her seat before addressing Stone. "The chief will see you now."

Beaumont looked up from his desk as Stone entered. "So what can I do for you, Sergeant?"

"I have a suspect in the Winters murder."

"You do?" Beaumont seemed less than enthusiastic. But then again, he always seemed this way. Stone no longer took it personally. There was some kind of major excavation underway inside the man and it scoured out any trace optimism before it could take root.

"I'm meeting with LaFrieniere to go over the evidence and see if we're ready to make an arrest and file a charge."

"You really think you have a case?"

"I do. I've got a key witness and enough supporting evidence to make it all stick together."

"Then what's been the holdup?"

"The suspect is Walter Sumner."

"As in Sumner Irrigation Systems?"

"The very same."

The chief stared off into some remote region of speculation.

"I wanted to give you a heads up before I went ahead," Stone added.

The chief turned steely. "You're sailing off into some very troubled waters. You know that, don't you?"

"I know that."

The chief clasped his big hands to together in front of his perfectly pressed tie. "I'm not going to stand in your way. But I'm not going to stand behind you, either. Understand?"

"I understand."

Beaumont's eyes took on a tiny trace of compassion. "It's the best I can do under the circumstances."

"I'm sure it is," Stone said. "I don't have any problem with that. You live here. I don't, not really."

"When are you meeting with LaFrieniere?"

"In about an hour."

"Let me know how it goes. If he wants to move on it, then I'm interested. Otherwise, I've got better things to do. And so do you."

"Right."

· · ·

"Walter Sumner?" LaFrieniere said. "You've got to be kidding. Tell me you're joking. Please." The district attorney shifted his ample belly to try to find a position of comfort. It wasn't going to work. The afternoon heat in the courthouse only added to his suffering.

"No doubt about it," Stone confirmed. "My witness made a positive ID. She was only a few feet away when he did it."

"So let me summarize," said Thomas Gilford, the head investigator. "You find some matches from the Rancho Vista in the Winters girl's bedroom. You go out there and run into this teenage tramp in the restaurant. She tells you Sumner and Winters were fighting in the next room over from her and that Winters came barging in with this sob story about Sumner's bad attitude."

"That's about it."

"How do you know it was on the night of the murder?"

"I don't. But even as it is, I'd say it's highly incriminating. Especially when you combine it with what the waitress told me out at the country club."

"Ah yes, the country club," Gilford said in a most dismissive tone. He ran a couple of fingers through his thinning red hair. "I dunno. It all seems just a little flimsy to me given that we're talking about a murder rap. Does this girl have a last name?"

"Wentworth. Linda Wentworth." Fortunately, Stone remembered the alias he'd given the girl.

"And where might we find Miss Wentworth?" LaFrieniere asked.

"I booked her in juvenile detention on a shoplifting beef." Stone felt slightly queasy about revealing Rhonda's whereabouts, but didn't really have any options. He started to get that strange sensation of sliding down a well-greased funnel.

"I'm going to have to talk to this Wentworth person myself, one on one," Gilford said. "But I can't do it for a day or two, so keep her on ice."

"Not a word of this can get out," LaFrieniere cautioned. "Not a word. No charges, no arrest. No nothing. We can't move on this until it's airtight, and right now it's anything but. We'll meet again after Tom's talked with this Wentworth girl."

. . .

A dozen rows of empty desks faced Stone went he got back to
the office. Mrs. Crenshaw seemed oblivious to the vacancy and
typed yet another report in triplicate. Only Brainard remained at
his desk, hunched over his typewriter.

"What's going on?" Stone asked Mrs. Crenshaw. "Where is
everybody?"

"I really don't know," she said as she twisted her typewriter's
platen and hit the carriage return.

Stone put the issue aside and continued on to his desk, where
he picked up the phone. The long distance operator put him
through to the LAPD's Hollywood Division who in turn connected him to his old partner, Sgt. Murphy.

"Murphy, it's Stone."

"Well I'll be goddam go to hell," Murphy exclaimed. "Long
time, no hear. You still up there in the turnip fields?"

"You got it. Now here's the deal: I'm working a murder case
and I need a little help from your end."

"Oh yeah?" Murphy said suspiciously. "And how little is
little?"

"You got a pen?" Stone asked.

"That's a bad start," Murphy said with a wink in his voice.

"I have a teenage runaway in custody named Rhonda Savage.
Says she's from LA. Claims to live in an apartment in Westwood,
a place called the Sunset Terrace, number twelve. Also claims it's
rented by some movie guy named Ray, who's taken an interest in
her."

"Aha," Murphy said. "Fuck pad deluxe."

"Sure looks like it. Can you check it out for me?"

"Yeah, I suppose I can do that."

"Thanks. Anything else you can dig up on the girl would be
a real bonus."

"Alright, but let's not get too excited, okay?"

"Okay. So how are things going?"

A sarcastic chuckle from Murphy. "How do you think?"

Stone nodded. "Got it. Well let me know, okay?"

"Hey," Murphy said, humor aside.

"Yeah?"

"I'll do what I can. We owe you. I know that."

"Thanks. Talk to you later."

It was good to hear Murphy say it out loud. Stone hung up and took in all the empty desks. What was the deal?

"Hey Stone," Brainard said as he walked toward the door. "Let's go. We're gonna be late."

"Late for what?"

"It's Ernie Wheeler's retirement party, over at the Pyrenees Café."

Wheeler. The desk sergeant who had the night desk on the evening that the evidence locker was looted.

"You know the deal, right?" Brainard said as he gingerly descended the stairs ahead of Stone.

"I'm not sure I do," Stone said. They reached the ground floor and pushed through to the parking lot out back.

"He took the hit."

"The hit for what?" Stone had a pretty good idea, but wanted Brainard to verify it.

"The big evidence fuckup. Somebody had to go down, and he was the guy. Doesn't really matter. He was going to retire next year anyway."

"Will he still get his full pension?"

Brainard reached his car and stopped. "Oh yeah. They did whatever they had to do and made it all work out."

"Well good for them."

Brainard climbed gingerly into his prewar Plymouth coupe and let his back settle into place with a sigh of relief. "Know where it is?" he asked Stone.

"Hold on and I'll follow you," Stone said.

A two-story building housed the Pyrenees Café on its bottom floor at the intersection of Sumner and Kern Streets. If nothing else, the location gave Stone a good idea of how far back the Sumner name went around here. A lone diesel locomotive crept by on the tracks across the street. The ominous mutter of its big engine bounced off the café's front wall and out into the industrial storage yards beyond. Bricks, gravel, rusty I-beams and rolled wire.

. . .

They pulled around to a parking lot in the rear. It held a couple of dozen cops' cars, which were a lot older than actual cop cars. They went in the back way to the bar, where a cloud of booze, testosterone and cigarette smoke fouled the air. Stone followed Brainard past old wooden tables full of cops and half-drained pitchers of tap beer. One such table held Ernie Wheeler, surrounded by a half-dozen old timers, guys hovering close to retirement. Even though it was Ernie's party, he seemed none too happy about it, which confirmed what Brainard had told him.

Stone felt slightly conspicuous. He only knew a handful of these people, but they all knew him, the LA cop, the guy from the big time. Someone snagged Brainard and sat him down, so Stone went on alone to the bar and ordered a beer. He gazed out at the double chins, the ample bellies, the slacks from JC Penney's, the receding hair gone gray. This was it. For James Stone, this was as good as it was going to get.

"Hey, you're Stone, right?" A cheery voice rescued him from a sliding into a terminal funk.

"Yep. That's me."

It was a young guy, mid-twenties, probably a patrolman. Clean shaven with a stylish flat top. One of his buddies, another young guy, stood next to him. "I'm Withers, this is Coyle."

Stone raised his glass. "Pleased to meet you."

"I know you probably get a little tired of this," Withers said apologetically. "But what was it like to be a cop in Hollywood?"

"I bet it wasn't like it is around here," Coyle added.

Stone smiled and put down his glass. "It wasn't anything like it is around here." The pair nodded their heads eagerly. The signal to go on.

The beer flowed. The pitchers foamed. The glasses stayed amber. The cigarettes piled up like fallen white timber in the ashtrays. Stone spoke of celebrities high on pot, of hidden porno studios, of jazz clubs awash in heroin, of million-dollar jewel heists, of actresses turned whores and vice versa.

They loved it. And so did he. When the pair finally excused themselves, he looked up to empty tables and a vacant bar. He left a dollar tip and headed out.

In the parking lot he winced at the mean light pouring out of a hot and hazy sky. A slight beer buzz enveloped him, but nothing too serious. He'd spent most the time regaling and not drinking. He felt good, better than he had in some time. He'd reconnected with the brotherhood. The bush league version, but the brotherhood nevertheless.

Except for Stone's car only one other remained in the lot, an old Dodge from the thirties. A lone figure stood by the driver's door and randomly thrust a key at the lock under the handle. Ernie Wheeler. He wobbled like a dying top while he did it.

"They should've baked a cake," Ernie mumbled to no one as Stone walked up.

"Yeah, that would've been nice," Stone offered.

Ernie turned his old bulldog face to Stone. "Yeah, a fuckin' cake." He nearly went over, and steadied himself with a hand on the hood.

"Tell you what, Ernie," Stone said. "I'm gonna give you a lift home. You can come back and get your car tomorrow. Okay?" He declined to mention that Ernie was too drunk to drive. It made certain people belligerent and stubborn about their driving skills. He didn't know if Ernie was one of them and didn't want to find out.

"Yeah, and then I can go get the fucking cake," Ernie declared.

"Yes, you can. First thing in the morning." He gently removed the keys from the old cop's grasp and steered him toward the passenger side. "So where do you live, Ernie?"

"Werner, off Buckner."

Stone unlocked the passenger door and oozed Ernie on in. "Here you go, buddy."

Stone got in the other side and pulled the old coupe out onto Kern and went right. "Fuckin' cake," Ernie mumbled. "Know what I'm gonna do with the fuckin' cake?"

"No I don't think I do," Stone replied.

"I'm gonna stuff it in Gilford's face. And I'm gonna keep it there until he chokes on it."

Stone turned to Wheeler. The aging sergeant stared out into a future that ended somewhere short of the windshield. His jaw sagged. His flesh smoldered in a deep twilight pink.

"What's Gilford got to do with it?"

"I took the hit. Know what I mean?"

"For the evidence?"

"Twenty-five years," Ernie declared. "I'm there twenty-five years. Good years. Put away a shitload of bad guys. And you know what they're gonna remember me for?"

"The missing evidence," Stone suggested.

"You know what they're gonna say? They're gonna say that Wheeler took his eye off the key and the evidence walked. Biggest police fuckup in years. That's what they're gonna say."

"So how does Gilford fit into this?"

"When he retires, they're gonna have a cake. A big fancy one from some bakery downtown. They're gonna have speeches. They're gonna say what a great job he's done."

Stone knew that it was time to venture a very big guess. "He was there the night the evidence walked. Right?"

Ernie nodded. "Fuckin' A."

"But he didn't sign in, did he?"

"What for?" Ernie said with a snort. "He's the big cheese. The big cheese does what the big cheese wants. Same as always."

"So who knows about this?"

"Just me and him."

"And he set up your retirement deal for you?"

"Yeah, somethin' like that."

"Ernie, I could be wrong, but I get the feeling that you weren't supposed to tell anybody about this."

"Fuck him," Ernie spat through the booze fog. "I'll tell anybody I goddam well please." He nodded, but jerked back upright. "Anyway, you don't count. You don't live here."

Stone knew precisely what the old sergeant meant. The Bakersfield Police Department was a closed system, a sealed political sphere. It assimilated newcomers very slowly, if at all. In Wheeler's drunken eyes, he was simply a non-entity.

"Well I wasn't going to tell anybody anyway," he told Ernie. "So it's no big deal."

"Turn here," Ernie said, and pointed right.

Stone dropped Ernie at a modest house halfway down the block, with potted plants on the little porch, all pruned and well-watered. Wheeler's wife came out with a sympathetic smile as Stone led him up the empty driveway. "He doesn't get like this very often," she apologized.

"I'm sure he doesn't," Stone said as she took his arm.

"Come on, honey," she said. "Time for a nap."

"Time for cake" Ernie mumbled.

• • •

The June sun wasn't going to give up without a fight. It flung a smothering blast of heat into the Juvenile Hall parking lot from its smug perch in the western sky. Stone watched the exchange of uniformed men in front as the shift rolled over. Who was bought and paid for? He had no immediate way of knowing. It hadn't been a pressing issue until now.

Wheeler's revelation about Gilford gnawed incessantly at him. The head investigator had cleaned out the evidence in the Fancher case. A very risky move. He had willfully sabotaged any possible prosecution, which kept the case out of court, and thus out of public view. It appeared that he was another member of the Cradle Club, or at least heavily entangled with those that were.

Rhonda would know.

Stone went to the service door, used the phone, and gained entrance. He went through two new guards and had Rhonda brought to the visitor's room. Once again, they conversed under the benevolent and paternal gaze of Dwight Eisenhower. Rhonda led off.

"When do I get out?"

"Maybe right now," Stone answered. "I've got a question about Dick Fancher's parties, a really important question. Do you remember a man showing up there with red hair and big muscular arms? He also has a really high voice."

"Yeah, there was guy like that. Red hair, high voice. He liked to wrestle you and pin you down."

"Do you remember what people called him?"

"Yeah, they called him Gil."

Stone clasped his hands and exhaled deeply. "We've got to get you out of here. Right now."

"Don't you need a lawyer or something to do that?"

"I hope not. Wait here."

Stone went out to the counter, where the guard was drinking a Coke and chewing on a piece of beef jerky. "I want the prisoner released in my custody."

The guard put down the Coke. "You sure about that?"

"Yeah, I'm sure about that."

"I mean like it's way past quitting time. What are you going to do with her? "

"I'm taking her down to the station to see if she can ID a couple of burglary suspects we just brought in."

The guard shrugged. "Your call. You're going to have sign your ass away to do it."

"That's my problem, not yours. Let's get it going."

• • •

Rhonda retreated into sullen silence as Stone drove up Chester Avenue into Oildale. He'd tried to explain to her how dangerous her situation had become. The man named Gil roosted near the top of law enforcement tree. If she went back into custody, there was a very good chance she'd never come out. A faked suicide, a staged assault, a fall in the shower. His admonishments seemed to bring out a hidden streak of fatalism in her. This current crisis ranked no higher than God knew how many others in her short and troubled life.

Stone had to wonder how big a lead they had. He'd booked Rhonda under the alias of Linda Wentworth, but Gilford would see through that in no time. Stone was one step ahead, but had no idea right now how make it two steps. "To be honest, Rhonda. I'm not quite sure what to do with you. We'll just have to make it up as we go along."

After taking a left off Chester onto Arvin, he pulled up in front of Christine's clinic. She was out front with a gallon can of Sherwin-Williams, painting over the racist graffiti left by the KKK. Unfortunately, the new paint didn't quite match the grimy shade of white underneath, leaving a series of overlapped brush-strokes on the siding. "Wait here," Stone instructed Rhonda.

At Stone's approach, Christine put the brush down on the can and looked over his shoulder toward the car. "Let me guess who your new friend is," she said.

"Sorry about this," Stone said as he reached her. "But I didn't have a lot of options."

"I'm sure you didn't," she said.

"The kid's in real trouble," Stone warned.

"And so are you."

Stone nodded. "And so am I."

Christine looked at the car again and sighed. "Well she can't just sit out there. It's too damn hot. Bring her in."

After a brief introduction to Dr. Harmon, Stone led Rhonda out to the little patio in the rear of the clinic and sat her down with a can of soda. "You getting hungry, Rhonda?"

"Starting to."

"Well let me talk to Dr. Harmon for a couple of minutes and we'll get you something to eat."

"Yeah."

Stone returned to the front room and sat on the old couch next to Christine.

"You know Tom Gilford, right?" he asked.

"The DA's Head Investigator? He's been around for years. He's an asshole."

"He was also a big time buddy of the late Richard Fancher."

"I didn't know that."

"Very few people do. And I'm sure he'd like to keep in that way."

"He was one of the party people?"

"That's what Rhonda says. And Rhonda ought to know. Needless to say, the kid's in big trouble if she stays locked up. So I sprung her. She's been released in my custody."

"For how long?" she asked.

"For as long as I can get away with, which won't be very long at all. If I don't get her back later this evening, I'm in deep shit."

"So what are you going to do in the meantime?"

Stone shrugged. "Get something to eat. And then have a long chat out back with Rhonda. I need every detail I can get about what went on at Fancher's and the Rancho Vista and how Gilford figures in. I'll have to take her back later tonight while I think up a new excuse to check her out again tomorrow."

"You can't keep this up indefinitely," Christine said.

"No," Stone admitted. "I can't." He rose slowly off the couch. "So where can I get some takeout food around here?"

"There's a Chinese place a couple of blocks south on Chester."

"That'll work." Stone headed down the hall toward the patio. "Go ahead and figure out what you want." He walked out the back door.

Gone, gone, gone.

No Rhonda. Just a vacant chair and an empty pop bottle on the table.

"Shit!" Stone hissed. He ran to the back fence and looked up and down the alley. Nothing but bare dirt and burnt refuse.

He charged back through the clinic. "Rhonda took off," he exclaimed to Christine and bounded out the front and into his car.

· · ·

As he drove, Stone steadied himself and fought off the urge to dwell on the potential consequences of Rhonda's disappearance. Instead, he focused on a methodical search of the surrounding blocks. No good. Only barking dogs and scowling neighbors. Cops were less than popular around here. No use stopping and asking about a stray teenager.

Christine was waiting just inside the open door to her clinic when he returned. At this hour, the sun still blazed with evil intent and demanded shelter. "I've got to find her," Stone declared.

"Right now, that might be rather difficult, wouldn't you say?" she calmly asked.

Stone walked past her and sank down onto the couch. "Could be. But not nearly as difficult as what'll happen if I don't."

She sat down beside him and put her hand over his. For no good reason, it felt immensely comforting. "Would you care to elaborate?"

He took a deep breath. "Not quite yet." She didn't know any-thing about his quasi-blackmail maneuver with Delfort. Or his dubious confrontation with Sumner. Or how Rhonda's absence would reduce his grand strategic edifice to pitiful rubble.

"There's a couple of places she might wind up," he told her. "I'm going to need to check them out."

Christine got up, went to her desk and wrote something on a prescription pad. "Here's something that might help," she said, and handed him the top slip.

He furrowed his brow as he read it. "I don't get it. It's an address."

"It's where I live. Come by when you're done looking. I'll wait up."

• • •

An intermittent procession of headlights streamed through the darkness outside the front window of the coffee shop at the Rancho Vista Motel. People, gas, beans, oil, beer, machinery, coffee mugs, and all the rest of it, moving north on Highway 99.

Stone ignored the traffic and stared at the prescription note with Christine's address. He marveled at the irony of it while he sipped his coffee. Why would she reach out just now, when he was absolutely flat on his back? But then again, why did anybody do anything? It was all beyond him and floating loose in the infinite expanse of the human condition.

After leaving some change to cover the coffee and tip, he headed out into the parking lot. He'd already wound his way through the entire complex several times, and had seen no sign of Rhonda.

So Rhonda, just where would you go? Not out on the street. You're too smart for that. It might get you a one-way ride out into the desert instead of jail. You wouldn't take off without some kind of plan. You knew in advance where you were headed. And just where might that be?

Stone's speculative reserves were spent. The answer would show up when it was good and ready.

Two highway rigs roared by in tandem out 99, punching into the moonless night toward Fresno. Stone watched their taillights recede and finally wink out. He climbed in his car and headed south toward town.

. . .

Dr. Christine Harmon's porch light welcomed him as he pulled up to the curb on 21st Street in the central part of the city. The night had shed the day's brutal ration of heat and left a pleasant smell from the flowering shrubs in the front yard. He hesitated for a beat before ringing the doorbell but went ahead anyway. What the hell.

Christine answered wearing tan slacks, high heels, and a loose silk blouse the color of new cream. So much for white lab coat, plaid skirt and sensible shoes. Only the attitude remained. Implacable. Firmly centered.

"I know it's late," he apologized. "Sorry about that."

"No need," she said. "Come in."

He surveyed the living room. Stylish, but not showy. Precisely what he'd expect from her.

"Let me take your hat and coat," she said. "Go ahead and have a seat."

Stone sat in a chair opposite a generously upholstered couch done in avocado. It felt like an upscale version of burlap to his touch.

"Did you get something to eat?' she asked while she put his things in the front closet.

"Yeah, I'm fine," he lied in the timeless male tradition.

She crossed and sat on the couch. "You don't look fine. You look like you could use a drink."

He nodded. "Maybe I could."

"It didn't go well, did it?"

"No, it did not."

She stood. "Come in the kitchen. Let's see what we can get you."

Stone followed her in and checked out the appliances. All new and seldom used. Even a dishwasher. You didn't see many of those. She opened a cabinet to a shelf holding a modest supply of liquor, and stood aside. "See anything you like? I don't entertain a lot, so there's not much to choose from."

Stone spotted a bottle of Irish Whisky. "A little bourbon, would be fine. Straight up."

Christine fetched two glasses from an adjoining cabinet and poured them both a shot. She raised her glass slightly. "I'd say cheers, but under the circumstances, it doesn't seem appropriate."

"No, it doesn't." Stone took a sip. The buttery burn felt good going down.

Christine took a sip and silently led them back to the living room, where they assumed their previous seating, which was as close as Stone wanted to get right now. He stifled an impulse to tell her the whole truth, the magnitude of his transgressions, the potential damage, the ruinous consequences.

Stone took another sip, a much bigger one. "So why did I come here?" he asked out loud.

Christine appeared amused. "To Bakersfield? Or to my house?"

"Either one." The half glass of whiskey was definitely on the job.

"Let's start with Bakersfield," Christine proposed. "You've already told me what happened in LA, and where it left you. Given everything that went down, this place was your best shot, right?"

"Right." Stone took another sip, the biggest yet.

"As for my house, I hope the reason you came here is because I asked you to. If you hadn't, I would've been at least a little disappointed."

"Really?"

"Really." She patted the seat cushion next to her. "Why don't come over here where I can see you a little better."

It seemed like a really good idea. Stone did it. The rest was easy.

19.

Mrs. Crenshaw stopped typing the morning report the moment that Stone came into view. She broadcast a toxic radiance and her thin lips contorted into what some might call a smile. Stone saw it as a nasty little squiggle of rose lipstick beneath cat's eye glasses.

"The Chief wants to see you immediately," she proclaimed.

"You mean I can just walk in? Unannounced?" Stone asked. "Is that the new rule?"

"No it's not. I'm simply relaying a specific request," she said. "How you respond is entirely up to you."

"Do you go to church, Mrs. Crenshaw?"

"Of course I do."

"And what church might that be?"

"Southern Baptist."

"Do you pray for the delivery of sinners into the arms of Jesus?"

"Every Sunday."

"Would you offer up such a prayer on my behalf on this coming Sunday?"

Her mouth opened, exposing a lifelong void. Stone turned away toward the chief's office before she could think to close it.

. . .

Chief Beaumont wore a suit instead of his usual uniform. No matter. The face on top was still mined from a rock quarry.

"Stone. Come in. Sit." His chilly blue eyes stalked Stone as he crossed the office and sat down opposite the chief.

"Got a call this morning from the Juvenile Hall," he said and reached for some notes. "It was about a prisoner you booked for shoplifting. A girl named Linda Wentworth."

Stone flinched inwardly at the mention of the alias he'd dreamed up for Rhonda. Maybe it wasn't such a good idea.

"It seems you took custody of her last evening." He looked up at Stone, blue eyes boring and tunneling. "That right?"

"That's right."

Beaumont looked back down at his notes. "You told the duty officer you were bringing her down here to ID some burglary suspects. That right?"

"That's right."

"So how'd that go?" the chief asked.

"It didn't."

"What happened?"

"She got away from me."

"She escaped?"

"Yeah. I left her in the back of the car, but I forgot to lock it. I stopped at a gas station to take a leak, and when I came out she was gone." For the first time in his career, Stone was on the wrong side of an interrogation. And like all perps, he was spontaneously improvising a chain of lies and fervently hoping it wouldn't collapse of its own weight.

"So did you report it?" the chief asked.

"No, I didn't. She's just a kid. She's not a menace to anyone, except maybe herself. I figured it would keep until morning."

"You fucked up. You know that, don't you? You should have reported it immediately." The chief leaned back reflectively in his chair. "If you're really lucky, I'll find some way to duck a formal investigation. But for now the cat's out of the bag. The people

over at juvenile want to know what happened, and I'm going to
have to come clean with them."

The chief softened slightly. His face went from granite to sand-
stone. "You haven't left me any room to move, Stone. I'm going
to have to suspend you until this thing gets settled up."

"And then?"

"And then, if you're lucky, you still have job. If not, you're on
your own. Understand?"

"Understand."

"Yes sir." Stone quashed an urge to spew out the truth about
Rhonda Savage, about Delfort, Fancher, Gilford and Sumner. Out
of the question. He'd like to believe that the chief stood apart
from it all, but had no way to be sure.

On his way downstairs, Stone passed Mrs. Crenshaw, who no
longer had any idea what to make of him.

"Sunday. Don't forget," he told her.

· · ·

Stone stood in a little patch of shade in front his apartment where
it butted up against the parking lot. The late morning sun had
baked its paved surface into a thermal purgatory. All was very
still, save for the whoosh of an occasional car out on 4th Street.
The ticks and pings of the agonized engine in his parked Chevy
were clearly audible. He'd seldom been here at this hour, when
everyone was out doing battle with the world at large, except for
a few bitter women who sealed themselves inside with old cop-
ies of *McCall's* and TV soap operas and trickles of sweat rolling
down their pale skin.

Stone trolled along the bottom of his sullen disposition,
looking for bits of optimism. In truth, his encounter with Chief
Beaumont could have been much uglier. He hadn't been fired outright and he was still on the payroll. In his own stentorian way,
the chief was signaling a hint of sympathy and compassion. Stone
knew that his boss would do what he could to salvage the situation – as long as it wasn't at his personal expense.

Up on the roof the swamp cooler rumbled to life, and it promised a slightly diminished temperature inside, so he unlocked his door and entered. As he did so, he felt something extra in his pocket and pulled it out. The key to the safe deposit box glared up at him in reproach. What a dumb thing to be carting around something that critical in his pants pocket.

He scanned the room, searching for a hiding place, and spotted one: the stove, an old GE model with a scratched top and burners on their last leg. A quick pull on the front left burner and it came free with a groan from its electrical socket. He reached into the vacated spot and lifted the grease pan out, exposing a hole that punched through to the metal frame below. It let him place the key on the frame's surface and push it back out of sight, but not so far that he couldn't feel around with his finger to retrieve it.

After putting the burner back, he draped his coat over a chair at the kitchen table and walked to the refrigerator and looked in at his beer stock. He'd saved a single bottle of Miller High Life for a special occasion. The label depicted a girl in festive garb perched on the crescent of a gibbous moon. She raised her glass to toast to a black starry sky, as if to acknowledge a universe of infinite potential. Stone hoped she was onto something. He took the bottle out, opened it, and plunked down on the lumpy old couch, where he took a deep swig. A cool yellow tingle enveloped his tongue. Very gratifying.

So now what? Back in LA his personal road map would have stretched over thirty years, from patrolman to lieutenant, and then on out. A tidy pension and a million stories to tell at parties and family gatherings. All gone. And now it looked like a replay here in Bakersfield. So what about his third act? His police days were most certainly over if the city let him go. Then maybe, money aside, he just might do something that he really wanted to.

Like something with the music, the boisterous, electrified sounds coming out of little bars up and down Chester Avenue. He recalled Travers saying how Nashville had gone soft, with lush strings and smooth rhythms. And how the music right down the street would ultimately prevail because it was closer to people's hearts and hardscrabble lives.

Travers was right. But how did James Stone fit in? He didn't sing, he didn't play pedal steel, he didn't pick lead guitar. But he did one thing extremely well and that was to listen. He heard nuance, he heard detail, he heard the difference between a good performance and a really great one. Ultimately, this knack might take him somewhere. But maybe not. Right now, any kind of dawn seemed permanently parked over a very distant horizon.

Several swigs later, he heard a car pull up outside. A big car, judging by the strength of engine's idle. He considered going to the window to check it out, but decided against it. The world was now officially passing him by, so why bother?

One final swig as a knock registered on his door. He went to the front window and gingerly parted the curtain. None other than Samuel Delfort stood out front. The attorney rocked nervously from foot to foot, and looked back to see if anyone was watching.

Stone took his time answering the door. When he did, it framed Delfort in a brilliant rectangle of sun, pavement and sky.

"We have to talk," Delfort announced. "Right now."

"You're sure about that?" Stone asked from behind a slight beer buzz.

"Yes, I'm sure," Delfort answered. He gave his shirt collar an irritable tug. "It's hot out here. I'd rather we did it inside."

Stone shrugged. "Sure. Why not?"

Delfort entered as Stone stepped aside. "I'd offer you something," Stone said. "But I can't think of a single reason why I'd want to."

Delfort ignored the barb and took in the drab room, but refrained from comment. He turned back to Stone. "Since we made our deal, the situation has changed substantially. We need to renegotiate."

Stone shrugged again. "Whatever for?"

"I've heard from the DA's office. It seems that you took a young teenage girl into custody and then managed to lose her. That wouldn't happen to be your witness, would it?"

"The DA's office, huh? Well let me guess who told you. Just maybe it was your old party pal, Head Investigator Gilford. You know, I hear that in his spare time he's made a hobby out of investigating young girls."

"All that's beside the point," Delfort said. "The only thing that counts is that your key witness is now out of the picture. It leaves you with no compelling evidence against Mr. Sumner. Your case collapses. You've got nothing, except maybe your job back, if you're lucky."

"Oh but I do have something," Stone countered. "I've got all your party pictures, and I'm sure I can find a way that they get to the right people."

"And just who might the right people be?" Delfort said with a smile.

"Hard to say. It might be someone here in town that's got a clean bill of health. Or maybe someone in LA. Someone who works for the *Times*. You and your prominent pals could be a big story, counselor. You could be Pulitzer material."

"You seem to forget that you've withheld evidence in a capital murder case, sergeant."

It was Stone's turn to smile. "That's a little story. You're a big story. I'll take my chances."

"Okay, enough of this," Delfort said. "We all know what the bottom line is here."

"Oh yeah? And what's that?"

Delfort reached in the breast pocket of his suit and pulled out an envelope. "This is a thousand dollars, a down payment on a settlement for the return of the photos. The balance of nine thousand will be split into two installments. The first when you hand over them over, the second when you leave town permanently."

"Wow," Stone said in a solid deadpan.

"To use a tired metaphor, sergeant, you've stirred up a real hornet's nest. This is your last chance to settle this thing on a reasonable basis. If you don't take it, all bets are off. It's out of my control."

"Gosh, I don't know what to say," Stone quipped.

Delfort tossed the envelope over onto the dining table. "Then don't say anything." He turned and headed for the door. "You know where to find me."

"Yes, I do," Stone said to Delfort's retreating figure.

Stone stood in the little patch of remaining shade outside the door and watched Delfort climb into a big Lincoln Continental. The swelter of the overhead sun had turned its interior into a kiln made of glass and steel. The lawyer yanked his tie loose and pulled his shirt open. All the windows descended at once with an electrified hum to expel the heat. Impressive.

Stone went back inside and shut the door. The envelope, plump with currency, rested on the dining table. He sat and looked at it, but didn't want to touch it. If he did, he might become infected.

· · ·

Stone waded through the harsh fluorescent light that saturated the county morgue. "So what have we here?" he asked when he reached Christine, who stood over a gurney occupied by a dead male in his twenties.

"He's the classic single-car collision," Christine observed. "Hit a telephone pole out on Hwy. 58 heading west. I estimate the speed at about sixty-five. No booze. Just stupidity. The crash pitched him forward into the steering post, which caved in his sternum and blew out his heart. He was dead before his head hit the dash and flattened his frontal lobe."

"That means he's in almost as bad a shape as I am," Stone said.

"Rhonda?"

"Yeah, Rhonda," Stone said.

"What now?" she asked.

"The juvenile people screamed to the chief. He suspended me pending an investigation. I'm on my own."

"Not good," Christine said. She looked down at the corpse. "But better than this guy. He kind of puts it all into perspective, doesn't he?"

"Yeah, I guess he does," Stone admitted.

"You got a plan?" she asked.

"I'm going to keep after Rhonda. She'd better hope that I find her before they do."

"And then what? Are you going to take her back into custody?"

"Can't do that. I'm not a cop right now. I've got to get her out of town while she's still in one piece."

They both stared down at the deceased accident victim and Stone said "I don't know what else to tell you. It's a real mess. I'm sorry I dragged you into it."

Christine turned away from the gurney. "I've got news for you," she said. "Nobody's ever dragged me into anything."

"I'm glad to hear that," Stone said. He reached over and gently brushed her hand for just an instant. It felt warmer and softer than he expected. "I've got to get going."

He was almost to hallway door when she spoke from behind him.

"When will I see you again?"

His heart quickened, but just a beat or two. Only enough to remind him that they all lived somewhere outside the bounds of true sensibility.

"Hard to say. I'll let you know."

• • •

"Captain Video rallies men of good will and leads them against the forces of evil everywhere."

Stone slumped on his couch in front of the TV, which was tuned to the Dumont Network. "Hey Captain," he said to the screen. "Where were you when I needed you?" Why hadn't the captain descended from his craggy mountain headquarters depicted in fuzzy black and white and taken on the dark side of Bakersfield? All he'd needed to do was rally a few men of good will. Stone snorted.

Captain Video faded and the Dumont Evening News came on. A somber Morgan Beatty announced that a coup in Guatemala had just toppled the current government, thus ending the so-called Guatemalan Revolution. Stone toasted the screen with his open beer. "Go get 'em, Morgan."

The phone rang. Stone answered with a laconic "Yeah."

"Sergeant Stone," a male voice said, "I understand you've lost something."

Stone sat up straight and turned down the TV. "Who's this?"

"Doesn't matter," the voice intoned in the lazy remnants of an Okie drawl. Thing is, I just might know how to find it."

Stone was good with voices, and was sure he'd never heard this one. "So what do we do about that?"

"Clover Club. One hour."

"Let's say I show up," Stone speculated. "How will I know you?"

"Don't y'all worry about that. I'll know you. That's what counts."

The caller hung up. Stone sunk back on the couch. He turned the TV sound back up. Morgan Beatty was saying that a colored woman in South Carolina had been kicked off a bus for sitting in the whites-only section.

"Goddam it," he muttered as he stood up. Once again, he had that bad feeling about sliding down a funnel. Didn't matter. He was out of options. He had to go.

· · ·

The June sun hovered near the looming horizon on the far side of the valley. Its light slipped from yellow to orange as it raked the Edison Highway in front of the Clover Club. A long shadow had consumed the parking lot by the time Stone got out of his car and headed toward the entrance. Out front a highway rig emitted a deep growl as it shifted gears on its way east.

He found the place about half full, which was normal for a weeknight. The band was on a break, and the clientele clustered around wooden tables full of beer pitchers and drained shot glasses. Their cigarettes fed a blue cumulus that pressed against the ceiling.

Stone stood by the bar and scanned the faces. No eye contact. He pulled up a stool and ordered a beer. The band had mounted the stage and was getting ready to fire up. Lefty Frizzell with Jelly Sanders on fiddle.

Stone grasped his beer mug and took a swig as Lefty launched into "If You Got the Money, I've Got the Time." Stone liked the tune but was too distracted to savor it. He scanned the room once more. Nothing. Somebody was jerking him around, and he found that supremely annoying.

His blood pressure rose a couple of points with each passing song. By the end of the set, he was ready to hurl his beer mug into the mirror behind the bar. Instead, he simply got up and stalked out.

The night was out in full force by the time he reached the parking lot of packed earth shrouded in dust. A solitary light with a metal hood cast its feeble glow out into the lot. Old Fords and Chevys sat in crooked rows and their shadows jabbed out into the darkness beyond. A tree in the back hung limp in the heat, its leaves sagging in distress. And close by, a group of men stood in a semicircle behind the rusted bed of an old GM pickup truck. Lean men, shaped by lives of arduous labor, with greased hair and biceps exposed under rolled up shirtsleeves. A bottle of Charter Oak whiskey circulated amongst them and patiently brought their collective demon to life.

Stone failed to notice them. He was too caught up in being played for a sucker.

"Hey there, buddy. Where you think you're goin'?"

He instantly recognized the voice. It belonged to the jerk from Blackboard, the one who bullied Fatalia, the one he gut punched when they moved on him.

That time, guy had two buddies. This time, he had a half dozen.

Stone suddenly realized that the anonymous caller wasn't just jerking him around. Rather, he was setting him up for a massive beating. At the very least.

He considered how useful his revolver would be right now, but it was a hopeless ten yards away in his glove compartment. Because of his suspension, he was just another civilian and didn't have a concealed weapons permit.

Without a word, he turned and headed toward the north side of the parking lot, which was open to the highway. Whatever they were going to do, he'd make sure they did it in plain sight.

"Now what you up to?" the jerk said.

Stone stopped and turned to make his stand. It prompted the men to halt abruptly about six feet from him. They expected a frightened rabbit and now faced determined opposition. A pack of wary dogs bound together by the jerk, who stood at their center.

"I'd like to introduce you to a little club we got here in town. It's called the KKK. That ring a bell?"

Stone glanced over toward the entrance to the bar. The band had started up. No one would be leaving right now. He was on his own.

"You know what we heard about you? We heard you're from LA. Now that ain't so bad, but we also heard you're a nigger lover. Now that's real bad. One thing we can't stand around here is a nigger lover."

"Oh yeah?" Stone said. "Well why don't you and I have a little talk about that?" His only chance was to isolate the jerk. If he could cut off the head, the body would wither.

The jerk saw right through the ploy and smiled. He motioned with his arms, and the pack spread out to encircle Stone. "Thought I told you: We're a club, and that means we stick together. Now as I recall, me and you tangled over at the Blackboard, and you had a buddy with a gun. Looks like he's all gone this time. Too bad about that."

Stone knew he was in big trouble when two of the advancing pack went out of his peripheral vision. But he wasn't going to go down with getting off at least one shot. He charged the jerk with a startling burst of speed and knocked him off his feet. The pack froze in place, dumbfounded by Stone's audacity.

The two of them hit the ground at an angle that favored Stone. He came up on top and launched a right at the jerk's head, but was off balance and the punch only grazed the man's nose.

"Get him!" the jerk screamed to the pack. He pushed his long arms into Stone's chest to keep him out of punching range.

Stone felt a fist crack into his cheek and knock him sideways. A foot smashed his ribs, and then another. The jerk squirmed free and came to his feet. "Pull him up!" he commanded. "He's mine!"

A pair of powerful arms grabbed Stone around his chest and yanked him upright. Calloused hands clasped the back of his neck to pin him in place. The jerk brushed his nose where Stone hit him and regained his composure.

"You know, last time me and you tangled, you taught me a new punch. Now it's time to try it out on you."

The pack members on each side of Stone reached in and locked his arms at the elbows. The jerk now had a clear and defenseless target. And he was going to make a show of it. He danced around Stone with fists up, like it was a fair fight. "Yessir, I did learn my lesson," he said.

Stone fought to stay focused. The blows had inflated big, hot balloons of pain in his head and ribs. He saw one last chance to gain an advantage, and focused on the jerk's shifting feet. The man was once again underestimating his speed.

The jerk's right foot came forward to plant the gut punch. In a flash, Stone drew up his legs and delivered a lightning kick to the man's lower chest. His arms came open and he flew backward in an awkward sprawl and skidded to a dusty stop.

He lay there, momentarily stunned, while the pack held their breath.

The jerk struggled to his feet and looked wildly about in a boiling stew of rage and humiliation. The ante had just been dramatically raised and he needed to match it. He saw what he needed. One of the pack had brought a baseball bat along as a backup. "Gimme that," he screamed and the man handed him the bat.

Stone felt himself slide into a strange and unexpected perspective. He abandoned the calculus of survival, which no longer held any promise. The jerk, the pack and the parking lot all receded into some internalized distance. Only the bat held his attention. It was nearly new, with the oval stamp of a Louisville Slugger burned into its ash shaft. Near the head, the brown cursive of some star player's signature played out along its length. But which player? He couldn't quite resolve it. So there it was, his final issue, left unanswered.

The bat came to life in a brilliant glow. The yellow of its ash, the brown of its contoured grain.

The bat went deep red in a hellish retreat.

The bat turned bright again, then back to red. In the background, a deep mechanical burble rose into an ear-splitting snarl before subsiding. The eyes of the pack left Stone and turned toward the highway.

Lincoln Jefferson dismounted from his big Harley-Davidson motorcycle. He walked toward the pack in silhouette from the flashing lights on his bike. All that could be seen was his enormous size, his leather jacket, his holstered automatic, his jodhpurs and his boots.

Stone felt the quick release of the arms restraining him. The jerk dropped the bat, but not before Jefferson spotted it.

"So what's going on here?" Jefferson asked in his thunderous baritone. "You guys playing a little a ball?"

"No sir," the jerk said. "We were just fixin' to leave."

Jefferson now came into full view. The lights no longer masked his color. The pack appeared stunned and thrown into hopeless confusion. They looked to the jerk for leadership and saw nothing but a hateful husk.

"Well don't let me stop you," Jefferson said.

Without a word, the KKK melted away and headed for their cars, each marinating in their own odious brew.

Jefferson turned to Stone. "You okay?"

Stone took the luxury of a deep breath, even though it hurt his ribs. "Yeah, I'm okay."

"I heard what happened with that kid at juvenile," Jefferson said. "So they let you go, huh?"

"At least for the time being."

Jefferson gave his forehead a thoughtful scratch. "Well personally, I think that's bullshit."

Stone smiled through the pain. "Me too."

"You got your car here?"

"Yeah."

"Okay then." Jefferson started back toward his bike. "You be careful."

"I owe you," Stone said as Jefferson climbed onto his Harley. "I won't forget this."

"I'm sure you won't," the big black cop replied. "You're not that kind of guy."

He touched his boot to the clutch and twisted the throttle. The bike's beefy engine put out a strangled roar and he disappeared into the darkness down the highway heading east.

20.

JUNE 23

SOUTH BAKERSFIELD

Stone flipped the rearview mirror down so he could see the right side of his face. Not too bad, everything considered. No dramatic changes in its topography, just a little swelling around his cheek and eye.

When the light turned green and he turned the wheel, his ribs clamored for their fair share of attention. A sharp pain traversed his side as he headed south on Stine Road, but it felt more like muscle than bone.

Duke Snider, he thought. That's it. Duke Snider. The name stamped and burned into the Louisville Slugger, the bat they were going to use to kill him. Snider played for the Brooklyn Dodgers and averaged 42 homers per season. Plenty good enough to get him emblazoned on God knows how many bats in sporting goods departments across the country. Stone wondered how Snider would react if he knew that he was nearly an agent of death, that his name had almost merged with a human skull targeted for destruction.

He slowed halfway down the block and spotted the house on his left. Its driveway curved in a semicircle behind some trees that partially hid it from view. A porch light illuminated the front, which had a distinctly European feel that threw it out of cultural synchrony with its neighbors.

He swung into the driveway and saw the MG parked in the rear in front of the garage. No surprise, not at this point. Rage trumped the pain as he got out of the car and marched to the front door while drawing his revolver. The door had a security grille embedded into its wooden surface at eye level, the kind with a little metal gate that opened to present a view of anyone standing on the porch.

Of course. As Head Investigator of Kern County, Thomas Gilford had accumulated more than enough enemies to warrant such a feature.

Stone rang the doorbell, which set off a quivering stream of dog barks from within, each identical to the last. A smaller dog, maybe a Sheltie. He brought his revolver up level with the grille. After a brief moment, a slight clack registered as the grille gate opened and an eye appeared from behind the brass scrollwork.

"Open right now, or I shoot!" Stone yelled.

The gate slammed shut. A big mistake. Gilford should have left it open, and stepped out of view, like he was going to open the door. It would have bought him a little time.

Stone aimed at the spot where the doorknob met the frame and fired. Splinters flew and the door sprang open. He shouldered it aside and headed immediately for the hallway beyond the living room. People don't keep weapons in their kitchens; they stash them in their bedrooms to deal with nocturnal intruders. Gilford would be no exception.

The dog, indeed a Sheltie, continued its frantic barking and bravely blocked Stone's path until he was within kicking range, then leaped aside. He charged down the hall toward an open bedroom, where he found Gilford opening a drawer in a nightstand to retrieve a pistol.

"Freeze or you're dead!"

Gilford turned slowly and brought his hands up. His mouth sagged open in alarm and his eyes spewed panic.

Stone brought a pair of handcuffs out of his pocket. "You know the drill. Up against the wall, spread eagle."

Gilford silently complied while the dog barked itself ragged out in the hall. Once Stone had him cuffed behind his back, the Head Investigator turned around and all his arrogance, contempt and disdain were back in full force. "You're not a cop anymore, Stone. And you know what that makes you? A common criminal. You're gonna go down for this."

Stone smacked him across the face with a backhand delivered at full force. Gilford's head twisted and his mouth flew open. His eyes clamped shut and his lips distorted in pain as he rebounded.

Stone grabbed him just below the collar and pulled him in close. "Yeah, go ahead and call the cops. I'm sure they'd like to know what the ruckus is all about. Maybe you and Delfort and Blitz could give them a few lessons on how to put on a really swell party. Maybe you could share some snapshots." He tightened his grip on Gilford. "You should've brained me a little harder when we were in Fancher's basement. Because from now on, I'll be a real nuisance. Count on it." He reached into the nightstand drawer, pulled out a revolver and emptied the bullets onto the rug.

"You'll do time for this," Gilford warned.

"Turn around," Stone commanded. Gilford complied with a disgusted sigh. Stone kicked the small of his back and he crashed down onto the floor, stomach first. He barely managed to twist his head to one side and avoid a head-on collision between his nose and the carpet. Stone pulled out the key to the handcuffs and unlocked one side while Gilford was still stunned. He clamped the cuff around the leg of a large brass bed, and stood back. As Gilford looked on, he dropped the key in the doorway to the hall. "It's gonna take a little work, but I bet a big strong guy like you can move that bed over to here. Good luck with that."

"Fuck you!" the Head Investigator screamed as Stone went down the hall on his way out. The dog had gone strangely silent, which was a good thing, because Stone had been tempted to deliver a swift kick to shut it up.

He'd just upped the ante considerably. He didn't care. Some atavistic chorus had sung to him and made it quite clear: It had to be done.

On his way home, he methodically assessed the situation. He still had the pictures stashed securely in a safety deposit box at the bank. But he didn't have Rhonda, which was once again problematic. The pictures would provide hard evidence of criminal behavior, but Gilford wasn't in them. Only Rhonda could place him at the parties.

· · ·

When he pulled off 4th street into the parking spot in front of his apartment, he was still burning off the adrenaline reserves that he'd taken on in the encounters with the KKK and Gilford. Maybe a beer would bring him back down. He needed a decent night's sleep for more reasons than he cared to think about.

He paused on his doorstep under the porch light and looked up and down the street. Dark, quiet and empty. Only a dim trace of sky glow hanging on the horizon like a spent fog bank. Bakersfield was too small to own the night.

He got out his key, but when he pressed it to the lock, the door swung open of its own volition. The darkness of the interior stared out at him with bad intent. He felt for the switch inside and turned on the overhead light. It gave a stark and brutal accounting of what had happened within.

His entire life had become an ugly sea of flotsam and jetsam floating on the apartment floor. Family pictures. Cancelled checks. School diplomas. A pen knife from his boyhood. A pair of cufflinks. His birth certificate. Commendations from the LAPD. An old deck of cards. A scattering of plastic poker chips.

All violated in an effort to find the one thing that really mattered.

He tore his eyes away from the floor, and centered them on the stove. Each burner had been ripped from its socket, along with its grease pan. He held his breath as he went to the cavity for the left front burner. He carefully poked his finger into the hole leading to the frame below and felt for the key. Nothing. Only cold, greasy metal. He collected himself and tried again. Nothing.

He sagged into a kitchen chair. A tiny breath of wind pushed the front door open, exposing the pavement outside in a circular bath of porch light. A cat walked into view. It had fur of a chalky gray that differed only slightly from the darkness beyond. The top of its right ear was mangled and curled. It stopped in the middle of the doorframe and turned its head to look in at him. It saw nothing of particular interest and moved on.

• • •

The music was so damned good that it nearly made a difference. It bounced with a savage delight off the knotty pine walls of the Rainbow Gardens down on Union Ave. It tumbled over the tables, the bottles, the dancers and the drinkers. It turned longtime losers into the temporary winners. It elevated Stone to where the hopeless mess smoldering out there in the night seemed almost manageable.

Haggard. That was the kid's name, according to Ron Travers, who occupied the bar stool next to Stone. Merle Haggard. Broad face, high forehead, expressive mouth, all topped by a full head of swept-back auburn hair. He sang with a power and conviction beyond his years, backed by the inimitable bark of his Fender Telecaster. He couldn't have been more than eighteen.

The song ended to explosive applause and the bandleader, Lefty Frizzell, announced a break. Travers turned to Stone. "So what do you think?"

"He's good," Stone commented. "Really good. Is he as young as he looks?"

"He has to go outside when he's not on stage," Travers noted. "It's the liquor laws. How'd you know he'd be here? He's just sitting in. He's not on the bill."

Stone took a quick pull on his bottle of Schlitz, his fourth. "I didn't. It just wasn't a good night to stay home, that's all."

Travers nodded thoughtfully. "Yeah. Some nights are like that."

"I've a got a question for you," Stone said. "Let's suppose for a minute that you had a thirteen-year-old daughter."

Travis chuckled. "I don't think that's in the cards, detective. At least not in this universe."

"Understand. But what if you did, and what if she was being chased around by a guy in his forties? Would you be upset?"

"Absolutely."

"Why?"

Travers looked down pensively at his beer. "Because it wouldn't have anything to do with love. The guy's not after affection or companionship or personal discovery. It's about predator and prey. It's about the thrill the hunter gets when he tracks down a vulnerable victim and closes in for the kill. Pretty cold, wouldn't you say?"

"Yup," Stone agreed.

Travers paused for a sip of beer. "So there you have it. Any more questions?" he asked with a trace of a smile.

"I'm all done," Stone said. "Thanks."

"Don't mention it. You gonna stick around for next set?"

Stone looked at this empty bottle. "Don't think so." He got up off his stool. "Take care of yourself."

Travers raised his glass in salute. "Always."

• • •

Stone stood in the phone booth on the far side of the Rainbow Gardens parking lot. Its dirty glass smeared the passing traffic into a transient blur. He thought about Rhonda and what Travers had just said inside. The professor was right. In the end, it was all about predation and power, about snuffing out the final vestiges of someone's childhood.

He lifted the receiver and put a dime in the middle coin slot atop the phone. The dial tone came to life and droned in his ear as he cranked in Christine's home phone. He rotated the coin return bin while waiting for an answer and looked inside. Sometimes you got lucky and bagged a nickel or dime. Never a quarter.

"Hello, this is Dr. Harmon." She always answered that way in case it was business.

"This is the former detective James Stone," he announced. He wondered if he sounded a little thick after four beers. "Are you available for consultation?"

"It depends," she answered. "What ails you?"

"When I got home tonight, I found my apartment turned upside down. Very thorough, very professional. Nothing left to chance."

"Oh my. You think is was the cops?"

"Either that or the best burglars ever to walk the streets of Bakersfield."

"Did they get what they wanted?"

"They wanted the key to a safe deposit box at the Bank of America, and yes, they got it."

"Do you want me to guess what was in the box?"

"Fancher's party pictures. The entire set. Every last one of 'em."

"Oh dear."

"That's what I say, plus a little more you don't want to hear. Look, my place is a total disaster, and I'm just not up to dealing with it tonight."

"Say no more. I'll see you when you get here."

"Thanks." Stone hung up and headed for his car. As he unlocked it, someone opened the door of a pickup parked next to him. It was the Haggard kid, who took the final swig on a bottle of beer before dropping it onto the floorboard at his feet. He noticed Stone as he climbed out, and gave a deferential nod.

"Good job," Stone told the kid. "You sounded great."

Haggard stopped, scratched his high forehead and gazed down at the toes of his scuffed cowboy boots. "Yeah, it was alright. But not good enough."

Stone found this amusing. "You sure about that? I was there. The crowd loved it. So how much better does it have get?"

"How many people you suppose were in there?" Haggard asked.

"I dunno. Maybe three dozen."

"Three dozen huh? Well that means there was maybe one genius listener. And they knew it wasn't perfect. That's all that counts. Y'all have a nice night."

Stone watched Haggard stroll back toward the club with the swagger of youth wrapped snugly about him. Genius listener. He'd never thought about it that way. He suspected that this rare creature would stalk Mr. Haggard throughout his life and pay a visit whenever hubris threatened to carry the day.

On the drive over to Christine's Stone realized that Haggard was right. There was at least one genius listener who took in his performance on this night in June of 1954. Ron Travers.

Stone pondered the gulf between the pair, and how the world occasionally conspires to create the most unlikely connections. Even in Bakersfield.

21.

JUNE 24

DOWNTOWN BAKERSFIELD AND OILDALE

Mr. Farnsworth at the Bank of America was less than pleased. The clock read 10:02 AM, two minutes past opening, and here was Mr. Stone back with a sob story about a lost key.

"You have a master key, right?" Stone asked.

"No, we do not," Farnsworth said sternly. "That would compromise the security of all the boxes. After you sign the appropriate forms, we'll have to drill the lock. There'll be a replacement fee, of course."

"Of course," Stone confirmed. "Now what if somebody found the key and came down here and opened the box? Could you tell? Do you keep a log or something?"

"I suppose you could call it that," Farnsworth said, implying that it would take countless years of banking experience to understand the requisite documentation. "You have to sign in with your key number before you can enter the vault."

"Could we take a look and see if the key was used yesterday? If nobody's gotten into the box, I'd rather hold off on drilling," Stone explained.

Farnsworth gave a fussy sigh. "I'm not sure what the bank's policy is on revealing something like that; but this one time I'm willing to make an exception."

"Thank you." Stone failed to inject any sincerity into his gratitude.

They walked to an alcove in front of the vault. It held a small desk and two file cabinets. Farnsworth produced a key and turned to Stone as to a wayward child. "You don't happen to remember your box number, do you?"

"Sorry," Stone said with a shrug. "They all look pretty much the same."

"That's the whole idea," Farnsworth said in retaliation. He unlocked the first cabinet, thumbed through some folders and pulled out a file. He fished out a single form and silently read it. "Could you verify your date of birth and social security number?" he asked Stone without looking up.

Stone did so. Farnsworth returned the form to its folder. "F-72," he announced. He unlocked the second cabinet and removed a large, bound ledger, which he placed on the desk and opened to a partially filled page. He ran his finger down a row of entries, and stopped near the bottom.

"Ah yes," he said. "F-72. Someone signed in for access just before closing and signed out shortly thereafter."

"What name did they give?" Stone asked, as if it would do any good.

"James Stone," Farnsworth replied smugly. "A friend of yours?"

"Apparently not," Stone said.

"Well in that case, Mr. Stone, I suggest that you contact the authorities."

"The authorities," Stone repeated. "You're right. Now why didn't I think of that?"

· · ·

The little boy appeared to be Hispanic, maybe four years old. Recent tears had puffed and reddened his eyes and he wore a bandage around his lower left arm. His mother smiled when Christine offered him an orange lollipop and told him "You're a very brave young man." She turned to the boy's mother. "Keep the dressing on for a couple of days and don't let it get dirty. He should be just fine."

The mother nodded shyly. Stone wondered if her English was good enough to understand, but stayed out of it. This was Dr. Harmon's clinic, not his.

Christine directed her attention to Stone as the mother and son left. "Staph infection," she explained. "I had to lance and drain it. You look like you could use a lollipop, too."

"I was just at the bank," Stone said. "Sure enough, someone showed up late yesterday and grabbed the pictures."

"Which leaves you with zero bargaining chips, right?"

"Not exactly," Stone said. "There's still Rhonda."

"Ah yes, Rhonda." Christine said with absolutely no optimism.

"Could I use your phone to make long distance call to LA?" Stone asked.

"Go ahead, if you think it'll help."

"I'm checking with Murphy, my old partner," Stone explained. "He said he'd look into Rhonda from his end and let me know what's out there."

Stone made his way through two operators to Murphy. "James!" his old partner exclaimed. "I was just going to call you. I know that sounds like bullshit, but it's true. Swear to God."

"If you say so," Stone shot back. Murphy was Murphy.

"Okay here's the deal:" Murphy said. "I checked the Sunset Terrace apartments. It seems that Number Twelve was very recently vacated."

"Can't say I'm surprised," Stone said. Blitz had probably phoned 'Ray,' his Hollywood pal, as soon as the murder went down. "Any rent checks, anything like that?"

"Nope. Always paid in cash. That's about it on the apartment. Sorry."

"What about the girl?" Stone asked.

"Ah yes, little Miss Savage. Not a lot, but a little. Female, born 1941. Picked up on petty theft two years ago. Charges were dropped and the case referred to Social Services. The mother retained custody subject to monthly visits from a social worker."

"You got a name for the mom?" Stone asked.

"Yeah, Cynthia Crawford. Last known location was up your way, in Oildale."

"Oildale?" Stone's brain did a summersault and landed upside down.

"Yeah, Oildale. But no address. Probably a drifter and a drinker. One more thing."

"What's that?"

"Social Services said they got a call from your neck of the woods just before I talked to them. Someone from the Kern County DA's office. Looking for the same stuff you're after."

Stone's brain turned right side up. "How long ago?"

"Maybe an hour, something like that."

"Murphy, thanks. I gotta go."

Christine returned just as he hung up. "Unbelievable," he told her.

"What?" she asked.

"Rhonda's mother. She lives right here in Oildale."

"And how did that come about?" Christine asked.

"I have no idea. They gave me her name, but they don't have an address."

"You know, Oildale's not all that big," Christine said. "What's her name?"

"Cynthia Crawford."

Christine smiled and headed toward a file cabinet behind the desk. "You just hit the jackpot. She's a patient – or was patient. I'm not sure she's survived."

"What's her problem?"

Christine pulled out a file. "Terminal stage alcoholism, with advanced cirrhosis of the liver. Not pretty." She opened the file and scanned it. "Here's the address. It's over on Linda Vista, number 1354, just a few blocks."

Stone stood up and grabbed his hat "I've got to go. Right now."

"Be careful."

"Always."

• • •

When does a house quit being house and become a shack?

The question occurred to Stone as he pulled up to the address of Cynthia Crawford, mother of Rhonda Savage. A ring of dry weeds surrounded her tiny abode and sprouted from a bed of hard, bare earth. Remnants of peeling paint clung desperately to the weathered siding. A partially collapsed curtain sprawled inside the solitary front window. The walkway was a sad procession of chipped and dirty flagstones.

Once at the door, he heard a woman's voice coming from within. An old woman's voice, all raspy and quack-like, rising and falling in an abrasive tide.

He didn't bother to knock. If Rhonda was inside, he didn't want to tip her off. He pushed the unlocked door open. After countless years as a cop, he thought he was prepared for what he might encounter. He wasn't. The stench took him to the edge of nausea, a mixture of human and cat excrement, the product of a hopelessly clogged toilet and animals free to urinate and defecate at will. Rhonda sat on a tattered couch to his right, with a sleeping pillow at one end. She stared at her mother and seemed oblivious to his presence in spite of the sudden shower of daylight from the open door.

Cynthia Crawford occupied a partially collapsed recliner to Stone's left. She wore an old robe open to a filthy nightshirt stretched taut by a grossly swollen belly. Diabetic ulcers punched red craters into her bare feet and a nervous palsy danced through her curled fingers. Her toothless face looked the color of clay, and her gray hair hung limp and lifeless. She gazed out the window through eyes of ancient glass and raged at a world far removed.

"Show me the sinner! Let me devour the sinner! Let me feast upon him!"

Rhonda slowly rotated her face toward Stone. She did it with an infinite grace that underscored a strange wisdom far beyond his reckoning. Her eyes spoke with a startling clarity and conviction.

"Now do you get it? Now do you see what's made me what I am?"

Her mother started up again. "What's happened to the potatoes? I can't do nothin' without the potatoes! There's a diamond in there someplace!"

A mound of garbage towered on the kitchen floor. A cat tentatively pawed at it, looking for something edible.

"Where's the ring? Oh lordy! I think I done lost the ring!"

An open bottle of whiskey rested on a little table next to her. No glass necessary. Not anymore.

"Gotta get the train. The one that's goin' north. I'm gonna take it all the way, yes sir, all the way."

She paused to catch what breath she had left in her ruined lungs. Stone took advantage and turned to Rhonda. "They know you're here. We've got to go. Right now."

Rhonda understood and slowly came up off the couch. "What about my stuff?"

It occurred to Stone that no matter how reduced your circumstance, the question of your stuff always persisted. For some, it might be a mansion in the Hollywood Hills; for others, a pair of used shoelaces. "We'll worry about that later," he told Rhonda. "Let's go."

Rhonda crossed the room to her mother, who was oblivious to her presence. She gave her a pat on the head. "Bye mom."

"The bumper got bent," her mother proclaimed. "Now it's no damned good."

· · ·

Just as they reached the end of the block to turn south on McCray Street, Stone glanced in his rearview mirror. He watched an unmarked sedan, a county car, pull up in front of the Crawford house. He lost sight of it when he turned the corner and relaxed a little. Rhonda's mom had pulled up anchor long ago and now drifted at random through a world entirely of her own construction. She would be of little help to anyone pursuing them.

"Where are we going?" Rhonda asked, in a way that suggested that all places shared some sort of mysterious parity.

"Know where Visalia is?" Stone asked, as they turned right onto Norris Road toward Highway 99.

"I think it's up the highway someplace," Rhonda said. "Why there?"

"Let me get us out of town," Stone said, with yet another glance in the rearview mirror. "Then I'll explain."

"What about my mom?"

"You worried about her?"

"Sort of."

Rhonda's mom. Stone had seen a lot of human wreckage in his years as a cop, and this woman ranked near the very top. It went beyond her wretched physical appearance and demented raving. She seemed almost like an apparition, a ghostly summation of misfortune and tragedy accumulated through boundless generations before her, all waiting for Rhonda to come along and add her own mass to an almost unbearable weight.

"I'll talk to Dr. Harmon and make sure that someone checks on her," he said.

Not that it would do much good. The damage to Mrs. Crawford was clearly irreversible. Hopefully, the same was not true of her daughter.

· · ·

Once on Highway 99, they rolled north through fields compressed into a thin green horizon that sweltered under the broiling sun. They cranked down their windows for relief but found little in the scalding rush of air rising off the pavement. The last trace of the town disappeared behind them, with its motels, fast burger joints, discount tires, and newly minted service stations.

Stone disrupted the silent linearity of their journey. "I used you, Rhonda," he admitted. "I played you as a chip in a bigger game, and I lost. So now I owe you."

"Owe me what?" Rhonda asked.

"An escape route. They almost had you back there, and it was just dumb luck that I beat them to the punch. Next time would have been your last time. Truth is, I'm out of options and so are you. I can't protect you and you can't hide, at least not around here."

"So what am I supposed to do in this Visalia place?"

"Nothing. They've got a bus station there. We're buying you a one-way ticket back to LA, and I'm giving you some money to keep you off the street once you get there. The rest is up to you."

Rhonda nodded thoughtfully. "The rest is always up to me."

Stone rotated her remark though as many planes of logic as he could manage. In every case, the girl was right. It was up to her.

• • •

Stone parked on Oak Street in front of the Greyhound Bus terminal on the main route through Visalia. Traffic was sparse, and the oppressive heat held the place in an almost silent stupor. "Well, this is it, Rhonda," he announced. It didn't sound very ceremonious but he wasn't sure what else to say.

The girl didn't seem very concerned about what might become off her back in LA. Stone could guess why. She planned to head straight back to Ray, whoever that was, and the apartment in Brentwood. Of course Ray and the apartment were now long gone, which would put her right back on the street. When she stepped off the Greyhound, he had to somehow make sure it was a soft landing. The bus ride to LA took twelve hours, so that's how long he had to set something up.

Once inside the station, he left her at the magazine rack while he went to a payphone and dialed Christine. Since he was out of town, he had to shove a dime and a nickel into their respective slots to make the connection. She answered on the third ring.

"What happened? Where are you?"

Her composure seemed slightly frayed. He couldn't help but like that. "I'm up in Visalia. Sorry I didn't phone sooner. I'm at the Greyhound station with Rhonda. I'm going to put her on the bus to LA. She'll be safe there – at least a lot safer than here."

"And what does she do then?"

"That's why I called you. Caring for teenage girls isn't part of my job description. I remembered that you used to run a clinic in the wrong part of downtown LA. I thought you might be able to give me a few helpful hints."

"You did, did you?" She went silent for a moment, and Stone hoped it wasn't out of displeasure. "This just might be your lucky day," she said. "I was on a board with the guy who's now the Director of Social Services for Los Angeles County. He found me kind of attractive, although his wife thought otherwise. I know he'd love to make a big impression, even after the fact."

"You think he might handle the case personally?"

"At the very least, she'll get the absolute best Social Services has to offer. How long until the bus gets to LA?"

Stone told her.

"I'm going to need the arrival time and the bus number," she said.

"Will do. Talk to you later."

"Be careful, okay?"

"Okay."

Rhonda was thumbing through a magazine when Stone returned with her ticket. He glanced at the cover. It was something called *Teen Magazine* and touted a feature story entitled Going Steady Is Not For Me. The girl, the magazine, and this transient place assembled themselves into a tableau of tragic proportion.

He was certain that Rhonda had never had the luxury of being a teenager like the ones within the pages she was scanning. And given what the lords of Bakersfield had visited upon her, she never would, no matter how much repair work was done.

"Someone from Social Services will meet you when you get to LA," he told her. "I've been promised that they'll take good care of you. So give them a chance, okay?"

"Yeah, okay." Her reply had a very dull edge to it.

The money. It pasted itself across his mind's eye. The envelope from Delfort, fat with a thousand in cold cash. By some miracle, it had survived his apartment being tossed when they came for the key.

"You know how much a thousand dollars is?" he asked Rhonda.

"A lot."

"Yeah, a lot. Know what I'm going to do? I'm going to talk to a lawyer. I'm going to put a thousand dollars in the bank for you. If you finish high school, you'll get the money, part of it in cash and the rest to pay for college. But you have to graduate from high school to get it. Understand?"

"I think so," Rhonda replied from somewhere inside a daze. Her expression reminded Stone that a sudden burst good fortune can be just as overwhelming as bad fortune.

He heard the deep gurgle of a diesel engine as the bus to LA pulled up out back and its door swung open. Not surprisingly, no one got off, and Rhonda was the only one getting on. He walked her to the open door, and fished two dollars from his wallet. "Here's some money for food. You have a good trip."

"Thanks." A fine mist settled over Rhonda's eyes, the kind that rises ghost-like from the morning sand on an empty beach. It lingered just a moment then lifted. Stone extended his hand and Rhonda shook it. "Good luck."

Rhonda released his hand, climbed the steps onto the bus and disappeared into the back.

Stone lingered until the doors closed and the bus rolled out onto the street. The brief vigil left him feeling sad and wistful. Is this what it's like? Is this what happens when you send your kid off to college or to a job in another town? He had no children of his own, so he couldn't be sure but suspected it was much the same. Love and loss all hopelessly intertwined.

So be it. He headed to his car.

· · ·

The drive back to Bakersfield took about an hour. It gave Stone some time to ponder some loose ends with Rhonda. They dangled like untied shoelaces, waiting for the perfect moment to trip him. Ultimately, he didn't know whether or not the girl had witnessed Fancher's murder. She said she left before it happened, but how could he be sure? The only other witness was the itinerant creep Willert, so the truth had evaporated into a dense speculative haze that would probably never clear. He'd intended to confront her about it but never did. Truth was it no longer mattered. Fancher's depraved photo collection had been a head-on collision for Stone, and moved the whole matter to some higher court beyond finite reason.

He punched in the cigarette lighter and waited for the spiral orange glow to light his Chesterfield. For Rhonda and friends it was all about falling under the horrible shadow of predation cast by someone old enough to know better. It prompted Stone to recall a high school biology class where they studied this thing called a chrysalis that started as a homely caterpillar and emerged as a full-blown butterfly. He imagined a preying mantis hovering over the process, patiently waiting to strike when the butterfly prepared to spread its wings for the first time.

An ugly thought. Almost as ugly as the mess that awaited him just over the boiling horizon in Bakersfield.

· · ·

He stopped at a Richfield in McFarland for gas. Twenty-four cents per gallon seemed a little steep, but he was close to empty and had little choice. The pump hummed through the thick air and channeled a small portion of the Arabian Peninsula into his tank. While he waited for it to fill, he spotted a pay phone and called Christine. She answered on the third ring.

"It's done," he said. "She's off."

"You don't sound too happy about it," Christine observed.

"It was hard," he said. "Harder than I thought."

"I'm sure it was," she said gently. "What are you going to do now?"

"For starters, I'm going to give you her bus number and arrival time, then I'm heading home to clean up the toss. Then I'm going to have a beer. Or maybe I'll have one while I'm cleaning and another when I'm done. Big decision, huh?"

She paused before answering, leaving only the quiet hiss in the receiver. "I'm going to come over and help you," she declared.

Stone could tell that she didn't consider her offer to be optional, which was just fine with him. "I'll be there in about an hour."

"Fine. I'll see you then."

. . .

Stone had never seen Christine dressed down for housework, but somehow none of her appeal was lost in the translation. She wore flat shoes, loose slacks and a cotton blouse. A blue kerchief reined in some of the stylish curl in her hair. "So how do you want to do this?" she asked Stone. "Your place. Your call."

"Step by step," Stone replied. He looked out the randomized clutter that covered the floor from wall to wall. "Let's try to organize as we go. First, we'll get stuff up on the table, and I'll sort while you pick. You ready?"

"Ready."

Soon they had stacks of sorted items covering the table. Snapshots, cancelled checks, tax forms, silverware and the like. They chatted amiably while they worked.

"You were right about Rhonda's mom," Stone said. "It wasn't a pretty picture. What caused all that swelling in her belly?"

"It's a kind of chain reaction," Christine explained. "It starts when the liver is overwhelmed by the amount of alcohol it has to metabolize. Pretty soon, you got yourself a case of hepatitis and a severely enlarged liver." She dumped some old snapshots on the table and went back to the floor. "Next thing you know, the compressed blood vessels inside start to squeeze fluid into the abdominal cavity, and swelling sets in. In an advanced case like hers, you can tap on the stomach and watch a wave ripple across."

"Pretty gross," Stone commented as he sorted the pictures.

"What's this?" Christine held up something about the size and texture of a small envelope with a tab on one end.

Stone took it from her. "Oh yeah. It's piece of that instant film from Fancher's. Never got used. It was in the box with the party pictures. I must have missed it when I took everything to the bank." He realized that whoever tossed his place had probably failed to connect it to the evidence in the safety deposit vault. Not surprising. They were cops, not photographic experts. "Oh well," he said as he stared at it. "Doesn't do me much good. There's nothing on it."

Christine took the picture back from him. "You're sure about that?"

"Well yeah. I mean look at it..."

Christine examined the film with surgical precision. She gently grasped the tab on the end with her thumb and forefinger. "Maybe it already went through the camera," she speculated. "Maybe he never took the time to look at it." She continued to pull on the tab and the gray cover gave away to reveal a developed image underneath.

"Oh my God!" she exclaimed.

"What?"

"It's Vicky Beaumont!"

Stone leaned in close. The picture showed a young girl sitting on the couch next to none other than Thomas Gilford, who appeared to be dozing or passed out. She wore only a bra and panties. Her mouth hung slack and her eyes had that smeared look of heavy intoxication.

"Beaumont?" Stone asked.

"Vicky Beaumont. The chief's daughter."

"His daughter? I didn't even know he had one."

"None of the cops ever talk about her. Especially when the chief's around."

"Why's that?"

"She's dead. I did the post-mortem. That's why I recognize her."

"Post-mortem? What happened?"

"They found her body in Beach Park down by the river. Just fourteen. Very sad. She died of hemorrhaging from a failed abortion. Out of respect for the chief, we kept it quiet. Only the family and a few cops know what really happened."

Stone took the picture from Christine. "And here she is, in the company of Mr. Thomas Gilford. Wouldn't you know it?" He slid the picture into his shirt pocket. "We're through here for now. I've got to go. There's someone I need to see."

A state of alarm spread across Christine's face. She clutched his hand. "You're not going to the chief, are you? Please tell me you wouldn't do that."

"I'm not going to tell you anything. From here on, the less you know the better."

"Whatever you're doing, please, please be careful," she pleaded.

"That goes without saying," Stone said. It was a lie, of course, a fabrication to assuage her fear. And she was right to be afraid.

If he paused and gave it too much thought, he'd be afraid, too.

After he saw Christine off, he went back inside, checked the phonebook and made the call.

"Hello." The chief's voice sounded like it emanated from the gravel on a dry riverbed.

"It's Stone. I need to talk to you."

"I don't talk business when I'm home, sergeant. That's what I have an office for."

"Just this once, I'd like you to make an exception."

"What for?

"It's a little complicated, but once we talk, I think you'll agree. Trust me."

An anxious interval passed. "Okay. But it better be good. In fact, it better be better than good. You got the address?"

Stone wrote it down and hung up. He looked at the neatly arranged stacks of stuff on the table, edifices of order emerging from chaos. Together they formed the blocks of a town called James Stone. Once a pleasant place to live, but not lately.

A giant wrecking ball now threw it all into shadow.

· · ·

Chief Beaumont lived off Panorama Drive in a home atop a bluff that overlooked the Kern oil fields. While walking to the front door, Stone noticed how well tended the lawn and shrubs appeared. Just like the chief's uniform when he was at the office. The pursuit of order in a world full of chaos. Just what you'd expect from the alpha cop.

"Thanks for seeing me," Stone said when the chief answered.

"We'll see about that," the chief responded.

One look inside told Stone that the chief lived here alone. The place had a distinctly male presence, the kind that few women would tolerate. Exposed floors, drab earthen colors, a gun cabinet in the living room and a deer's head over the fireplace. They moved out back to the patio, where a feeble breeze struggled against the heat. The pair sat down in lawn chairs that faced outward toward the scorched and barren hills covered with swarms of oil pumps that pecked into the withered ground.

"So what's this all about?" the chief bluntly asked.

"I'm betting heavy on you," Stone told the chief. "I'm betting that you don't know what's going down."

"What do you mean?"

"Let's start with the kid, the one I lost from custody. She wasn't just another street punk. She was my key witness against Sumner in the Winters case. Her name is Rhonda Savage. She saw Sumner and the Winters girl together in a room out at the Rancho Vista. Better yet, Winters told her a sob story about how Sumner wouldn't leave his wife and marry her. I took her out of the juvenile center because I didn't think she'd ever live to tell the tale in court."

"Why not?"

"Because she was shipped in from LA on a regular basis by Richard Fancher, who had a special taste for very young girls. Rhonda Savage was there the night that our friend Gary Willert stabbed Fancher. Seems that she and Gary had a thing for each other."

"You think she helped with it?" the chief asked.

"I don't know. But whether she did or not, certain people want to keep the case out of court. At any cost. That's why the all evidence against Willert walked off."

"What people?"

"It seems that Fancher and some of his friends shared a fondness for young adolescent females. Way under age. Borderline pedophilia. Rhonda told me about a stash of pictures from their parties. Really nasty stuff, the kind that would send you up for ten years or better. I found it and was ready to tag it as evidence. But then I recognized some of the faces."

"Such as?"

"Samuel Delfort and Jonathan Blitz. Two of our most revered and respected citizens. If Rhonda testified in open court about what went on at Fancher's at the time of the murder, they'd be in really deep shit. They weren't going to let that happen."

"So why didn't you come to me?" the chief asked.

"To be honest, I didn't know whose side you'd be on."

The chief nodded gravely "Fair enough. So what did you do with the pictures? Where are they now?"

"They're gone. Someone tossed my apartment and got them back."

"Any idea who?"

"The same person that looted the evidence room. None other than our very own Thomas Gilford. It seems that he was another regular at Fancher's parties. Cop by day, pervert by night. A very busy guy."

Stone could almost hear the horrible roar inside Beaumont's brain. "You're sure about this?" the chief asked.

"I'm sure. Rhonda identified him as a regular. And a source inside the department nailed him on the evidence theft."

"Jesus," the chief whispered.

"I've saved the worst for last," Stone said. "When they tossed my place, there was one party picture they missed." He pulled the photo of Gilford and Vicky Beaumont from his shirt pocket and handed it to the chief.

Beaumont examined the photo. A strange and terrible stillness came over him, like the kind that settles in just before a big earthquake or tornado. Nothing moves. Everything waits. He stood up ramrod straight, put his hands in his pockets and stared out at the oil pumps in the distance.

Stone felt the world stop. He could only wait and hope.

After a long and frightful silence, the chief began to speak. Slowly. Bitterly.

"I'm going to tell you a story," he began, "and I'm only going to tell it once and you're the only one that's ever going to hear it. So listen close."

Stone nodded, but Beaumont paid him no heed and held his gaze on the sunburned hills in the distance.

"Sometimes, you get lucky about stuff," he said. "I was really good at being a cop. Right from the get go. All I had to do was hang on for the ride. But when it came to family, I wasn't so good. I don't know why. I just wasn't. It's just the way things go."

In a sudden flash of cognition, Stone knew why Beaumont was talking this way. He had no choice. If he didn't, he would launch into an internal rage that would ultimately consume him and leave only a porous and ashen hulk to carry on.

"Vicky was ten when I divorced her mother," the chief went on. "She took it hard, which really kind of surprised me. I'd never really been tight with her and I figured it just wouldn't make much difference. But it did. By the time she was thirteen, she was in trouble pretty much nonstop.

"Don't get me wrong. I tried to set things straight. I took her bowling, took her hiking. Didn't work. I just couldn't connect. Ever had something busted and you couldn't figure out how to fix it? It's a bad feeling. After a while, you just don't want to have anything to do with it. But when it's your kid, you can't stop trying.

"The guys down at the station did their best to help. Whenever she got in a jam, they took her home instead of booking her at juvenile. But it got worse. By the time she was fourteen, she was out all night a couple of times. I warned her over and over that she was headed for real trouble, but she didn't hear me. A lot of kids are that way. They don't listen, they only learn. She was one of them."

The chief paused. Only his chest moved as he drew a silent breath of ominous proportion. His gaze remained fixed on the distant and barren hills.

"And then along comes Gilford. My ex-wife already knew him from social functions and he poured on the charm. Funny how an asshole can suddenly become Mr. Nice Guy when it suits his purpose. At first, I didn't give a rip. Why should I? Helen and I were history.

"But the longer it went on, the funnier it smelled. One time I went over to ask my daughter if she wanted to go to a ball game, and there was Gilford alone with her out on the patio. Helen wasn't even home. He made up some bullshit excuse for being there and took off. I told Vicky he was way out of line, and she blew up on me. Said he understood her better than I ever had. Said I had no business trying to tell anybody how to be a father. I sucked it in and left. There wasn't a damn thing I could do about it. I wasn't the custodial parent.

"Another time I saw them alone together in a burger joint out on 99. I don't know what they were talking about, but whatever it was, he had her pretty much in the palm of his hand. You would have thought that he was some kind of teenage idol. This time, I stayed clear. Good thing, too. I was in a dangerous mood.

"Later, I went over to Helen's and told her that I seriously didn't like what was going on. And you know what? She dumped the whole thing onto me. Said I was being completely paranoid, and jealous to boot. Now what could I say to that? Not a damn thing. It was so far off the mark I couldn't even get a shot lined up. After that, I'd made up my mind. Gilford and I were going to have it out."

The chief stopped again. Took another breath. A deep one.

"Never happened. They found her body a couple of days later."

The chief turned to Stone. "Know how she died?"

"Yeah," Stone said quietly. "I do."

The chief looked back out at the denuded hills covered with the feasting oil pumps. "So what was I gonna do? I had no way to be sure it was Gilford. Maybe it was somebody else, some horny little pup she knew from school. Who knew? Not me, that's for sure. I had to let it slide, had to let it go. But you know what? It's never gone away, not even for a day. Not a single day."

He gave the picture back to Stone. "And now I see this. So how do you think it makes me feel?"

"I can't even begin to imagine," Stone said.

"Neither can I," said the chief.

"I'm sorry," Stone said. And he truly was.

"Don't be." Beaumont seemed to return to a semblance of normalcy, much to Stone's relief. "We never had this talk, right? Not any of it."

"Not any of it," Stone confirmed.

"You're back on the job as of tomorrow morning," the chief declared. "Forget about the Fancher case. Keep after Sumner. I'll back you when you're ready for the DA."

"Thanks," Stone responded. The breeze died entirely, along with the conversation. "I should probably go now."

"You probably should," the chief said.

• • •

"So now what happens?" Christine asked Stone.

"Nobody knows." Stone took another sip of his Manhattan. The lounge at the San Pedro mixed in a generous portion of vermouth that gave the drink a distinctive flavor. He rather liked it.

"I think you do know," Christine said. "Or at least you have a pretty good idea."

"Not really," Stone said. He couldn't tell her about his visit with the chief. He couldn't tell anybody. He couldn't announce that he'd likely triggered an avalanche of unknown proportion and consequence. He looked down at his drink and rotated the stem of the glass. "I like this," he said. "I think I'll have one more."

Christine gave him an amused smile; the kind one might give a slightly naughty child.

"As well you should."

22.

JUNE 26

DOWNTOWN BAKERSFIELD

"I prayed for you," Mrs. Crenshaw informed Stone. "Just like you asked. And I do believe that my prayers were heard. It would seem you have your job back."

"Well thank you," Stone said politely. "I appreciate all that you've done."

"Don't thank me," she declared. "Thank the Lord."

"I'll do that," Stone promised, and moved on to his row of desks, where Brainard was putting on his coat and hat. "Boy am I glad to see you," the old cop said. "My back's killing me. I gotta go lie down for a while. Anything comes in, it's all yours."

"Thanks," Stone said, with no hint of irony. He sat down, leaned back, and rolled a pencil between his thumb and forefinger. He felt the ripple of its hexagonal surface and examined the green bands surrounding the upper portion of its distinctive yellow paint job. He idly wondered how long pencils would look like this. Would they make it to the end of millennium? He doubted it.

He was still speculating when his phone rang and he picked it up. "Detective Stone."

"Dispatch. We just got a call from two officers over on Stine off of Stockdale. Double homicide."

"Got it. Tell 'em I'm on my way."

"Roger that."

Stone put down the pencil. He didn't ask for the street address. He knew precisely where it was.

. . .

Three patrol cars lined the east side of Stine Road at the crime scene by the time Stone arrived. The medical examiner's van occupied the front of the driveway. Neighbors gawked from their porches and stood in nervous clusters out on the street, forming little pools of rampant speculation. He wondered how much they knew about Thomas Gilford. Probably very little. The Head Investigator ran in different circles than they did. Circles they could scarcely imagine.

Stone showed his badge to a patrolman at the foot of the driveway and took charge of the scene. "You the one who called this in?" he asked.

"Yes sir. The neighbor next door went out to get his paper about 8 AM and heard a dog barking in the driveway."

Stone pictured the Sheltie, right down to the patches of brown and white in its fur. He even heard the beast's incessant barking as it bounced off the back of his memory.

"The guy looked over and saw the kitchen door standing open and thought maybe it was a burglary, so he called it in and we arrived a few minutes later."

Over the patrolman's shoulder Stone caught sight of a big black Lincoln parked directly in front of the house on the curved driveway. Delfort's.

"We went in through the open door and found two bodies in the living room, so we did a quick search and backed out. We called it in and secured the scene."

"Where's the medical examiner?" Stone asked.

"He's inside, along with the lab guy."

When he reached the door, Stone saw that it was new. No trace of his gunshot damage remained. Gilford must have been a finicky fellow and had it promptly repaired. Stone continued on in.

The watch. The Patek Philippe. Stone spotted it on the wrist of Samuel Delfort as soon as he entered the living room. Which was fortunate, because it resolved a potentially difficult ID since the lawyer's face was almost entirely gone. The body knelt in front of the couch and inclined back onto the seat cushions. Delfort had on a stylish sports shirt almost untouched by the violence just above it, where the head had been reduced to a hemisphere. Only the gray-streaked hair and ears survived intact. The balance was a ragged swamp of red pulp.

Stone turned to the second body, which was sprawled on the floor leading toward the hallway. It had a similar head wound, but at an angle that left half a face. The receding red hair on the remaining scalp left little doubt that it was Gilford. Had he been heading toward the same nightstand and gun? Probably.

"Twelve gauge. Double ought buck." Lavelle, the medical examiner, had come up next to him. "You get a spread of an inch per yard with that kind of stuff. The killer shot from about twenty feet, which would put him back in the kitchen."

Stone turned in that direction and saw the open door in the rear past the refrigerator. He went back and examined it. No sign of forced entry. The assailant had simply walked in and started blasting.

The assailant. He had to be careful to keep using terms like that, even with himself.

"Whoever did it was a really good shot," Lavelle added from his standpoint in the living room. "That's not an easy hit at twenty feet. See the corner over there?" He pointed to the end of kitchen wall nearest him. "There's a couple of stray pellets embedded in the plaster."

"What's that tell you?" Stone asked.

Lavelle pointed to Gilford's body. "It tells me that this guy tried to make a break for the hallway and almost made it. The killer brought him down on the run and nailed him with a clean head shot. Very impressive. You're probably looking for a military guy or a seasoned hunter."

"Could be," Stone said. "What about the other body?"

"I can't be sure, but my guess is that the guy dropped to his knees and was begging for deliverance when he got it. Piss poor way to go."

Stone had a personal policy for reverence for the dead at crime scenes, regardless of which side they might be on. In this case, he was willing to make an exception. "So you think the killer caught them by surprise?"

"Sure looks like it."

"What about the spent shells?" Stone asked.

"Gone. Probably carted off by the killer."

The muffled barking of the Sheltie intruded through the open door in the back. Someone had stowed it in the garage.

"I'm going to take a look outside," Stone said. "Let me know if you need me."

"Will do."

Stone walked out into the pale morning heat and around to the rear of the house, where a cement patio stretched back to a cluster of shade trees. Twin teak chairs and a low table faced a brick-lined barbeque pit. A half dozen empty beer bottles and a big glass ashtray full of butts sat on the table.

Stone moved closer to the barbeque pit. A squeezable can of charcoal lighter rested next to its blacked grill. Something caught his attention in the ashes below. He tilted the grill up and retrieved it. Unmistakable. The glossy texture, the white border, the tiny bit of remaining image inside the charred edge. The remnants of a Polaroid photo.

The Sheltie started up again in the garage. The sun got earnest about the heat. A curious neighbor stood on tiptoes to get a better view. Stone pocketed the photo fragment and moved into the shade of the trees bordering the patio. It seemed that Delfort had done exactly what Stone had suggested when they were first dickering over the pictures. He barbequed them.

Stone looked at the two empty chairs and beer bottles. The pair had incinerated the pictures and gotten a little drunk to celebrate. Delfort had probably even told Gilford about Stone's original proposition, and they shared a good laugh about it.

All the while, the assailant had watched them from concealment in the darkness afforded by trees. When they returned to the house, it was still hot so they'd left the back door open. The assailant followed them in and shot them just as Gilford was about to see Delfort off.

But what then? Someone might have heard the shots. If so, how would the assailant retreat? Not out on the street, which was the first place the neighbors would look.

Stone continued on through the trees to the back of the property, where a wooden fence about six feet high ran almost the entire width of the lot. But not quite. It contained a gap near the north end, a break in the steady march of cedar planks.

When he reached the gap, an irrigation canal appeared on the far side. Stone knew about the canals, which channeled water from the Kern River, but had never seen one up close. The earthen cavity in front of him had a span of maybe seventy-five feet, with walls of sandy dirt that slanted down to the flat bottom, which was now bone dry.

At the gap in the fence, a set of footprints ran down the incline to the canal's bottom and turned north. Soft, clumpy footprints set in loose earth. The kind that left no particular signature. A closer look told Stone that it was actually two sets of superimposed footprints, one coming and one going. He stepped through the fence and descended along their path to the waterway's arid bottom and looked north. The Rosedale Highway crossed the canal a hundred yards ahead, and he began to track the footprints in that direction. Above him, a series of fences on each side blocked any view into the property behind them. Even in the light of day, he had the canal all to himself.

When he neared the highway, the footprints turned right and went up the dirt bank to a low-slung chain link fence that bordered a small parking lot. He followed their path to the top and felt the gritty sand filling his shoes. He easily scaled the fence and took in the lot. The back of it was concealed from the highway by a one-room barbershop, where a large billboard loomed overhead. He looked for security lights and saw none. At night the lot would have been deserted and lost to the shadows.

"It was all settled up," he said to himself. "So you just got in and drove on home. Nobody saw you come, nobody saw you go. Perfect."

He went back over the fence and down to the bottom of the canal, where he walked south down its center, piling his own footprints onto those already there.

He stopped when he reached the embankment below Gilford's backyard. A sound caught his ear, dim and distant. It came from somewhere to the north down the canal. He scanned the length of the earthen channel and saw nothing. The sound ceased in his ear but persisted in his head.

It sounded almost like the clink of jostled beer bottles.

• • •

It took until late afternoon for the office to finally settle down. It seemed like every cop in the whole department had to come by his desk and casually ask about the double murder over on Stine Road, the one that took out the big-time lawyer and the DA's top cop. Stone listened patiently to endless speculation about how it went down and who was behind it. The majority favored someone just released from the state pen, and Stone conceded that that just might be true.

All the distractions had put him behind on his initial report, and by the end of the shift he was nowhere near done. The big floor fan in the rear now buzzed into a nearly empty room. He stood up and stretched. Time for a little coffee, which Mrs. Crenshaw always brewed in a little room down the hall with its own sink and a refrigerator for those that packed their lunches.

He passed the chief's office on the way to coffee room, and the door stood open. Beaumont silently beckoned him in.

"You working late tonight?" The chief's face possessed the neutrality of an ancient escarpment that had withstood eons of weathering with no visible change.

"Yeah, we had a lot of distractions around here today. I'm way behind."

So what do you make of it?"

Stone shrugged. "Hard to say. I've got a general idea of how it went down. Somebody walked along the irrigation canal and came up on the back of the property. They went in the through an open door and caught the victims completely by surprise. One shot each. Then they went back the way they came and drove off. Simple as that."

"Did they leave any evidence?"

"Doesn't look like it. We dusted for prints, but I doubt we'll get any. We also didn't find any spent shells. There were footprints in the canal, but they were way too messy to tell us anything."

"Tough break," the chief said. "Neither one of those guys was ever going to win a popularity contest. That leaves you with maybe a couple of hundred suspects."

"I'm afraid you're right," Stone said. "Know what I think?"

"What's that?"

"This thing has cold case written all over it."

"That could be," Beaumont admitted. "But don't give up just quite yet, okay?"

"Of course not." Stone strongly suspected that they would never speak of it again. And they didn't.

23.

NOVEMBER 2
OILDALE

"Bring up the bass," Stone commanded. "I need more bottom end."

The engineer twisted a knob-sized dial on the mixing console. Stone often brought him in from Los Angeles for sessions like this one. If record sales kept going up, he'd soon bring him on full time. The Kern label had already penetrated the LA market, with several solid hits on country radio, and was starting to draw some serious national attention: "Just who the hell are those guys out there in California?" Some in Nashville had started referring to it as The Bakersfield Sound.

He looked out through the recording booth window to Jimmy Harper and his band. Pedal Steel, lead guitar and one of those new Fender basses, plus Jimmy strumming a big Gibson J-200 acoustic. They were nervous, just like Stone knew they would be. The only place they'd ever played was a little joint called Bob's Lucky Spot out on the Edison Highway. But his ear told him they were the right stuff. After a little rehearsal and a couple of takes, they'd settle down nicely. If not, he'd send out for a six pack from the bar next door.

Jimmy sang a tune about being one step ahead of the law and one step behind in his doomed marriage. His voice had power and conviction, along with a slightly rough edge. People would instantly recognize that he was the real deal. Stone knew just how to coax it out of him. Sometimes he recalled his encounter with that Haggard kid, who spoke of genius listeners. At the time Stone never dreamed that he might be one of them. But every new record made him think that at least he was headed in the right direction.

More often, he thought about how these guys were like buried gems waiting to be extracted from the hard, dry earth. Jimmy sanded fenders in a body shop. The steel player pressed slacks at a drycleaner's. The lead player loaded produce onto boxcars. The bass player met weekly with his parole officer. To Stone, they were like an intricate puzzle awaiting just the right musical solution.

In the studio Jimmy and the band ended their tune. Stone pushed the intercom button so they could hear him. "Okay guys, let's do one more. Keep the tempo relaxed. We're not in any hurry." He'd learned that anxious neophytes always played the first couple of songs too fast and wound up stumbling their way through.

As they played, he admired the recording equipment in the booth. Reels, tapes, levers, knobs, speakers and switches everywhere. All courtesy of a capital infusion provided by none other than the Castle family, led by Fatalia, who had developed a genuine entrepreneurial streak. Just the jumpstart his little enterprise needed. His law enforcement background also turned out to be a valuable asset. The distribution end of the record industry was a little less than honest, and often stiffed little labels like his. But once they learned you were an ex-cop, you got paid on time and in full.

Christine showed up as they were playing back the take. She stood behind where Stone sat, put her hands on his shoulders, and listened thoughtfully. When the tune ended, Stone punched the intercom again. "Sounds fantastic, guys. Let's take a little break and then we'll do a couple more just for fun." Yet another ploy: as soon as you took the heat off, everyone loosened up. He swung around and faced Christine. "What do you think?"

She gave him a knowing smile. "I think it's perfect. And I think you're the perfect one to be doing it. I'm going to be late at the clinic. Multiple cases of the mumps. I just wanted you to know."

"I'll walk you out," he volunteered.

When they reached the sidewalk, he paused and looked down Chester Avenue toward downtown. It seemed very distant, in both time and space. He put his arm around Christine's waist and brought her close. Her scent mingled with the autumn air in a most pleasant manner. Close but cautious: That was the best way to describe what they had grown into. Both were too far along in life to afford a stumble of the heart, but their regard for each other seemed to endure and had become a thing worth nurturing. They used to talk about tomorrow; now they talked about next month.

The heat had come and gone, along with the fallout from a summer full of murder. As expected, the *Bakersfield Tribune* gave it all scant coverage at best. It also failed to report that Jonathan Blitz, its publisher, had come down with liver cancer and left town on a desperate odyssey to find a cure, no matter what the cost. Several of his celebrity acquaintances had recommended some kind of mystical clinic in Brazil.

Stone's cop days were officially behind him. For the chief's sake, he'd hung on long enough that his resignation had no plausible connection with the ongoing investigations. Brainard had taken over the Gilford-Delfort case, which naturally brought the entire business to a permanent standstill. Conversely, the guy who took Stone's job pounced on the Sumner case as a way to make his mark. He quickly formed an alliance with the new Head Investigator at the DA's office. Somehow, it got out that they had Sumner's fingerprints on Charlene's matchbook from the Rancho Vista and on a pricey perfume bottle as well. With Blitz gone, the paper ran with the story and saw a noticeable increase in circulation. The evidence wasn't enough to charge Sumner, but it was more than sufficient to motivate his wife to file for divorce and relieve him of half of his net worth.

And the Fancher case, the crime that started it all, took an ironic turn and simply faded into oblivion, just as Delfort and friends had originally intended. Gary Willert, the nasty drifter, was arraigned on car theft and then jumped bail and disappeared out onto the endless highways of central California.

Occasionally, Stone's business took him north on Highway 99 past the Rancho Vista Motel, and he thought of Rhonda. Had he put the money to good use? He'd asked the attorney in charge of her funds to check on her occasionally, and it seemed that she was still in school. A good sign.

Stone walked Christine to her car and watched her drive north toward the clinic. It looked to be a good night. When he was through producing the session, he'd hop on down the street to the Blackboard. Bill Woods had promised him that Buck Owens would be playing lead tonight.

It didn't get any better than that.

CPSIA information can be obtained
at www.ICGtesting.com
Printed in the USA
BVHW04s2011130818
523998BV00008B/147/P

9 780986 377075